CURSE OF THE DRAGON SHADOW

Dedicated to

Angela, Carol, Charlotte, Ellen, and Shanna
for cheering Riony on through all her trials,
and making this story a joy to write.

Shadow Dragon Saga
Curse of the Dragon Shadow
Legend of the Dragon Soul
Rise of the Dragon Sworn
Blood of the Dragon Throne
Reign of the Dragon Born
Secret of the Dragon Crown

First Edition
Published by Fairies and Fantasy Pty Ltd November 2023

ISBN: 978-1-922390-71-4 (paperback)
ISBN: 978-1-922390-73-8 (hardcover)

Curse of the Dragon Shadow copyright © 2023 Selina Fenech
Cover art and interior illustrations © 2023 Selina Fenech
Editing by Zero Alchemy

www.selinafenech.com

CURSE OF THE DRAGON SHADOW

SELINA A FENECH

BOOK ONE OF THE

SHADOW DRAGON SAGA

CONTENT ADVICE

Coarse language: Rare/mild
Violence: moderate-to-high fantasy violence
Sex: References only

Contains references to or descriptions of:
Slavery, animal cruelty, torture, blood and gore, kidnapping,
scars, fire, ableism, corpses/undead, birth, murder.

CONTENTS

ELUNDRAE
EIGHT WINDS OCE.
TAEN HIGHLANDS
Nord Halfort
Heithorn Estate
Treede Wild
EYLE TAENESK
Eldisun Grove
The Great Wing
Vesland Plains
EYLE TAENUSH
Longtail River
Unicorn
(11)
Abandoned Quarries
(1)
Lorg Cornis
WESTERN ALDERKIN DEPTHS
(Ewess Deemfret)
Midsun Dale
(2)
Snowshimmer Ric
Yeonard's Passage
Vasthome Reach
Lorg Blessun
Sturmfell Peaks
(12)
Lorg Nisk
(10)
Tallesis Shores
(16)
Sut Myrr
EYERSUNN SEA

Dragon Keeps

1. Braigwenkeep (Trade Hub)
2. Nevrynkeep (Mining)
3. Ardahnkeep (Trade Harbor, Old Rolanian Capital)
4. Tjollaskeep (Mining)
5. Salixkeep (Fishing)
6. Ulfrenkeep (Mining)
7. Ylvakeep (Farming)
8. Leskakeep (Farming)
9. Pryshakeep (Farming)
10. Dastmyrkeep (Glass)
11. Tarrickeep (Mining)
12. Gerichkeep (Lumber)
13. Skaellakeep (Farming)
14. Idrakeep (Penal)
15. Hjelzahnkeep (Training)
16. Eslindekeep (Incomplete)

NORTHERN
ALDERKIN DEPTHS
(Nerrun Deemfret)
Gris Hofen
(15)
Sunborn Range
Stonewing Crest
(4)
CENTRAL
ALDERKIN DEPTHS
(Luns Deemfret)
Eishowl Peaks
(6)
Bovin Steppes
(13)
(5)
Unicorn Tears River
The Red Cliffs
Erst Hofen
SOUTHERN
ALDERKIN DEPTHS
(Sons Deemfret)
Talon Bluffs
Lorg Sesstra
(8)
Lorg Eldstrom
Lorg Draeka
Draeskull Crags
Starris River
(3)
Grand Hofen
Nord Myrr
(9)
Serpents Run
Seasong Shores
EYLE NORDCREST
(14)
Mestra's Horn
EASTERN
ALDERKIN DEPTHS
(Ilst Deemfret)
DRAEKHAN'S REST
(7)
Etherflame Plains
DRAEKHANHELM
SKYBREAK SEA

ALDERKIN DEPTHS
Relic Lower
Wet Descent
Whisperwind Passage
UPSLOPE
DragonMaw Descent
Stores
1.
Upper Flats
The Curtain
2.
Relic Upper
12.
3.
9.
The Grand Arch
11.
Flowstone Steps
Delver's Circuit
Crystalline Reservoir
STONESHIELD GATE
Livestock
Roo Far

THE UNDERCITY
Mushroom Farms
CURSED DEPTHS
DOWNSLOPE
phans' Den
UNICORN GATE
FIRSTMAN'S PASS
5.
7.
10.
4.
8.
6.
1. Temple Tower
2. Grand Column
3. Frostwork Column
4. Dragonwing Tower
5. Satinstraw Tower
6. Slowflow Flats
7. Rimstone Flats
8. Shimmervein Tower
9. Grand Arch Markets
10. Downslope Markets
11. Curtain Markets
12. Sinking Stream Lake

ONE

O ne big consequence of stealing a baby was having to then raise the thing. Riony Eyfarr had learned that lesson the hard way. She was only ten the first time she acquired a newborn. She never intended to repeat the experience. Eight years on, her first charge was more than a handful already.

Riony glared at the simple room carved from limestone. It didn't hold much. They didn't have many belongings. It also didn't contain her adopted sister.

I told her to stay at home. So, of course, she's gone. Better if I told the little spitfire to go catch cave spiders with her bare hands, then maybe she'd be here taking a nap.

Riony had only been away a short time, trading for

food at the mushroom farms, but Lyrrin played a game of doing the opposite of what she was told. The kid thought she knew everything and drew trouble to her like a magnet to dragon-forged steel. Riony prayed to the stars that she wouldn't find her sister in too deep this time. There had been a lot of talk in the undercity lately of kids going missing. Riony and Lyrrin's small two-room dwelling was in the undesirable highest tier of the Dragonwing Tower stalagmite, keeping the rent cheap. The immense limestone formation had been carved and hollowed into multiple homes by the previous inhabitants of the caves, but few humans enjoyed climbing to the highest rooms, including Riony. *So many stairs. That I just came up.*

Grumbling under her breath, Riony stepped back outside and pressed the stone button that rolled her front door closed. She eyed the twisting pathways at ground level far below. At least descending was faster than ascending.

Riony vaulted over the ornate stone railing and slid down the smooth slope until she hit the level below. She jogged along her downstairs neighbor's balcony, dodging some hanging laundry, then leaped across a gap to a lower flat-topped limestone formation below.

The surface was slick beneath her boots, wet by tiny drips from a craggy ceiling far above. Riony angled out over the edge to check her landing was clear, then dropped the short distance to the street level below.

Now, where did you go? Riony aimed for the small local market first. Lyrrin had no sovs to spend, but could sometimes use her big blue eyes to be gifted treats in sympathy. Riony grasped the hilt of her sword, the scale-patterned metal biting into her palm as she barged through the maze of crystal-lit pathways between rock-cut buildings.

The warm, earthy air was heavy in her lungs. It had been three years since she and her sister had fled underground and Riony still wasn't used to the bustling slums of the sprawling underground metropolis that was now her home.

Thousands of human refugees had made the Alderkin ruins their own, filling the expansive cavern to bursting. But only that cavern, the one closest to aboveground, as though the humans there still tried to be as close to the sun and sky as they could, even if they could never see it.

There were other levels below, more than even the bravest of delvers had managed to map, but they felt too dangerous, too haunted, to be habitable. Riony's skin shivered at the thought of the dark, cursed depths beneath her, both terrifying and thrilling. The delvers told wild tales of their scavenging adventures, and she hoped she'd soon set her own eyes on those treasure-filled spaces, both for her sake and for Lyrrin's.

They needed the money delving would bring in. Riony

wouldn't mind the status it would bring either. She just had to convince the delvers to let her into their ranks. Riony's gaze scanned the buildings and homes stacked up the huge stalagmites and cliffs, tracing every surface. The dwellings stretched right up to the distant ceiling, jagged with stalactites, like the toothy maw of some gigantic beast.

Tracking down a missing child in this mess was like finding a flea on a full-grown dragon. Riony pushed a flop of red hair away from her eyes and searched the crowd filling the small street market she'd marched into. An easy view from her vantage point of standing a head taller than most.

"Lyrrin?" she called, hands cupped around her mouth.

Nearby, a spice seller did a roaring trade offering overworld delicacies to add flavor to basic undercity fare. The scents of curry and cake filled the street. Riony's mouth watered as she passed his stall, and her empty stomach growled. As she forged onward, her gaze snagged on the story seller's shop, offering up the newest serials in press-printed booklets brought in from the dragonkeeps. It had been ages since Riony had the sovs to spare to buy and read those romantic adventures. A pang of longing stabbed at Riony, but she ignored it and kept walking.

From the shadows of an alleyway, a hand struck out and grabbed Riony. A woman with a motherly face and missing front teeth leaned close to her. "Got any need for

silvernix? Only fifty gold sovs."

Riony tugged her arm free and shook her head. She moved away fast.

Unicorn blood that cheap? Who is she kidding?

She rubbed her thumb over her acorn pendant, its surface polished smooth from the worry-born habit.

Spotting a street vendor Riony sometimes took Lyrrin to for fried rope worm, she touched his shoulder in greeting. "Have you seen my sister?"

"Little hooded scamp? Ran off that way not long ago." He pointed, then held a sizzling tray of sausage-like meat cooked on metal skewers under her nose. "Got some good juicy worms today if you want—"

"You know I love the juicy ones! But can't. Sorry!" Riony rushed by, eager to lay eyes on Lyrrin again and confirm she was safe, so she could skin the kid herself.

She couldn't afford meat now, anyway. Her last sovs went to the mushroom jerky she'd just bought. She'd been doing what she could to earn enough to keep her and her sister fed, but selling herbal remedies was a tricky and wildly unreliable business when living underground.

If she could convince Master Brishan to take her on as a delver, she and her sister would never have to worry about going hungry again. Trials were coming up soon, and Riony had been training so hard she had aches in muscles she didn't even know she had. And she knew most of her muscles, very fondly. She was strong enough to join, she knew that much. She just had to make a good impression on the other delvers and she'd be in. But until then, the situation was dire enough without Lyrrin running off.

The direction the vendor had sent her went right toward the orphans' den. *I should have figured she'd go there.*

Lyrrin could generally be found either trying to turn some random animal into a new pet or at the orphans' den, seeking company with others her age who had lost their parents on their journey to the Alderkin undercity too.

The memory of ragged, ravenous skeletons, and the raw, final screams of her amma cut through Riony's heart. Clenching her jaw, she shook off the visions of her past and pressed on. Glow crystals lit the crooked pathway through the caves, casting a soft cyan light over Riony as she barged past other comers-and-goers. A man in ragged brown hides and layers of dirt sat sprawled at an intersection. Riony's gaze lingered on him for too long and he met her stare with a sharp, cunning look. His eyes were red-rimmed and marked around the left one with a badly healed burn scar. Bowing his head, he reached out a beseeching hand and mumbled desperate pleas. Riony flicked her gaze away and marched on. Everyone in the undercity suffered. Everyone here had lost. She couldn't help him. How could she when she had nothing? She had to focus on keeping herself and Lyrrin safe. The glow crystal at the entrance of the orphans' den flickered dully, almost out of charge. A young man with bronze skin and a tumble of golden curls took it from its sconce and replaced it with another, tracing the carved rune in a single swift motion to activate it.

Bright light washed over him, filling the area, and he turned around, spotting Riony. He greeted her with a friendly smile. Riony had met him a few times before, since he was one of the regular helpers for the younger orphans. She admired him for that, and also for how he always managed to be well dressed and presentable in neat, new clothes. Not the sort of ragged hand-me-downs that were all Riony and Lyrrin could scrounge up.

He had a genuinely happy smile and somehow seemed to find it more freely than others in the undercity. Riony wondered how he did it, looking after others and himself with such apparent ease and joy. Maybe she could ask him to give her some pointers one day.

"Hey, Zade. Have you seen—"

"I am NOT clumsy!" A piercing, shrill voice answered Riony first. "I can do anything you could shado and better!"

Riony winced. "Aaand that'd be her. Sorry, she's not supposed to be here."

Zade juggled the old glow crystal and chuckled. "We

don't mind. Happy to have her around if you need someone to help look after her at times."

Riony fought down the bristly feeling at the implication she couldn't look after her sister herself.

Offering a smirk, she waved the offer away. "You might have made it your mission to rescue every orphan you see, but it's okay, I've got this one."

"It's no trouble. The more the merrier. The other kids enjoy her company."

There was another squeal from Lyrrin, then the gruff mumblings of a boy.

"Sounds like it."

"Kids, right?" Zade shrugged. "Think you can manage the extraction?"

"Sure. I'll go and grab her. Listen for my screams, in case I need backup. Stars shine upon you!"

"And you!" Zade's smile widened, and he waved as Riony stepped into the dormitory.

The smell coming from the orphans' den twisted Riony's nose. Unwashed, unhealthy children from babes to working age filled the space beyond capacity. The wide, low-ceilinged cavern seemed more suited to housing livestock than humans. Carers stepped gingerly between the little napping bodies crammed together on the floor, soothing where they could. The community came together to provide for the children, when possible, but that only helped to a point. There were just so many of them. And that care couldn't replace the parents lost in the overworld to fire or slavers or shadow revenants.

"It's not my fault. It's the gloves." Lyrrin's voice carried across the room from the play area.

Riony beelined for her.

A boy replied, "Then why are you always wearing them?"

As most of the smaller kids were resting, there were only two in the play area—an alcove to the side with a few patchwork dolls and games.

As they came into view, Riony's guts turned cold. She swore under her breath. The boy was Benjin, little brother to people Riony did *not* want to be on the bad side of.

Reaching them, Riony lifted her hands in a gesture of peace. "Okay now. Seems to me like a good time for making up and being friends."

Lyrrin shot a tempestuous glare from under her oversized hood.

Benjin ignored Riony, a smirk dimpling one brown cheek. "If your hands worked right, maybe you could look after those pets of yours better—"

Something squirmed under Lyrrin's shirt, and she clutched it protectively.

"—and stop them ending up in people's stew pots."

"That was you?" Lyrrin shrieked and threw herself fists first toward Benjin.

For the love of stars. Riony stepped into her path, greeted with a hailstorm of tiny, gloved hands pummeling her chest.

"It wasn't me! I'm trying to help you. You're just too tamebrained to get it." Benjin leaned around Riony toward Lyrrin as though he wanted a black eye.

Riony grasped Lyrrin's wrists, wrestling with her until she stilled, then shot back to Benjin, "Don't talk to her like that. The only dumb thing she's done recently is get into a conversation with you." The moment she let go of Lyrrin, the child sprung into attack again and Riony had to push Benjin a few steps back to safety.

A voice whispered in a husky breath close to Riony's ear, "What, exactly, are you doing to my brother?"

Oh sparks. Riony grabbed Lyrrin by the collar, then turned to see the young woman who had snuck up behind her.

There weren't many who could look Riony in the eye. Aishena barely came close, but somehow seemed to loom over her through attitude alone. She was made of all thin, rigid angles, her ashy-tan face curtained by steel-toned locks.

She had Taen features, in the sweep of her eyes and

sharpness of her nose, but Taen normally braided their hair in intricate patterns, and Aishena left hers hanging free. The way it shimmered and glided around her added to her ghostly presence. She moved as though sound offended her and had a habit of lurking in the shadows like a vengeful spirit. Sly, confident, effortlessly capable. In other words, totally hot. A shame she and her siblings were all ice-hearted bullies.

Benjin straightened out his tunic with a huff. "She pushed me."

Riony held her palms up innocently. "It was for his own benefit, I swear."

The promise of swift retribution was clear on Aishena's pouted lips. "What possibly benefit could anyone get from being manhandled by a thug like you?"

As much as Riony wanted to say, *ask your amma*, she managed to suppress the impulse. "If I can just explain—"

"What's going on?" A new voice boomed from across the cavern.

Riony's mouth curled down as Yoskar, the eldest brother, approached. His bulky muscles were mismatched with how he studiously pushed spectacles back up his nose. Like his little brother, his silver-gray hair was clipped close to his scalp, sparkling against his cool brown skin. Not a braid in sight.

Both he and Aishena wore dusty leather armor covered with straps, buckles, and harnesses. Their belts held the tools of the delving trade: cave-silk ropes, athames, multiple personal glow crystals, and more that Riony could never afford. Not unless she became one of them.

Exhaling slowly, Riony spread a friendly grin on her face. "Look, the kids and I were ... playing a little game, that's all. How about we go and talk about it over a drink or—"

"If Benjin takes one of my pets again, I'll stab him in his sleep!" Lyrrin howled.

"I didn't!" Benjin whined back, and the flurry of tiny fists began again.

Riony sighed and pinched the bridge of her nose. *This child is going to kill us both.*

Aishena, unaware that Lyrrin was all bark and no bite, lunged one big step toward the girl, arm raised.

A flash of protective instinct flared through Riony, and her hands shot out before her brain could catch up. They slammed into Aishena's chest, thrusting her backward.

The delver drew a long, outraged gasp as she stumbled. Yoskar caught and steadied her, then held her shoulders tight when she tried to rush back at Riony.

"Aish," Yoskar snapped.

A chill fell over Aishena's expression. She stilled and

stood at attention like a soldier. The command in his words also stilled the two quarreling children, who froze, hands still entangled between them.

Yoskar looked Riony up and down. "I've seen you before, sniffing around Master Brishan. You think you're going to become a delver?"

"I *know* I'm going to become a delver."

"No. No, you're not. Not after assaulting my sister like that."

"Whoa, slow down a second. I didn't mean ..."

"Which is exactly why you'll never be a delver. Brute strength is nothing without the brains to back it up. Master Brishan might have been considering letting you take trials, but you'll never be one of us. I'll make sure of it."

A trickle of cold sweat raced down Riony's spine. "I'm sorry. Please ..."

His roving, disapproving gaze stopped, and he leaned close to Riony, lifting a hand toward her face. Then he lowered it again. His fingers lingered near Riony's neck and landed on the acorn she wore tied on a leather strap there.

No ...

"What even is this ridiculous thing?" Yoskar's words were slow and mocking.

"Nothing. An acorn. Just a small reminder of life above." Riony tried to back away, but Yoskar's hand closed

around the pendant.

From behind her brother's shoulder, Aishena simpered, mockingly. "Why? Do you still dream of returning one day? Dream of seeing the sky and stars? Feel the sun browning your skin?"

"Only when I'm not dreaming about being a better delver than you." Riony tried to keep the tone light and ignore the lump in her throat at how Yoskar's grip tightened.

Aishena scoffed. "You should know by now that dreams are like the mushroom farms. Full of sh—"

"Could you try not being a complete ass in front of the littles?" Riony snapped.

Yoskar's eyes narrowed, and he jerked his hand, snapping the leather thonging. He flung his hand sideways, and the acorn clattered against the stone wall and fell into a dark corner.

"No!" Lyrrin yelled out.

Riony shot her a warning glance.

Body shaking and shoulders slumped, she spoke in a flat tone. "Did that make you feel better? You can pretend all you like that you don't dream, but look at you, still acting like overworld nobles. Yet here you are, hiding in the dark with the rest of us losers."

Benjin stepped over to his big brother's side, puffing out his chest. "We're not like you. You have no idea how important our family is. We're Hjelz—"

"Benj! Silence!" Yoskar snapped.

Aishena's eyes had widened, and she had one hand resting on the hilt of one of the many athames on her belt, ready to strike.

What the sparks did I do to deserve this? Riony put her hands up in a calming gesture.

"Is everything all right here?" Zade stepped right between the opposing sides.

Bravely, Riony thought, considering she and Yoskar were both slightly older and significantly bigger than him.

He tilted his head toward Riony. "You need backup?"

"Did I scream?"

"Well, no, I guess not. But ..." He looked skeptically between the two sets of warring siblings.

Riony sighed, then through gritted teeth said, "Everything is fine."

"Yeah. Fine. We were leaving." Aishena gave Zade a look of utter disgust, then wrapped an arm over Benjin's shoulders in a way that made him wince as she dragged him away. Yoskar shot a final condemning look back as he pushed up his glasses again and followed after his family.

Lyrrin stared at Riony, her bottom lip quivering.

"Hush," Riony warned again.

She stood still and waited as the delvers disappeared

from view. Zade offered only one concerned glance back before he hurried after them. Then Riony bolted over to where the acorn had fallen. The flea-ridden cot there was empty, just a tangle of threadbare rags, and Riony clawed through it, patting the edges and raking her fingers over the surrounding filth until the smooth, hard shape pressed against her palm. She held her breath as she brought the acorn up and brushed it clean. With a look over her shoulder, she held the acorn close, acting as though to retie the leather about her neck. Instead, she carefully twisted the top of the acorn free and inspected the miniscule glass vial held within. It shimmered, a silvery rainbow, the glass unbroken, despite the markings scratched into the side.

Lyrrin skittered up next to her. "Is the uni—?"

Riony slapped a hand over her sister's mouth. "It's fine. Our precious *acorn* is safe."

Lyrrin reached out and touched the etched lines with a gloved finger. "I'm sorry I made the glass more fragile. I just wanted to make it pretty."

Tears glittered over her vivid eyes and Riony pulled her in close. Anyone who saw them in person would never confuse the two of them for real sisters. Riony, a brown-skinned, flame-haired tower of muscle, and Lyrrin, diminutive and pale, with black hair and eyes a brighter blue than a sky clear of dragon-smoke. But in this place, where everyone had fled to from the perils of the overworld, there were many who ended up in families that weren't those they were born into. Riony closed the acorn pendant and tied the cord around her neck.

Patting the hood over Lyrrin's head, she said, "Didn't I tell you to stay at home?"

Lyrrin turned her face up, her expression petulant. "I'm not useless. I can look after myself and can't sit around waiting for you all day. This is where all the kids are. It's safe here."

Riony squatted in front of Lyrrin and took the child's gloved hands in her own. The leather was worn and cracked.

"It's entirely the opposite of safe. Safe is with me, or when I have to go, safe is in our home which you should be grateful to have. Which we'll be lucky to keep if Yoskar follows through on his threat to stop me from becoming a delver."

Lyrrin's lips wavered. "I'm sorry I got in a fight with Benjin."

Riony stood and extended her hand. "Come, I'll walk you back home, and I want you to stay there this time."

Lyrrin wrapped both arms around Riony's offered limb. "Why, where are you going?"

"Up above."

"Nooooo. I don't want you to."

Lyrrin tugged back, but Riony pulled her along to walk beside her, heading down the dimly lit path toward their home.

"I have to go. It's the only place to find green-leaf herbs, you know. They don't exactly grow around here. And we need trade."

"Can't you get some other job?"

"I know herbs. And they might be hard to come by, but even just a very few pieces of the right kind of green is more valuable than most jobs down here."

"Except delvers."

"Except delvers." Riony sighed. "Maybe we'll get lucky and Aishena and Yoskar will fall into a bottomless pit or get eaten by cave spiders soon, then I might get a chance. Until then, I'm going to need to sell some more herbs and fast."

Riony had hoped that her last harvest would have been enough to get them through until after delver trials, but Lyrrin was going through a growth spurt and eating like a bovin.

"Don't worry though. I've found a new foraging place. Safer than picking around near where the breachers go scavenging."

The land close to the Alderkin depths exits had been scraped bare anyway.

"Where?"

"I've found a warm spot. Up high above the snow line. There's a meltwater stream and I saw some green but haven't had a good search yet."

Lyrrin leaned away but didn't let go of Riony's arm. "A warm spot? They say dragon's nest in warm spots."

Riony swung her captive arm back and forth, dragging Lyrrin with it. Each swing grew a larger smile on the child's face.

"Who says? Wild dragons are practically extinct. I'd be more worried about the shadow dragon."

Lyrrin's eyes widened.

"Don't worry, if it shows up, I'll punch it so hard it will disappear in a puff of smoke." Riony brought her arms up to flex her biceps, lifting Lyrrin from the ground. "The trip is worth it. Just a quick harvest will keep us going until delver trials. I think I saw some shillgrue up there, too. I can make some more leather conditioner with it."

"My gloves are getting stiff again," Lyrrin conceded, hanging in the air and giggling. With one big swing, she jumped back to the ground, and her hood fell from her head.

Riony brushed a hand over her dark hair, seeing a slight cyan sparkle along the scalp, then quickly pulled the hood back up. "And I need to find more hair dye, too. We're almost out."

Lyrrin thought for a moment, then nodded. "Just be safe, okay? Also ..."

"What?"

"I'm huuungry," Lyrrin sang mournfully, eying the rope worm merchant as they passed. Riony felt a tight ache in her own stomach as well. On the long climb back up the stairs to home, she reached into the satchel at her side and handed over the hard strips of mushroom jerky.

"Just for you. Not for any pets." She eyed the bulge of Lyrrin's shirt just above her belt.

Lyrrin nodded and waited for Riony to open their door. Another reason their dwelling had been cheap was that the rolling, circular stone that formed the door often got stuck. The clever Alderkin mechanisms that made the solid weight slide easily were failing after decades without anyone with the knowledge to repair it, much like a lot of things in the depths. Lyrrin could squeeze through the gap, but Riony had to put her shoulder against the heavy stone and heave to get it open enough to go in herself.

Riony followed her sister into the two small rooms they called home. She grabbed a pair of gloves, then threw on an extra shirt and thick, fur-lined cloak over the sleeveless tunic she usually wore in the temperate caves.

She slung her backpack over one shoulder. "Now please, please-please-please, stay here for me? Kid snatchers have been around again."

"Yeah, sure." There wasn't even the attempt of submission on Lyrrin's face. "Just don't take too long, or I might get bored."

Riony pushed the front door open again, shaking her head. She was tempted to take Lyrrin along to keep an eye on her but couldn't put her in that kind of danger.

Glancing back, she saw a small, furry snout poke out of her sister's shirt to nibble on some offered food.

Riony ran a hand through her short, wild hair. "You live to defy me, don't you?"

Lyrrin stuck her tongue out. "We should always try to help others when we can. That's what Amma always said."

Yeah, and that's what got her and Pabba killed.

Keeping just herself and one child alive since then had been hard enough for Riony alone. That's all she could focus on, those two lives, one step at a time. Keep them housed. Keep them fed. Make sure her next trip to the overworld didn't get her killed.

"Take care of yourself. I won't be long." Riony turned away with a brave smile, doing her best to comfort Lyrrin, but her insides churned.

Every time she breached the overworld, she risked not coming back alive. And in a world where coming back dead was entirely a possibility, Riony didn't like the odds.

Two

Riony kicked at loose rocks along the crumbling tunnel and created a mental list of the herbs she hoped to gather on her trip. It helped to calm her nerves as waves of past trauma set upon her in anticipation of heading aboveground.

Corpsefoot and shillgrue should be around; they grow like weeds anywhere. Some hennan or tinctoria for Lyrrin's hair might be less likely. They grow more on the plains. But anything with some pigment in the leaves will do.

Anything is better than letting her natural color grow out. We'd be in trouble then.

The voice in her head sounded so much like her amma's, and she recalled her many times crouching in gardens or over a candlelit table strewn in leafy bundles as her mother told her how to identify each herb and its medicinal properties.

They would talk about which herbs were safe for expectant mothers, and which they were learning to use for wider purposes now that the cure-all silvernix was scarce.

It was important for midwives to understand herbal remedies since the use of unicorn blood on pregnant women had been prohibited for decades, due to it causing strange birth defects. They didn't know for sure, but Riony and her parents speculated that was why Lyrrin was the way she was.

"Learn your midwife skills well, and you'll always have good, secure employment under a dragonlord family," Amma had said, her voice full of hope and promise. "And with the knowledge of natural remedies we've kept while everyone else relied on unicorn blood, who knows what fortune our future might bring?"

Riony sniffed away the sensation of wetness in her nose and kicked at a larger chunk of stone, like a challenge between it and her toes.

The twisting path was separate from the major transit tunnels humans used to get in and out of the main cavern, and the carefully carved walls, decorated with organic swirls and knotwork patterns were dusty and cracking.

The tunnel was already picked bare of anything valuable by delvers long ago. Riony walked alone through the darkness, lit only by her personal small glow crystal hanging from a netted pouch on her belt.

Trailing her fingers along the intricate carvings on the wall, Riony felt the catch of tendrils of cave spider silk. She wiped her hand on her pants to scrub the gummy strands away.

Cave spiders were just one reason most humans avoided exploring the massive cave system and carved tunnels beyond the one inhabited cavern.

When the Alderkin realized they had lost the war and their home, they collapsed and destabilized whole areas, and scattered the remaining levels with traps, making venturing into the abandoned depths a risk only delvers took.

Riony had only explored this tunnel due to running around trying to recapture one of Lyrrin's escaped pets for her.

That little owlette had been determined to be free. Riony could relate.

The crumbling fractures in the walls grew worse as Riony continued higher, creating large holes in the stone. It was through one of these gaps that Riony had discovered a path into a natural cave system, which lead out to the overworld.

Reaching that gap again, Riony found it bigger than she'd last seen it. Debris lay across the ground around it, and Riony sucked air through her teeth and stared at the rocky ceiling. After making a silent plea that the mountain didn't collapse on top of her, she hefted one of the larger rocks out of her way.

Something glinted in the space where it had been. A short crystal blade half buried in the dirt.

"Whoa. Is that—?" Riony snatched it up greedily.

An Alderkin athame. She'd never held one herself. They were way too expensive—if they still held a charge.

It must have only been revealed by the crumbling walls since the last time anyone had been through. Riony brushed the silty dirt from the knife, holding it close to her glow crystal to see what sigil the athame was imbued with.

There was the standard harden rune that engraved almost all Aldkerin artifacts, to toughen the brittle crystal. Beneath it, a couple of curved lines, intersected by a third, were etched into one flat side of the dagger.

A cutting rune! Nice! Her excitement wavered as she racked her brain.

How does it go?

Riony hadn't seen this rune activated before. Spying on rune usage and trying to memorize all their activation sequences was more Lyrrin's thing. But with only three strokes, Riony figured it was worth having a guess.

She traced the lines with her finger, one, then another, then another. Nothing happened, so she tried a variation on the sequence.

Each line had to be traced in the right direction, in the right order, to activate an Alderkin sigil, and those wild inhuman people had never shared that knowledge. Anything humans had worked out how to activate had been through trial and error.

On her third attempt, the blade hummed briefly to life, glowing a dull yellow, then faded out before Riony could test its capabilities. She tried to activate it again, but nothing happened. She pouted and huffed. It was out of charge.

With an active cut rune, even a tiny blunt blade like this could slice through nearly anything. But without a charge, it was basically useless.

Sighing heavily, Riony dropped the athame into her backpack anyway. Lyrrin might like to see it, even if it didn't work anymore.

Riony climbed through the gap in the tunnel and marched through the adjoining natural cave. It held the musty smell of guano, but if any bats or owlettes made the rocky nooks and crannies their home, they were asleep now.

She put on her gloves as she went and pulled her heavy woolen cloak closed as icy wind whistled toward her. It grew strong, as though pushing her away, a warning that the overworld wasn't a place for her anymore.

Natural daylight filtered in, pale blue, through the curtain of frozen water that rose high before her. She traced the light rune on her glow stone to deactivate it. Glow stone charges lasted for ages, but she still tried to conserve its energy as much as possible.

A waterfall had frozen, forming a wall across the cave entrance, all rivulets and icicles, dripping with water that still ran in just a few places and tinkling like wind chimes.

The hole Riony had pushed out through last time had already begun to seal up, with lines of dripping ice like cage bars spreading across the gap. She tried to clear it away with protected fingers that already felt cold, but the ice wouldn't snap.

Ice was always harder than she expected. But she was strong, too. Wrapping her cloak around one arm, she cracked her elbow against the icicles.

It had been her time as a slave to the Heithorns that had made her strong. The work she'd been forced into, the weight she'd carried from such a young age. That strength had saved her life more than once.

Sometimes she felt like she should be grateful for that, except that she completely sparking hated every moment of that time.

With two more hits, she managed to clear away enough ice to squeeze through.

The sword hanging at her belt caught against the side of the hole and she had to readjust the scabbard midway.

The ex-dragonguard longsword often got in the way, but she'd go skinny-dipping with carnivorous olm before she went anywhere without it.

Frosty wind gusted around her, meeting her face with a pinching chill. Her cheeks tingled as Riony crawled through the gap and stepped out into the overworld.

This high into the mountains, snow was all she could see. Her path led to a place between peaks, so she couldn't look down onto the rest of the land, to see the scarred and burning hellscape it had become. She couldn't see the dragonkeeps looming in the distance.

Up there, she could pretend the world was healthy, peaceful, not plagued with death.

But the ever-present scent of dragon-fire hung in the air.

The sky was relatively clear, just a soft haze of smoke lingered, dulling the brightness of the sun.

Riony stood for a moment, turning her face to its warmth, relishing the feel of light on her skin. Her years underground had turned her complexion ashy. She missed how the sun had browned her skin to a warm, rich sienna.

Riony stomped out into the crunchy-slick snow, following the slow drip of water until that flow grew stronger, warmed by a hot patch of the mountain's molten heat under the surface.

Soon, along that meager flow, the snow cleared entirely, and a narrow stream emerged, rushing down the steep slope, surrounded by lichen-encrusted stone and just a few weak yet resilient green-leaf plants.

Riony smiled. She loved that color, that life that crept between the cracks, in even the most impossible of places.

Careful to not end up with a foot dunked in the icy water, she stepped around from rock to slippery rock, inspecting the plants.

Corpsefoot and shillgrue—as expected. She pinched off a generous number of sprigs from both. The shillgrue she'd keep and make into a leather conditioner, and the corpsefoot had value among women who didn't want to fall pregnant, so she could trade it well, too. A little bit of it went a long way, and overdosing had unpleasant side effects.

Riony was surprised to also find a small tuft of carrowmy (culinary), a patch of trailing genjermint (for sleeping tea— good for trade, too), and ... Hennen! Riony recognized the thin bronze leaves immediately.

But the plant was scrawny, far too small to provide enough to dye even just the roots of Lyrrin's hair.

Carefully, Riony scooped some extra dirt around the base of the plant, that had been exposed by the melting snow. Hopefully the next time she came back it will have grown large enough to harvest.

Riony stood from her crouched position and arched her back, stretching it out and rubbing her numbed hands together. Her breath puffed out in a cloud. She watched it with a smile, and as it cleared, up on the white ridge above her, something moved.

The hazy silhouette of something big, four-legged. A long, low howl carried to her on the wind.

A wolf? So far up here? Maybe it had been driven into the mountains by the shadow revenants and burning vengeance of the dragonlords like the rest of the mountain's inhabitants. Riony squinted at it, checking it wasn't headed her way.

She patted the hilt of her sword. *I won't bother you if you don't bother me, pup.*

Riony turned back toward the stream, when a larger, darker shadow flashed over her. Something massive, flying right above.

It could just be a bird. Don't panic.

Riony tensed, working hard to keep her footing as she looked up, terrified of what she might see.

Terrified that it would be the shadowdragon.

A leathery wing flapped, lifting snow crystals in gusts. A piercing scream burst into her ears.

It wasn't the shadowdragon. But it was a dragon.

Riony stood frozen, awestruck. A dragon, a huge one! Not one of the smaller steed-like crossbreeds the dragonriders mastered.

Riony's amma and pabba had held to the Rolanian belief that dragons were born from the souls of their ancestors that had fallen from their path to the stars, tragic creatures born to suffer and bring suffering.

But Riony wasn't so sure. That might have been some of her previous master's enthusiasm for dragons rubbing off on her, but Riony always thought there was something beautiful about the powerful beasts.

Riony shielded her eyes, trying to get a good look.

A seasong dragon, maybe, based on the size, although it was much paler than they normally were and farther from the ocean than it should be. There was no sign of a harness or saddle showing.

Another cry emerged from its wedge-shaped head as it lifted high into the air again, shimmering against the clear sky. It was immense, large enough to take Riony entirely into its mouth if it chose to.

Its snakelike neck led to a body that seemed unhealthily skinny and a long tail that was crooked and boney. Armored scales of silver with a few specks of black covered the beast, and Riony's breath caught as she watched its elegant swoop through the air.

A dragon. A true, wild dragon. Untamed. Unbound. It was beautiful.

And it was coming her way.

It changed angle midair, looping around and directing itself for her.

No, thank you. This is not the day I get eaten by a dragon.

Riony wasn't sure it had seen her yet, and she didn't want to wait and find out. She filled her lungs with frozen air and ran.

The dragon's shrill cry chased her as she crashed over slippery, slushy ground. Her boots skidded dangerously on the steep slope. She pushed on, faster, toward the safety of the caves.

The beat of the dragon's wings grew closer and a gust of wind knocked Riony off her feet, throwing her onto her side on the slick ground. She skidded like a sled, back the way she'd come. Spinning, she tried to slow her descent, but her hands only grabbed uselessly at loose snow.

She slid fast on her back, headfirst, down, down.

The ground disappeared beneath Riony. She grasped for anything to halt her fall. Her gloved fingers brushed against slick, frozen edges as she tumbled roughly into a narrow chasm.

The deep crevasse of ice swallowed her. She crashed against the hard walls as she fell. Screams were knocked from her burning lungs in a painful percussion.

Bones cracked.

She landed hard and faded away.

THREE

R iony awoke to a deep, dreadful sense of cold.
A thick, heavy cold, so encased around her bones
that shivering couldn't shake it free.

She'd never been so cold. And there was something
else there, too. Another withering sensation.

Pain.

Ouch. Wincing her eyes open, she looked up at the
thin ribbon of sky showing between the glassy walls that
enclosed her. A warm, golden light shone down.

Sunset, already? Riony tried to sit up, and agony jolted
through her. Her right arm throbbed and hung uselessly.

Her eyebrows rose at how she seemed to have acquired
an extra joint, a new bend between her elbow and wrist

where one shouldn't be. She looked away before the bile that was rising could escape her mouth.

A dull ache filled the back of her skull, and her hips and legs felt stiff and pockmarked with bruises. And there she was, some hundred or so steps straight down in a hole in the ice.

Well, this situation isn't much fun.

She muffled a groan as she brought herself into a sitting position. The pain from her arm made her eyes water, and the tears seemed to freeze instantly to her lashes. With an extra grunt, she got to her feet and reviewed her surroundings.

The crevasse ran like a gash in the glacier, narrow and disappearing off to either side. The walls were slick, clear, solid ice, hard as any stone. Climbing out seemed impossible, a dumb idea to try even with two good arms.

"Of course, I'm going to try anyway. What am I? Someone who doesn't try to do dumb and impossible things?" she said to her reflection in the ice.

She put on a brave smirk, but it faded quickly. She had to get out of there, one way or another. She was going home, no excuses. She was going to get home to Lyrrin.

Riony held on to the ice with her functioning hand and tried to support her weight with it enough to bring her feet up into footholds.

She balanced there for a moment, then tried to raise

herself again. Without her second arm to support her as she reached for a new grip hold, her feet slipped on the slick surface and she tumbled back down, smacking her broken arm onto the icy ground.

Her scream of pain echoed through the long, thin crevasse. Attempting to climb had not been a good idea. Dizziness threatened to take her away from consciousness again. She heaved in a deep breath.

Nope. Don't you dare pass out!

Riony sat up again, leaning her back against the sheer ice wall. She shook her head to clear it, her wild, red hair tumbling over her eyes.

Riony's good hand went to her neck, grasping for the acorn. Still there, not lost or damaged in the fall. She still had some luck on her side.

The temptation to use the precious, silver fluid the acorn contained was hard to resist. Although barely more than one drop, it would be enough.

It could be enough to save a life though. What was a broken arm compared to a life? That single drop of silvernix had been in her family for decades. How could she use it now?

I can't. It's too precious. I might need it one day, for Lyrrin, for saving a life. This is just a stupid little broken arm. Nothing I can't handle.

Also, how dumb would I feel if I fixed my broken arm and still couldn't get out of here?

Riony took stock. She still had her acorn—last resort. She still had her sword—another small miracle she hadn't landed on it. It was too long to splint her arm with, and the athame in her backpack too short.

She had a few handfuls of fresh herbs tucked into the pouches on her belt. No food. No water. Her clothes weren't suited for being out in the cold this long. She was supposed to have been home hours ago, but nobody knew exactly where she had gone.

She rolled her head left, then right, taking in the length of the crevasse.

There had to be another way out.

Up on her feet again, Riony found the way to the left quickly dead-ended around a corner.

She shuffled along the other way, through the thin crack between mountains of ice. If that orange glow over her shoulder was the setting sun, she was heading back toward the stream where she'd started.

She stumbled a couple of times, feet unable to grip properly on the satin-smooth ground. She slouched to her left, leaning her less painful shoulder against the wall for stability.

The crevasse narrowed into a sliver so thin that Riony

had to shimmy through, panicking partway when she thought she was stuck. She considered using that narrower section to prop herself between the walls and edge herself to the surface, but it widened out too quickly above head height.

On the other side of the tight section, the crevasse opened up again, finishing at another dead end.

No. No, I refuse to go out like this. How lame and boring, to freeze to death in a hole in the ice.

Riony wondered if she could pose herself in her final moments in some interesting and lewd way so that when someone found her rock-hard corpse in the distant future, they could at least have a laugh.

Giggling to herself, Riony had to admit that she was getting dangerously delirious. She turned on the spot, looking up and around, hoping for a smooth slope, somewhere easier to make the climb.

The dead end itself was less ice and more crumbling chunks of dirty snow. Maybe she could climb there.

Riony pressed her hand toward it, testing for purchase. It shifted dangerously. A small avalanche smashed around her feet. She dodged back. Rocks and mud mixed amongst the snow, landing hard.

She could only try to climb up there if she was ready to be buried alive. Which she was not.

Riony swore long and loud. When the landslide had

stilled, she stepped forward again to inspect the muddy mess. She must be close to the stream, where the solid ground emerged from beneath the snow, but where she stood, she stood on ice only, surrounded by ice left and right.

Bright, clear ice.

Riony ran her hand over the ice on one side, moving her face close to it. It looked thin, like a glass window. There was something behind it, the shadows and shapes of a hollow space, blurry through the wavy, frozen water. A snow cave? Tunnel? She had to hope it could be another way out of there.

Her body moved before her brain and Riony kicked at the thin ice. Her foot hit hard, sending shock waves through her. Every busted and broken part of her screamed with agony, and she wilted onto her knees, gasping with pain.

"Shut up, Yoskar! I can so think before I act. Sometimes. Sparks! Why do I always forget how hard ice is?"

Shaking off the pain, Riony wiped away tears. When she could see clearly again, she checked her efforts.

Not even a crack.

She put her face close to the transparent wall, angling side to side, trying to gauge the thickness.

Riony didn't know a lot about ice. She didn't know whether she was looking at something as thin as a dragonglass sheet window, or a wall so thick she'd be chipping through it for a year. The frozen water was deceptive in its clarity.

But she was sure there was a hollow on the other side.

It would still take work, but she couldn't think of another option with her broken arm making climbing impossible, and that climb remaining improbable even with both arms. She had to do something, and fast. As much as she pretended sheer willpower could fight against the bad blood shooting through her body from the injury, she was fading.

She had to break through.

Her longsword felt clunky in her left hand as she drew it. Weighing her options, she decided not to ruin the blade more than she already had by attacking the ice with it. She gave it a solid whack with the sharp pommel instead.

Happily, the ice chipped away. Unhappily, the impact made every part of her ache and her head spin.

The sword worked. It was her body that was the problem. If she could just deal with the pain somehow, she could chip through the ice easily, and hopefully crack right through.

She patted the pouch on her belt where she'd put the herbs she picked earlier, and a thought formed.

Okay, that's not a bad idea. It's more like the kind of idea that makes a bad idea feel good about itself.

Corpsefoot, when too much was taken, had the side effect of numbing an entire body. Along with also quickly leading to vomiting, organ failure, and death.

But if she took just enough, enough to work without pain but not kill herself outright, maybe she could get home in time to counteract the overdose.

And if not, at least she wouldn't feel herself die.

"This is fine. This is going to work. You're just poisoning yourself, just a little," she muttered, as she pulled the herb out with shaking, gloved fingers, and plucked one large fleshy leaf. No, maybe two? Definitely not more than two.

This is such a bad idea.

She placed them on her tongue, then chewed. Her lips twisted at the tart tang.

Then she sat and waited. If it worked, it wouldn't take too long. Then she could make her way back, use plumeberry tea to clear the toxins, and work on healing properly. She just had to stay awake. Stay focused. Not let the sick dizziness take over. Easy.

It was only a few minutes before the pain noticeably lessened, and soon Riony could move without any pain at all. She had to remind herself how damaged her arm was, unbandaged as it was, lest she risk damaging it further. She still couldn't properly move the hand on that side, but the numbing effect was all she needed for now.

The cold didn't bite at her anymore either and her shivering had stilled. Her eyelids felt heavy as she pulled her cloak off and wrapped it around the blade of her sword. Holding it at that point in her left hand, she swung it like a bat, smashing the hilt into the middle of the thin ice.

It jarred, shaking her whole body, but she felt nothing. White chips flew from the point of impact, and the pommel punctured the ice. A hairline crack spread from that hole. She struck again, and again, each blow chiseling away more ice, growing the hole larger, spreading the cracks out like a spiderweb.

She bared her teeth in a grim smile. She was doing it. She was going to get through. She felt no pain. Maybe she had taken just enough corpsefoot that she wouldn't—

Her stomach contracted, a violent sense of pressure without the pain, and she doubled over, vomiting onto her feet.

Oh no.

Sweat dripped down her forehead and she had to wipe it from her eyes. Maybe she hadn't taken just enough after all.

Riony turned back to the wall, sending all her strength into the swing of her sword, her eyes wide with fear. She had to work fast.

Again, and again, and then *crack*. The sword blade slipped from Riony's grasp as she tried to wrench it back for another swing. The hilt and pommel had broken through and stuck fast into the hole.

Riony stared at the cracking wall for a few deep breaths.

With a primal roar, she charged shoulder first into it. She felt the pressure of the collision, and then the ice gave way. It fractured and broke, falling in clear crystals around her.

She toppled through the newly created hole. Her sword, freed again, clattered at her side. She grabbed it with her good hand, clinging to it like a doll to her chest as she stood. Vomited. Fell. Stood again.

Keep moving.

The space that opened in front of her was vast, a smooth, curved cave of ice, with a solid rocky floor. The light of sunset filtered through the frozen water, mixing a rainbow into the cool blues. The cave extended off into the distance, past where Riony's rapidly blurring eyesight could see.

She stumbled through, desperately hoping for an escape. Her vision darkened, with spots and stars shooting through the murkiness.

Her body was so numb, she couldn't feel her feet moving underneath her, couldn't feel her tongue in her mouth. But her insides now felt both hot and cold, and twisted the wrong way as though wrung between unkind hands. Sweat ran down her chest.

For a moment, she couldn't remember where she was, just that she had to keep moving. Get home.

Something glinted in her path, tucked into a nook on one side.

She thought it was her imagination at first. Or maybe the glow of Alderkin magic. Maybe she'd made it back into the depths. *Where am I?*

But the shiny, metallic shapes were head-sized, oval, nested together in a pile of carefully arranged stones.

Eggs? What could make an egg that big? Not even the largest carrion bird. The answer seemed both impossible and so entirely clear at once.

Dragon eggs.

There was no time to be in awe, as sickness surged again through her, spilling the spatters of an empty stomach onto the ice. The world swayed.

Riony stumbled on. She followed a gust of air and shambled out like the living dead into the overworld again. Over one crest of deep snow, then another, unsure which direction she'd find home.

The final blood-red rays of the smoky sunset glared off the bright ground, blinding her.

Woozy and completely wrecked, she collapsed.

Her consciousness faded in and out.

Pain returned, shooting through her gut and chest, as though a giant had reached a hand into her rib cage and squeezed. Riony put every effort into standing, but her body only twitched and gagged in response. Her head felt clamped in a vise, ever tightening, bringing darkness with it.

No. I'm not dying here. Lyrrin needs me.

Her body moved again, and she couldn't tell if it was through her own effort or some other force. Was she still stubbornly moving forward, one step at a time? She couldn't make sense of anything. She felt like she was flying.

Then it became clear she was being moved, carried on something soft and warm. Fur tickled her nose. Then she was dumped, unceremoniously, onto rocky ground.

She managed to crack her eyelids open, gaze rolling loosely around, seeking her savior.

The wolf was there.

It spoke to her with a voice from her past.

"Don't ever come back here again."

FOUR

Lyrrin paced the claustrophobic confines of the quarters she shared with her sister.

Why hasn't Riony come home yet?

There were so many perils aboveground that could have given Riony a reason not to return home. Lyrrin's stomach flip-flopped, and she shook her head, trying and failing to shove those intrusive thoughts away.

She squeezed her eyes shut, huffing out a grunt of frustration. She didn't want to think about *reasons*.

Instead, she pouted.

Lyrrin didn't grieve the absence of sky the way Riony and the older people in the undercity seemed to. Maybe it was because she hadn't had many years of it that she could remember and miss before moving underground.

She did miss playing, though. She missed playing with Riony, back when their parents were around to be the parents, and Riony wasn't such a fun-killing tyrant.

It's been ages. I'm so bored.

They owned no clock, and there was no sunrise or sunset in the undercity. Sometimes, when it was quiet enough, Lyrrin could hear the bell of their neighbor's clock downstairs, but the air was currently filled with the sounds of bats, marking the coming of night in their own way, chorusing a shrieking, chittering cacophony as they awakened and flew out to feed.

Lyrrin lay on her back on the floor of their bedroom, the few thick blankets and bovin furs that made their bed barely cushioning between her and the limestone floor.

She dragged her arm backward and forward, pinching a little strip of mushroom jerky in her fingers. Sir Butterfur Spelunkychunks chased it in lithe, pouncing leaps across the roughly knitted wool.

At least since coming to the depths there had been lots of interesting animals to play with. Like cave otters. Lyrrin loved how they moved, like slick, shiny ribbons, whether diving through the underground pools or skittering up rocky walls.

Sir Butterfur was a young one, only about as long as

Lyrrin's leg, and a sweet pale caramel color, similar to their limestone surroundings. The adults could get as big as Lyrrin and plagued the markets and public baths in search of food like adorable furry thugs.

Owlettes were also high on Lyrrin's list of favorite cave creatures. She didn't like the bats, with their scrunched in, angry faces. Some cloud mice would be nice to have, though. But they were so fast.

If only there was more room in their home to keep pets, maybe she'd have more luck in actually *keeping* them.

She'd been secretly feeding Butterfur for weeks before she managed to lure him into having snuggles, but he still came and went as he pleased if she didn't keep him buttoned up in her too-large tunic.

There wasn't much space for anything in the quarters Riony had rented. Only two rooms, each so small Riony could lay lengthways across them and reach out and touch the walls. Lyrrin wasn't tall enough to do that trick yet, but she was still growing.

A moth-eaten patchwork curtain separated one room from the other, defining a living area and a sleeping area, both lit by a single dimming glow stone.

The Alderkin amenities built into the living area and small bathroom to the side still mostly worked too, which was good in a city where so many facilities were failing.

They had hot and cold ventilation, running water, and a little area they could cook over a crucible marked with a burn rune. The bathing area was broken though, so they had to go and use the public hot baths.

Lyrrin had filled their one large pot with warm water, hoping Butterfur might like to splash in it, but he didn't show interest in getting in.

"Go on. I'm not trying to cook you. I promise."

Some of the bigger apartments that the delvers got to live in had their own hot spring baths big enough to swim in. Benjin had bragged about theirs. If Lyrrin had something like that, Sir Butterfur Spelunkychunks could swim around all day without fear of becoming a meal.

What if Riony can't become a delver because I fought with Benjin?

Then she'd never get a home with their own hot bath for pets to swim in. Lyrrin pouted. Benjin was an infuriating brat though. And if she found out he was the one who ate one of her pets she held fast to her promise of vengeance.

Lyrrin lured Butterfur close with the treat, then pulled him in for a hug. He wriggled in her grip, pointy teeth gnashing at the hard jerky. He was always so hungry, like she felt lately. She'd eaten almost all of what Riony had given her already and her stomach still grumbled.

She got up to see if there was anything else to eat in

their small dwelling.

The previous Alderkin residents of these rooms had carved shelving into the rock walls of both rooms, with beautiful, flowing curves and leafy patterns framing them, but Lyrrin and Riony had few belongings to store there.

Lyrrin checked through their supplies. One jar had a handful of root flour in it, but Lyrrin wasn't allowed to cook while Riony was out and wasn't very good at making flatbread anyway.

There wasn't much else. Some old cutlery and dinted metal bowls, their ratty, secondhand and ill-fitted clothes, plus some multipurpose rags. One shelf held a line of mostly empty glass jars that Riony kept her herbs in, and Lyrrin had some bottles she'd scavenged that she liked to play at potion making with.

She didn't have much to put in them, but liked to scratch pretty patterns and Alderkin runes on the sides and imagine they were magic. Riony had taken their backpack with her, the one that had carried everything they'd owned as they had escaped the overworld into the depths.

There wasn't much in it anymore, none of the cool ropes and tools like delvers had that could help on her journey, but Riony always took it with her when she went out scavenging for herbs. Not that she ever filled it. It seemed to be getting harder and harder to find green things growing.

On the highest ledge of the shelves sat a doll made of corn husks and fabric remnants which Lyrrin pretended she was too old for now. But sometimes she got it down and held it close to her nose so she could smell the way the earth above and time with family used to smell, before she'd lost them both.

A small anxiety brewed within Lyrrin as she stared at that doll. That loss could happen to her again.

No. Riony will be home soon. She's not late because of reasons. Not bad reasons. Some other reason I can be angry at her about.

Lyrrin tucked her worry down deep. Better to huff at the boredom and tease Butterfur with the last of her food than to think about how Riony should have been back by now. She sat down again on the blankets and tore another tiny strip to dangle in front of the otter.

Lyrrin considered returning to the orphans' den to play. It wasn't so late that she couldn't find a friend to spend time with. Zade never scolded them for playing into the evenings. It would serve Riony right for making her wait so long if she came home to find her gone again.

We have to be extra careful, because of how you're different. Riony's warning came to her. Because it was, at least in part, Lyrrin's fault she couldn't go and play, couldn't be with the other children.

The stories of kid snatchers were real. Benjin had told her all about some of his friends from the orphans' den that had gone missing.

He really liked to boast, even about awful things.

Lyrrin hated that because of how she looked she might be a more tempting target. Her unnaturally blue eyes did attract attention, and that was even with the effort they put in to keep her hands and hair disguised.

All because Lyrrin had been born different. A mix of distant races with a complexion and features not normally seen in these parts where Taens and Rolanians were the norm, and strange even beyond that.

So she should be grateful to have a private room, and she should follow Riony's guidance and rules. But it was all just *so unfair*.

"This is the place, up here!" A muffled voice came through the stone front door. It sounded like Benjin.

Lyrrin stilled to listen better. Butterfur tackled her unmoving fingers, pulling at them with his grabby little claws and nipping at the jerky with his pointy fangs.

"Ouch! Naughty!"

There was a thumping knock at the door, and Lyrrin sat bolt upright. She herded the cave otter into a corner and threw a blanket over him.

Nobody is eating you! Then she pulled her gloves on and hood up before going to open the door.

It only rolled halfway, sticking again, and without Riony's help, she couldn't push it wider.

Benjin stood there, bouncing from one foot to another, face flushed with excitement. The light of the glowstone glittered off the expensive trim of his neat, fitted shirt.

Lyrrin fidgeted with her baggy, rolled-up sleeves and turned her nose up at him. "What do you want?"

"We found something that belongs to you!" He grinned badly, lips shaky and more agitated than happy.

Lyrrin frowned, checking her gloves, then her pockets. She didn't have much she could lose. Only her handkerchief and a pretty rock she'd picked up, both still there. "What are you talking about?"

Heavy footsteps and heavier breaths drummed up the stairs.

"Right at the top? Of course this peasant lives right at the sparking top," a female voice muttered.

Benjin puffed out his chest. "It's your sister. Delvers found her, collapsed in a tunnel. She's real sick. My brother and sister are bringing her up."

Lyrrin's eyes opened wide as she took in Benjin's news. "Riony's sick?"

She should do something, prepare, be ready to help her.

But how? She turned on the spot, trying to think about what Riony would do. She dashed about, straightened the blankets, grabbed some washcloths, then put them down again. Went to fill a cup with water and then put it back.

What do I do? Flushed and flustered, she turned back to Benjin again. There was nothing she could do but wait for Riony to arrive.

Maybe it wasn't so bad.

"Stop looking so happy about it!" she snapped at Benjin.

"Hey, we're the heroes here today. You want your sister back or should I tell them to turn around?"

"No way I'm carrying this dead weight a moment longer." Aishena reached the top of the steps, carrying Riony by the legs. Yoskar followed behind, holding up the rest of her under her armpits. His glasses had slipped and were balanced precariously on the end of his nose.

Riony hung limp and bowed between them. Her red hair clung wetly to a face that was mottled mauve and yellow and she smelled like off meat.

Her sword was stuck crookedly through her belt and the tip scraped along the floor. The backpack she'd worn before was off and balanced in the bend of her stomach and lap, her cloak gone.

"Where can we put her?" Yoskar asked.

Feeling light-headed, Lyrrin stepped back, clearing the

doorway. She pointed to the bedroom.

The delver siblings grunted and swore as they squeezed through the doorway and dropped Riony on the blankets in a not-gentle way. She groaned, dry retched, then stilled again.

"What's wrong with her?" Lyrrin asked in a small voice.

Aishena rolled her eyes. "Razed if we know. Don't know what she was doing up that disused tunnel. Only found her from her groans echoing out. Niskina thought she was an Alderkin ghost."

"Count yourself lucky we found her." Yoskar brushed himself down, then stood still, staring at Lyrrin.

When she only stared back, Yoskar sighed and gestured with upturned hands. "Generally, we get *paid* for the things we find when delving."

"*Yoskar*," Benjin whispered, looking mortified.

The older brother gave him a reproachful glare. "This is how the system works and it's how we earn the money we need to survive. And keep you alive, Benj."

He turned back to Lyrrin. "We're owed something for carrying this cumbersome body all the way up here."

Aishena put her hands on her knees, bending over to take a few deep breaths. "Seriously, how does she weigh so much? And stink so bad?"

The flames of anger heated Lyrrin's neck. "You want me to *pay* you?"

"Of course," Yoskar said flatly.

"Well ... like Benjin said, my sister already belongs to me. You're just returning her, so I'm not paying you anything!" Lyrrin stomped toward them, trying to get them to back out of the doorway.

They didn't move, and she had to stop before her face ended up pressed against Yoskar's armor-covered stomach.

"Wow, is this really all they have?" Aishena craned her neck, taking in the rooms.

Yoskar ignored Lyrrin, looking over her head. "That sword she carries around is decent enough. I'd take that as payment."

"Get out!" Lyrrin pushed at Yoskar, an immovable wall.

Aishena watched the futile battle for a moment, then grabbed Yoskar by his shoulder. "Come on, leave them be."

Then in a voice Lyrrin suspected she wasn't meant to hear, she said, "Let the kid say goodbye."

Benjin must have heard too. His head whipped toward Aishena, jaw dropped.

"GET OUT!" Lyrrin shrieked, tears running now over her hot cheeks.

The delvers stepped back, and Lyrrin slammed her fist against the door's closure mechanism.

Benjin stared back at her, pale-faced, as the door rolled closed.

Yoskar's voice carried in, muffled by the stone. "We'll come back another time for what we're owed. A debt must be repaid."

Lyrrin drew two deep breaths, quelling the shakes that were building within her, then raced over to her sister.

FIVE

The delvers had dropped Riony on her side, and she lay there like a lifeless doll.

Lyrrin carefully rolled her onto her back, tucked a pillow under her head, and straightened out her legs, then arms. When lifting Riony's right arm, Riony cried out fiercely, startling Lyrrin and making her let go. The arm flopped to the ground and Riony groaned again.

"What is it?" she asked, but Riony only moaned, her breath rough and panting.

Tentatively, Lyrrin touched the arm again, and saw the hints of bruising peeking out from the cuff of Riony's long shirt. She moved the arm slower this time and saw there was something wrong with how it bent within the clothing.

"Shh, I'm sorry. I'll try to be more gentle."

Riony didn't respond. Her head lolled, sweat running in rivulets all over, and she smelled of vomit and worse.

Lyrrin touched Riony's forehead with the back of her forearm and found it hot. She'd had enough of her own fevers in the past to know how Riony had cared for her then, so she opened the vent in the side of the room that had cool air flowing through and brought the bowl of water closer, still clean, since Butterfur hadn't swum in it.

She dipped a strip of cloth in it to dab Riony's forehead with, and as she did, Riony's eyes fluttered open.

"Plmmmbriss." Riony shifted, her left arm lifting, then falling again.

"What?"

Riony grunted, eyes winced closed, and brought her hand up to point at the shelf of herbs.

"Plumeberries?" Lyrrin asked.

Riony nodded in a wobbly way. "Tea. Hot. *Now*."

"For your arm?" Lyrrin frowned, she didn't understand. Riony had a fever, and something wrong with her arm, but plumeberries were for poisoning.

"Is broken," Riony murmured, mouth slow and slurred. Her eyes were bloodshot and yellow-tinted, unfocused.

"Broken?" Lyrrin's voice came out high.

"Mmm."

"What do I do?"

"Straighten. Bandage."

Lyrrin reached a hand toward the acorn around Riony's neck. "Should we …?"

"No. Not … me. Not so bad." Riony gritted her teeth, closed her eyes, and was silent for a long moment.

Lyrrin failed to suppress a whining sob.

Riony stirred again, but her eyes didn't open. "S'okay. You can do this. First … hot tea."

"Okay," Lyrrin said, grateful for instructions, but unsure as to how to follow through on them. The long-sleeved shirt Riony wore was a thick, stiff fabric and had twisted itself tight around the broken arm, making it hard to inspect. Probably not good for the fever either.

"Can you take your shirt off?"

Riony's head had drooped to one side, and she didn't answer.

I have to do it then. No! First tea!

Lyrrin skittered across to the cooking area and traced the burn rune on the crystal crucible. It lit up, red and hot, and she placed a metal bowl of water on the top.

Then she went to the herb shelf, grabbing and checking jars—dropping one, kicking the broken pieces to the side, eyes blurry with tears—until she found one with just a few hard, dry berries in the bottom.

"How many? Is this right?"

Riony didn't respond.

Lyrrin sniffed and swallowed as she dropped all of them into the heating water. Her chest burned and throat closed as Aishena's voice echoed in her memory.

Let the kid say goodbye. Say goodbye. Say goodbye.

She knelt back by Riony's side. Riony still didn't move, but her throat pulsed with a rough heartbeat and panting breath.

She's too hot. Lyrrin tugged on the sleeve of Riony's good arm, inching the long shirt off. She had to pull, then readjust Riony, then pull, then roll, bit by bit to free Riony from just one side. And the other side she'd have to do even more carefully. Lyrrin let out a small, frustrated whine.

By the time she'd stripped off the layer, she'd worked up a sweat, and the water on the stove had boiled over.

Lyrrin ran over, grabbed the bowl off, and deactivated the rune. The heat warmed through the thick leather of her gloves but didn't burn. She poured the hot tea into a cup, spilling half of it as she sobbed at the wrong moment. She set it aside to cool enough for Riony to drink.

Returning again to her sister, Lyrrin inspected the bared wound. The sight of it made Lyrrin's lips twist into a crooked line, as crooked as the forearm itself. The hand was swollen and purple. The fingertips had turned black.

She backed away, scooting into the corner of the room and

pressing herself to the wall. For a long moment, she couldn't hold back her tears, and they came in messy, gulping sobs.

Say goodbye.

Butterfur popped out from among the blankets and came over to sniff at what was happening. She grabbed for him, cuddling him tight until he nipped her arm and wriggled free.

Say goodbye.

"No!" she screamed and rose back to her feet in a fury.

She wasn't useless. She chose to listen to the echo of Riony's words instead.

You can do this.

Lyrrin wiped her eyes hard. "Tea. Hot tea."

Holding the cup in one hand and squeezing Riony's mouth open with the other wasn't easy. Lyrrin squealed in frustration every time a splash of tea missed and dribbled onto Riony's cheeks and chin. But some seemed to go down. Riony's throat worked, swallowing. And soon the cup was empty.

What next? Straighten? Eeeewwwww.

Lyrrin winced as she touched the puffy red and black skin of Riony's forearm, grateful for her gloves so she wasn't making direct contact. Then, whimpering loudly, she squeezed, pressing the arm into something more like a straight line.

As she pushed, she could feel the edges of jagged bone under her fingers. She tried to press those pieces of bone together as well, but Riony cried out in a wailing howl.

She couldn't do it, couldn't hurt Riony like that. It would have to be straight enough.

Bandage was next. When she and Riony had first come to the Alderkin depths, Lyrrin had more than her fair share of twisted ankles from racing around the uneven tunnels. She'd seen how Riony bandaged her many times, but trying it herself now, it just didn't seem to work the same way.

In her thick gloves she just couldn't get the bandage to hold, and it would loop loosely round and round. Every attempt jostled the fractured arm around more than Lyrrin thought was good, too.

With a glance over her shoulder to double-check the front door was closed, she slipped off her gloves.

She stared for a moment at her strange fingertips, the blue-tinted nails too dark and thick. Too sharp. Some strange affliction of birth, better hidden away.

Lyrrin tried again. The bandage went on tight and held when she tied and tucked in the end.

Sitting back with her legs splayed beside her, Lyrrin breathed out in a long sigh. Butterfur came over and sniffed around Lyrrin's pockets, but when they proved empty of treats, he went back to the corner, burrowing around and making a nest.

What do I do next? Lyrrin was tired. Her eyes felt hot as burning crucibles in their sockets. Riony was supposed to look after *her*. This was too hard.

Lyrrin bundled her knees to her chest and hugged them tight as tears broke free again.

Riony slipped between the seams of reality and dream. The few times she woke, she did so in pain. So much pain, she wondered whether living was really the thing she wanted to do.

But she would, for Lyrrin.

And every time she woke, Lyrrin would be there, bringing a bowl near her mouth to catch the endless rounds of sickness that spilled from her. Trying to get her to drink tepid, unstrained tea. Getting the bowl again when the tea inevitably came back up. Talking to someone ... *Sir Butterfur Spelunkychunks?*

Then the agony would be too great, and Riony would fade away.

She tried to hold on, turning her mind to the task of remembering where she was, what had happened.

She'd fallen into the ice, broken her arm. Poisoned

herself—not her brightest moment.

There had been a dragon. A mother dragon.

There had been dragon eggs.

Had that really happened? It felt like a dream from a lifetime ago. Eggs in the ice, a glowing cave, a talking wolf. No. Those must be dreams.

She slept and mumbled and remembered. Her parents were there with her, alive again, in a memory that felt as recent, as real as the others. They weren't happy that they had to flee, but the tiny, stolen bundle meant they couldn't stay.

The bloody sword in Riony's small hand meant they couldn't stay.

They weren't happy with her. But she was happy to see them. She tried to warn them of their future, as though she could travel back through time in her dreams and stop their deaths from happening.

Then she held them and cried.

Don't ever come back here again. The wolf spoke, startling her into consciousness.

That voice ... another hallucination.

Riony lay still, eyes unopened, waiting for the wave of pain to hit. It rose, but didn't crash over her and overwhelm her entirely. She stayed still longer, relishing the unexpected experience of consciousness, as voices drifted to her.

"I said come back when she's better." Lyrrin sounded like she did when she spoke through clenched teeth.

"Better? Honestly, I can't believe she's lasted this long." It was Yoskar. "I'm not waiting. I want payment now."

"We haven't got any money."

"You must have something valuable in there."

Silence for a moment. "We don't have anything. Riony's really sick. Just leave us alone."

"What did she do to get beaten up like that? Slip on a cave snail?" That was Aishena, her voice an icy, elegant sigh.

Yoskar huffed. "Proves that she never had what it takes to be a delver. She went wandering around where she shouldn't have been and paid the price. The depths aren't a playground."

"She is so tough enough to be a delver! She's sick and hurt 'cause she faced a dragon! A real brooding amma dragon!"

What? Riony's eyes snapped open. What had she said through her sickness? What did Lyrrin know? And why was Lyrrin telling the delvers?

Riony rolled onto her side, groaning as she got her feet underneath her. Since Lyrrin's announcement, things had gone quiet.

"She's lying. She's always making things up." That was Benjin.

"No. No, the entrance guards said they saw something

last week, too. Idiots said it was the shadow dragon, but whiter." Yoskar spoke again, low and thoughtful. "A wild dragon? A *mother* dragon? Brooding? You mean there are eggs out there somewhere?"

No reply.

Yoskar barked, "Where? Where did your sister see them?"

A squeak came from Lyrrin, and Riony moved faster, supporting herself against the wall as dizziness washed over her. Her legs moved waywardly beneath her, humming with pins and needles.

A grunt came from Yoskar as Lyrrin remained silent.

"Aish! Where did Niskina say they found her?"

Aishena replied, too softly for Riony to hear.

Yoskar said, "Because we can't let a wild dragon brood here. It could attract attention. Attention we don't want."

"But ... a wild dragon? I don't think I can—"

Yoskar sighed dramatically and ground out the words. "If we get rid of the *eggs*, we get rid of the *dragon*, and we don't have to worry about it."

Riony pulled open the curtain between the two small rooms and saw Yoskar standing in the half-open front door, grasping Lyrrin by the shoulder of her tunic.

Aishena spoke again, from somewhere outside, delivering a string of directions in some kind of delver slang Riony didn't understand.

Yoskar let Lyrrin go with a shove, and his gaze turned to meet Riony's. Fierce and predatory. "Thank you for bringing this to our attention. I'm pretty sure I know where to find the nest. We'll crush every last egg under our heels, and you can consider your debt paid."

"No, you can't!" Lyrrin's words matched those Riony spoke in her head, her mouth still too gummy and throat too dry to speak.

The delver turned away.

"Stop." The word came out of Riony as a gravelly croak.

Lyrrin turned at the sound, wide, crying eyes taking in Riony.

Yoskar and his siblings were already gone. On their way to destroy the eggs Riony had seen in the snowy cave.

SIX

Lyrrin's bottom lip wobbled. "They won't really break the eggs, will they?"

Riony opened her mouth to say something comforting, but it would have been a lie.

Most people in the depths hated dragons. They were the beasts the Taen dragonlords rode, using their power to turn the Rolanian people to slaves and their lands to ash. And Rolanians were the majority of the population hiding from that fate in the undercity.

Let alone the other draconic being that haunted the skies, the shadowdragon, bringing an undead blight wherever it touched the ground.

Whether from religious belief or personal experience,

dragons meant death or oppression and everybody in the undercity had lost something to a dragon one way or another. Most would take any chance they got to remove a few from the world.

Aishena and Yoskar were more of an unknown quantity. They had the look and bearing of Taen dragonlords themselves, but it certainly sounded like they wanted to see the eggs destroyed. And it was just the kind of thing a lightless jerk like Yoskar and his spooky sister would take joy in.

Riony cleared her throat. It felt ripped and raw, and her stomach made some provocative noises. She couldn't tell if the ongoing sickness was the corpsefoot poisoning about to knock her off for good, or the plumeberries doing their job in removing those toxins. Either way, her insides sucked right now, and her outsides weren't a whole lot better.

Riony pressed her forehead to the cool wall beside her. "Maybe they won't find the eggs. But now they know ..."

"I'm sorry. I'm sorry I told. I just didn't want them to think you weren't strong enough to be a delver."

Riony half smiled at that.

Fat tears splashed down Lyrrin's pink cheeks. "I didn't think they'd do something to the eggs. Can you stop them? Please? We can't let them kill *babies*."

Dispose of the newborn. It can't be allowed to live.

No! You can't kill a baby!

Old memories mixed like blurry dreams into reality.

Riony shook her head, more to try to clear it than as a reply. She was woozy and her arm felt wrong. The pain had lessened but it felt hot, tight, and crooked. Her fingers on that side wouldn't move.

That was my good hand, too.

"I don't think I can. If the mother dragon comes back ..." Riony didn't hate that dragon or her unborn eggs enough to want them destroyed, even if it had scared her into falling down that crevasse.

It was wild and free, and there was something so beautiful about that in a world where most dragons were tamed into utter subservience, simple tools to be exploited for their power in every way.

But when Riony's whole body felt like it had been broken into parts and put back together by an overenthusiastic toddler with a toy hammer, she wasn't sure what she could do.

"They can't break the eggs. They can't hurt the babies," Lyrrin pleaded again.

Lyrrin, who had brought home an injured owlette and hid it in her pocket for days before it flew away, who had been devastated when another of her pets was turned into a dinner by some hungry undercity dweller.

Lyrrin who cared about every creature big or small— how would she handle bringing about the deaths of unborn dragon babies?

Riony at least had to try to stop it happening. She could talk the delvers out of it, lead them the wrong way, something. She had no sure plan, still too addled from the effects of broken bones and vomiting up more than her own body weight to think it through.

But she could try.

Not like she hadn't taken extreme measures in the past in order to save a baby's life.

She gave Lyrrin a single nod.

"I want to come, too. I want to help."

"Absolutely not." Riony grabbed her long-sleeved shirt and put it on. She had to bite her tongue to avoid screaming as she bent her bad arm to put it through the sleeve.

She noted the bandaging there. Nice and neat, but no splint, and not tight enough. Lyrrin must have tried so hard, though. Riony's cloak had been lost somewhere in her previous misadventure. She hoped she wouldn't be out in the cold long this time.

What else did she need? She couldn't think straight, and her vision clouded and swam. She had to hurry if she wanted to stop the delvers in time. "Stay here."

"But—"

"*Stay,*" Riony growled.

Lyrrin watched her with scarlet-tinted, tear-filled eyes

as she turned away.

As the door rolled closed between them, a tiny shriek came through the stone. "I'm not useless!"

Riony took the stairs. She couldn't manage the fast way down when she could barely keep track of her own limbs. Her lucidity blurred in and out as she stumbled madly through the undercity tunnels in a haze of pain and fever, trying to catch up to the delver siblings.

More than once she had to pause, hold herself still and swallow back a swell of nausea. More than once, she failed, gagging up a disturbing pink foam from a raw and empty stomach. Her rib cage felt like it was on fire, slowly roasting everything within it.

It was easier to catalogue the parts of her that *didn't* bring her immense suffering. Currently: zero.

The cyan light brightening the pathways glittered off where she sweated right through her shirt, and people looked at her aghast as she barged around them.

The urge to just curl up on the cool cavern floor and sleep was overwhelming. Then she imagined Lyrrin's face if she returned having failed. She wiped her dripping forehead and pressed on.

Riony reached the tunnel leading to the frozen waterfall and hoped Aishena and her brother hadn't found the right way. All they knew was where she'd been found ...

wherever that was.

How she'd even gotten back and where she'd fallen, Riony couldn't remember, but it made sense it was somewhere along the same path she'd used before.

And Aishena and Yoskar were delvers. They knew all the tunnels of the depths and would know this one too. They had enough clues to give them some idea of where they were going. It wouldn't take them long to find the hole into the external cave.

How long have I been out of it?

If it hadn't been long, if it hadn't snowed since then, there was no doubt the delvers could follow her trail across the white plains back to the ice cave and eggs it held.

Riony picked up her pace through the rough, natural cave up to the frozen waterfall exit, and as she stepped out into the bright white of the snow-shrouded world, there were Aishena and Yoskar.

A moment of hope that she'd caught up, that they hadn't found the eggs, was shattered by the triumphant look on Yoskar's face as they walked back toward her.

Riony exhaled a misty breath. "What did you do?"

"We did what we had to do to keep our family safe," Yoskar said as he went by, then threw back at Riony, "That's what you do when you're worthy of being a delver."

Aishena followed right behind. She pretended as though

Riony wasn't even there, just scowled and bumped into her shoulder as she passed.

Riony steadied herself, watching them leave. A bitter taste filled her mouth. To crush unborn eggs ... did they really do it?

Riony had to see the truth with her own eyes. The snow, slippery and compressed from multiple passages marked a clear path for her and crunched as Riony plunged along the trail downhill. She tumbled like a twig in a stream all the way to the ice cave.

The entrance was large enough for a dragon, but obscured behind a drift of fluffy white that gathered as the wind buffeted more snow against it. Riony didn't feel the cold as wind gusted through her thin clothing, her body aflame with fury and sickness.

She hadn't had a clear look at the cave before, too ill and too rushed, and again it went by in a blur, nothing more than shining ice above and to her sides and crisp, frosty dirt beneath her feet.

Reaching the deepest part of the cave, Riony blinked and wiped at her burning eyes, seeking the dragon eggs.

Where the bright, metallic orbs had once sat, perfectly arranged in a nest of warmed stones, now there was messy carnage.

Shards of textured shell, coated in slimy red film, were

scattered around three tiny, fleshy lumps. Barely on the cusp of being grown enough to be recognizable as baby dragons, and small, too small. They spilled lifeless from their smashed shells. The air had a coppery tang.

Riony dropped to her knees in front of the broken creatures, mouth open in disgust, and a heavy, unexpected weight of grief descended on her.

They had done it. They had killed them.

The delvers wouldn't even have needed to touch the dragonlings themselves. They looked too underdeveloped to survive the harsh world outside their nurturing eggs. All it took was cracking the shells.

It wasn't the most terrible outcome, having three less dragons in the world. They were awful, destructive creatures.

These weren't dragonlord dragons, tamed and bound to do their bidding. But it didn't mean they would stay that way. They were likely to be captured by dragonlords and enslaved too, just another tool of oppression. And even if they managed to remain wild, they could still kill and destroy.

It wasn't terrible that they were gone. They were just three dumb dragons, in a land full of them.

But if their deaths weren't such a terrible thing, why was Riony weeping so hard?

Her previous master had berated her for having a soft

spot for dumb animals. But it was the Rolanian way. All creatures were siblings, all were to be treated with care and respect—all except for dragons. Them, and unicorns now long gone, stood apart.

But deep down, Riony couldn't shake the feeling that a life was a life, and it hurt her deep inside to see these tiny lives extinguished. And if it hurt her this much ...

What am I going to tell Lyrrin?

Riony bowed her head. She reached out her remaining functional hand and touched a broken egg. "I'm sorry I couldn't save you."

Her touch disturbed the tenuous pile. The remnants of shell cracked even more, and the contents flopped onto the ground, revealing a fourth, smaller egg beneath it. Also damaged, with large cracks running down the length, revealing a slowly leaking membrane. But not fully broken.

Riony's heart rate kicked up. She shuffled closer and rolled the egg carefully out from amongst the others, bringing it onto her lap. It was slippery with bright-red blood, but that seemed to be from the other eggs. The insides of this one still seemed fairly full, despite the leak. The egg still held its shape.

At the intersection of a few fractures was a larger hole where the membrane spread across, intact, like a fogged-up window. Riony peered at the softly churning liquids within.

Something squirmed, and Riony gasped back. The movement inside the egg sent a splash of gooey, clear fluid spilling out from the leak onto her hands.

More wriggling, then a slithery body pressed against the membrane window. Red-veined and translucent, the beat of a tiny heart could be seen, fluttering.

A heartbeat that slowed visibly, fading before Riony's eyes.

SEVEN

*I*t's going to die.
It was a fact. A simple, unchangeable fact.

It's going to die like the others.

And there was Riony, stuck as a useless observer in that moment between life and death, staring at the tiny, fading heartbeat, and wanting that fact to be untrue.

She shuffled the egg carefully off her lap, placing it back on the warm patch on the ground. The mother dragon had picked that spot for a reason, the one warm place in a world of frost and ice. It needed to stay warm. But Riony knew that wouldn't be enough to save it, as another dribble of fluid leaked from the broken membrane.

She couldn't fix that torn, protective skin.

Her good hand lifted as though possessed and wrapped around the acorn tied around her neck. An unconscious action, but it brought a shock of possibility along with it.

"Whoa, no, no, no." Her head shook. She wasn't really considering it, was she? She couldn't.

She lurched unevenly back to her feet, pacing away, as though distance could remove her from the tragedy about to happen. Remove any responsibility for it happening ... or not happening. Her thumb rubbed the smoothed side of the acorn.

It's going to die.

No. The silvernix was precious, too precious to consider using. Not to mention that it was forbidden to use unicorn blood on animals.

Riony scoffed. She'd always thought that was a dumb rule. She'd had that argument before as a child, screaming in fury at her parents to save the barn cat at their master's estate, back when they'd still lived aboveground. It had been burned by dragon fire and suffered in its last moments.

She'd adored that cat. It hadn't seemed right, watching it die when they could have saved it. A life was a life, that was the Rolanian way.

Her parents remained firm that their precious silvernix was for nothing but one of their own lives. Not that it had saved either of them, in the end. But their rules still rang like an off-key bell in Riony's mind.

Pacing back toward the nest, Riony eyed the broken egg.

Can I really sit here and watch it die when I could save it?

She grunted and snapped at herself, "You're not even sitting, tamebrain. Just walk away. It died with the others. You were too late to save any of them."

Riony imagined delivering that news to Lyrrin. Riony remembered how she'd cried for weeks about her cat. *Sparks, I still cry about that cat.*

Her pacing stopped and she clenched her hand around the acorn.

She returned to the egg, kneeling at its side.

Her fingers shook as she put the acorn to her mouth, and carefully opened the top with her teeth. She extracted the tiny vial from within and blew out a cold, wispy breath.

The acorn pendant fell to the floor and rolled away.

Riony could only stare at the silvernix. She didn't know what was going to happen. Generally, only dragonlords even had access to silvernix—their term for unicorn blood. Few others had seen it in use or used it themselves. Riony never had.

She'd heard the stories though, and hoped it would be enough, that it was even still potent after decades stored in that tiny vial.

That's what the dragonglass was for though, to keep the potency of the precious contents. As long as Lyrrin's decorations hadn't affected that.

Riony's skin felt clammy as she held the glass up to her eye. She rubbed the etchings on the side with a cold finger, checking the glass and looking at the opalescent fluid within.

Am I actually doing this?

She looked at the still leaking egg, the weak motions of the underdeveloped dragonling within. That life, fading away.

A life was a life. And the silvernix had been saved for a life.

Yeah. I guess I'm doing this.

She held her breath and let the single drop spill into the crack of the broken egg.

The thin liquid glowed as it ran like a teardrop through the split shell. It swirled about, coating the inner membrane, then was absorbed, disappearing.

At first there was no change, and Riony chewed her lip, watching, waiting to see the membrane stitch itself closed, waiting to see the miracle of magic that was legendary in their land.

Then the tiny creature inside shuddered and jerked, twisting violently within the shell, forcing more fractures into the egg. Riony swore and tried to hold the egg together with her one good hand. She fumbled, hand too shaky, and the shell shattered under her fingers.

The dragonling stilled completely.

"No, no! Please, it has to work." Riony's face scrunched up painfully.

She'd wasted it. It didn't even work and now it was gone. She was so stupid. She should have saved the unicorn blood, for Lyrrin, even for her damned arm, *something* other than this.

What had she been thinking? She slumped on the ground, broken and in pain, with fever rising again even against the cold of the ice cave surrounding her. She heaved in aching breaths and covered her face with her hands.

A dim shimmer flickered.

Riony peered between her fingers. A light glowed from the egg, growing into a steady beacon, cool and bright. Inside, the dragonling moved again, straining and stretching.

Each motion broke the shell further until it split in half and the tiny thing, still wrapped in the slimy membrane, spilled out in front of Riony's knees. The glow dimmed again, merely an occasional sparkle from within the milky lining encasing the baby.

It struggled then stilled, struggled then stilled. Sharp points deformed the membrane, but didn't break through.

After the creature's initial burst of movement, it was already slowing again, exhausted by its efforts.

"Um, oh sparks, what do I do?" What midwife training

Riony had from her mother didn't cover anything like this. The dragonling seemed like it was trying to hatch, maybe *needed* to hatch, but it seemed too early, too small. Its egg was gone though and while the membrane still held it, it wasn't the same protection.

The dragonling was coming out, one way or another.

Riony pinched at the leathery tissue, rolling it around until she found the punctured section. She couldn't tear it with just one hand, and her other was useless, so she shifted position to hold part of the skin down with the toe of her boot, then pulled with her good hand.

The membrane tore, and a pale, blood-spotted ooze dribbled from it, followed by a small snout. It opened in a tiny, tremulous whine.

"Okay, okay, little thing. We're getting you out."

There was a snuffle and a sneeze as it emerged farther, revealing two bulbous eyes, covered by eyelids not ready to open, and a forehead with a single horn in the center. It flopped forward, unprepared for a head too heavy for a world outside an egg.

Riony caught it, laying it on her lap as she worked to pull the rest of the membrane clear. It mewled in soft trills.

Something melted inside Riony. She scrubbed her face with the back of her forearm, as though she could rub her feelings away. *Stars, damn it. It's adorable.*

"Hey there, welcome to the world."

It lived. At least so far. She only hoped it would continue to, but that would be up to its mother now. As the last of the membrane was stripped off, Riony could see that it wasn't the same shape as its dead siblings.

Its moonlight-pale flesh had a soft fuzz to it and fewer scales. Where the others had an array of horn buds on either side of their scalp, it only had the single, central one, and floppy ears on either side. Its wings seemed more delicate and diaphanous and less leathery. Thin, gangly legs wobbled awkwardly, unlike the stout, sturdy arms of the others.

Changed. Different.

Did the unicorn blood do this? It wasn't meant to be used on mothers ... were eggs the same thing? Riony remembered the looks of fear and disgust in the delivery room when Lyrrin was born. Changed. Different.

Riony touched a hand to the side of the baby dragon's face, feeling the velvety skin, still slick and damp. "You weren't ready to come out yet, little one. But you'll be okay. You're going to be just fine."

Heavy breaths moved the creature's chest like bellows as its lungs learned how to work. Eyelids squeezed, then slowly peeled back, revealing lilac eyes. It cried softly against Riony's hand, and its cute, gummy jaws tried to suck and nibble at her chilled fingertips.

The thrum of its voice echoed in the ice cave.

Then it seemed to grow louder, louder, until it reached an ear-splitting roar.

Riony whipped her head around.

The mother dragon had returned.

Riony looked between the massive beast before her to the carnage of broken eggs beside her.

Oh sparks. She'll think I did it.

Did dragons care for their eggs? Did they feel about their families the way humans felt about theirs? From the way the dragon snorted jets of hot air and her eyes rolled wildly around, and the continuous growling shriek emanating from her throat, Riony guessed she must.

That was grief. That was dire, livid fury. And it was all directed at her.

"Listen, it wasn't me." She got up and held her hand high in a gesture of innocence, of surrender, but she knew the mother dragon didn't understand.

Huge claws stomped forward, talons squeezing and cracking the earthen ground. The dragon's horns and wings scraped the ceiling of ice, raining crystalline shards all around. Her tail whipped.

The one living dragonling tried to stand and flopped onto its side against Riony's foot. With one careful hand and one pounding with pain, she scooped it up.

"One lives! Here, one of your children lives!" She lifted it before her as the mother dragon's sword-like teeth stopped right before her face.

The beast stilled. Hot breath gusted from her mouth, engulfing Riony in a sulfurous mist. Shining silver and black scales made a shushing sound against each other as the dragon bowed its neck, dropping her chin to bring an eye as big as Riony's head close to the dragonling.

The pupil expanded and contracted within an icy blue iris.

She sniffed once, then again. Scaly lips rolled back over her deadly fangs and she growled. It was not a fond sound.

"It's yours, you must—"

The mother lashed out, sharp talons swiping at the strangely shaped baby.

Riony threw herself onto her back, taking the baby with her. The razor-tipped claws passed right over them. The dragonling shrieked. It writhed and wriggled free of Riony's grasp.

The mother roared.

Was it rejecting the baby? Because it was changed?

"No, please, it's your baby!"

The mother dragon ignored her, turning toward the scrambling infant. Riony pushed herself between them, standing to shield the dragonling's escape. The tiny thing skittered away, legs wobbling and scraping under it, dragging itself into a corner to hide between ice and rocks.

But there was nowhere for Riony to hide.

She reached to her side for her sword, but it wasn't there, left behind at home in her fevered rush. Not that it would have been much use, but Riony would have preferred to go down swinging.

The mother breathed in deep and opened her mouth, and Riony wondered what burning alive was going to feel like.

Seasong dragons don't flame. The knowledge drifted to her, in the same voice from her childhood that the wolf had spoken to her in.

Kess, that dragon-obsessed psychopath. Why was her voice the one that brought her comfort now?

And when the mother dragon breathed out, no flame emerged. But its breath filled the cavern like a wave, smashing into Riony and lifting her from her feet. She flew back, cracking hard against the wall behind her.

They have an air attack, tamebrain.

Thanks, Kess.

She didn't have even a second to prepare herself between slumping to the ground and having the dragon's claw close around her. It gripped Riony's entire chest and squeezed. Talons skewered through her flesh. Ribs cracked and all of the air was forced out of her.

Riony's eyes bulged, and she opened her mouth in a failed, breathless scream. The dragon replied, shrieking in her face, hot breath and pungent saliva flying. Then the claw released and Riony dropped like a sack of soup bones.

Riony wasn't sure how she was still alive.

Every breath wheezed and gurgled as her lungs collapsed, flooded with blood that spattered and spilled from her lips. Everything felt shattered and sharp-edged.

Burning might have been better after all.

The shining scales of the mother's tail whipped over Riony's face as the beast turned on the spot and left behind the cave full of the dead and dying.

EIGHT

Kess didn't think she'd ever see *Pony* again. Not since the servant brat and her parents murdered some dragonguard and ran away from Heithorn Castle before they could be strung up for their crime as they deserved.

That felt like a lifetime ago. A life Kess didn't care to remember much of.

The surprise of finding that the body lying passed out in the snow was once her slave was only overwhelmed by the surprise that Kess decided not to let the intolerable woman die there.

It had been hard work, dragging her floppy weight onto Griskin and dropping her off back in the tunnels the rat had emerged from. Kess had only done it to clear the area of other humans again, worried that Pony would spook the dragon mother.

Kess hadn't cared otherwise whether the ex-slave lived or died. She had bigger things to worry about.

But she cared now.

I should have buried you in the snow when I had the chance.

Half a year.

Half a year Kess and her wolf, Griskin, had been tracking that wild seasong dragon, following it from distant northern shores, learning its behaviors, carefully keeping her distance when it seemed ready to brood, and scaring any other humans away—not that there had been any up so high in the mountains, until Pony showed up—so the mother didn't spook and move on again.

And then, finally, payoff. Up in this blistering, frozen world, the dragon had nested. Four eggs—a good chance of at least one healthy hatchling from a clutch like that. She considered taking an egg early but knew that dramatically dropped its hopes of hatching successfully. She couldn't keep it warm like the hot patch in the cave could. So she bade her time.

It had taken her years before that to even find a wild dragon to track.

Half a year of anticipation, waiting for her chance, the best chance she'd ever had, the closest she'd ever come to the one thing she'd always wanted.

A dragon of her own.

After dumping Pony back into the underground tunnels and giving her a warning to stay away, Kess had taken up position again on a high cliff. Griskin's paws folded in front of him as he settled down in the snow on his belly, and they watched.

The mother dragon flew her normal patrol, as though unaware of the human that had just been near her cave and her eggs. Kess sighed in relief.

What was Pony even doing there, in the dragon's nest? It didn't look like she'd touched anything, wasn't trying to walk out of the cave with an egg herself. She seemed broken and half-dead of sickness, but not from dragon tooth or claw.

Moving the woman out of the snow probably lifted her chances of survival above zero, but not by much.

There weren't any other signs of life in the tunnel Kess had left her in. Nobody to help. There were rumors of an underground city in these parts, where refugees, ex-slaves, and other cowards hid beneath the earth. Maybe someone would find Pony in time.

Who cares though? Kess rubbed the dry skin on her lips and huffed out a cloud of white air. Seeing that damned redhead again had her rattled. As long as Pony died out of the way of Kess's goals, it didn't matter.

Kess settled in, tucking herself into the warmth of

Griskin's charcoal fur, running her fingers through the soft undercoat, then rubbing his ears. He leaned into her fingers for a better scratch, back leg twitching.

"Good boy, Gris," she whispered. "Not long now."

They had spent so many hours like this, together, watching and waiting, only interspersed with hunting enough to keep them both alive.

Kess was hungry now, but not as hungry as the mother dragon seemed to be.

Is she eating at all? Kess wasn't sure. Seasong dragons generally lived at sea, hunting huge schools of fish for their primary diet. There wasn't enough food up in the mountains to sustain a dragon of that size, even if it had a breath weapon adapted to hunting in this terrain.

Kess wasn't sure what type of dragon the father was; she hadn't been around for that part. It must have been before Kess began tracking the seasong.

Dragons didn't always lay directly after mating and could hold the fertilized eggs until the right time. It was only in factory breeding that humans had worked out how to force them to lay immediately for faster production.

It was strange that the seasong mother had come so far inland to lay her eggs. Maybe the offspring were hybrids, and the babies would need this climate to survive. Or maybe this is the one place in a world where almost all other dragons were tamed where she'd felt safe to finally nest. Even if it meant going without food herself.

And all the better for Kess if she was weak when the eggs were ready to hatch. She was half tempted to try to tame the mother instead, but the hatchlings were a safer bet. *Not much longer now.*

It had been a couple of days after the run-in with Pony that Kess returned from a hunt and settled into the snow on the lookout with Griskin again to keep watch of the nesting cave. With her hands buried deep in the fur of Griskin's neck, she felt his skin ripple and twitch, even before she heard him sniff at the air and whine.

Kess bolted upright, squinting at the white glare below. A couple of dark figures moved about and met another, who ran toward the cave.

"Raze it! Come on, let's—"

Another shiver ran under her fingers, the tension of a muscle as an ear swiveled back. Kess widened her eyes.

Grabbing the white blanket from the satchel at her side, she hissed, "Roll!"

Griskin was already moving. He knew the drill. He tipped on his side and rolled up small. Kess curled her chest around him and flung out the blanket to cover them.

They both lay frozen beneath the white sheet, breaths held, as the dragon passed over the top of them. The seasong mother hovered there for a long moment, breaking her normal patrol. And then she screamed.

Oh no, she must have seen the other humans too.

In a burst of air so strong it blew the blanket away, the seasong dove, speeding to her cave.

Kess followed her with her gaze, scowling as a flurry of snow landed over her. With a tap of a hand, Griskin rolled back to his feet, taking her with him as she clung to his back, feet strapped into the stirrups of her makeshift saddle.

They careened down the steep snow-laden slope. Icy wind tugged at her tangled hair, and she held her breath and closed her eyes against the bitter, whipping cold. With each stride, the wolf's strength and surefootedness propelled them swiftly toward their destination.

Finally reaching the entrance of the ice cave, Kess brought Griskin to a halt. She exhaled a billowing cloud into the frigid air.

Inside the cave, the dragon continued screaming.

Kess didn't dare follow in after her.

All she could do now was wait and grind her teeth and curse.

The dragon emerged, pale claws stained in steaming red blood. Her long head swayed as though drunk, and when she extended her wings and rose into the sky, she flew north. North, the direction of the sea she'd come from.

Her wings worked hard like a drum beating in the air.

She flew fast over the horizon and didn't turn back.

Kess watched, staring with her mouth opened and hands shaking. No, she wouldn't leave. She wouldn't leave her eggs, unless … Snapping her jaw shut, she leaned forward on Griskin. He took his cue, taking them on silent paws into the ice cave.

Kess's hands curled into fists so tight she cut her palms on her ragged nails.

Half a year.

All that time, all that cold and waiting and hoping, and she was back to nothing.

Broken shells. Broken bodies. And the only satisfying thing in this place of disappointment, a broken Pony.

Griskin sniffed and whined, looking to the corner of the cavern. Kess only had eyes for the bloodied mess of woman lying dead on the ground in front of them.

"I told you never to come back here," she muttered, wishing she'd made sure of that herself, that all her dreams didn't now lay crushed on the dirty floor because she'd had one stupid moment of sympathy. "You never could listen, even for your own good."

Pony wheezed and her eyelids popped open, scaring the shit out of Kess.

"Razing … You're still *alive*?"

Griskin recoiled too, yelping and pouncing back a step.

He knew as well as anyone that dead things that started moving again were a bad thing.

"Wha ... talking ... wolf ...?" The words came out between coughs and sprays of crimson.

Griskin lowered his head and growled.

Kess patted Griskin, reassuring him.

"Not a rev," she whispered.

He whimpered softly but straightened up from his defensive crouch.

"Just the biggest idiot of an intolerable human you've ever seen." Kess edged Griskin closer, angling the wolf to the side for a clearer view of the bloodied body before them.

Pony stared up at her face, making confused eye contact until Kess scowled and turned Griskin around again. The woman had the most infuriating irises that were gray or green or blue around the edge and warm brown, or maybe yellow, in the center, but all the colors played against each other and shifted in the light, making it hard to label any of them.

"Of course ... you. Always promised ... watch me die." Pony gave a sigh, a laugh, and a whimper of pain.

Alive, and still stupid enough to manage her ridiculous smile as her body lay smashed to pieces.

All these years, and Pony had barely changed. She still wore her scruffy red hair all messy over her eyes with that dumb little pigtail at the back. She still filled Kess with the uncontrollable urge to blacken both her eyes, then have her whipped for not crying out loudly enough when she got hit.

"Hi, Pony. You've really razed everything this time."

Her face scrunched in silent agony. "Right?"

Kess stared with heavy eyes. Maybe alive now, but not much longer. It was probably only due to the seasong dragon being half-starved to death that Pony had survived the attack at all.

Her punctured chest strained and arched. "Can you … help … please?"

"Help you? You want me to help you?" Kess barked out a laugh. Fury seethed like dragonfire through her veins. "You are the destroyer of my every desire. Why in all of Elundrae would I help you?"

Pony didn't answer. The stupid oaf at least knew there was no good reason.

"I helped you before and look what I got for it." Kess swung a hand at the smashed eggs, although Pony's glazed eyes didn't track the movement. "Why did you do it? Did you kill them all just to stop me getting what I want?"

As though hit by a surge of pain, Pony clenched her teeth, panting between them. As the breaths slowed again, Kess held her own, expecting to witness her end.

But instead, hot tears spilled from the woman's eyes, and she wobbled her head. "Not … me."

Griskin growled again, sniffing the air. His skin bristled beneath Kess's fingertips. The scent of death all around had him troubled. Kess only felt a dull, heavy weight in her chest. She snarled in contempt of that feeling of loss.

Unlike Pony, this wasn't the end for her. She'd get what she wanted one day.

"Just hurry up and die already. Put us all out of this misery." Kess cringed at her words, so small and petty. But seeing Pony there, in the moment when her greatest goal was lost, took Kess back to a life where small and petty was all she was.

She had escaped that. She had almost become something more, become what she was meant to be, and it was all made nothing by an awful Rolanian runaway slave.

Kess wouldn't help her. She wouldn't be sad this part of her past died.

"Goodbye, Pony."

"Please ... my sister ..."

A hot flush raced up Kess's neck. "We were never sisters. We were never even friends."

Between the spatters of blood on Pony's face, tears ran, streaming from the sides of her eyes and soaking the flame-red hair at her temples.

Kess glared down at her for a long moment, then turned away, leaving her to die alone on the frozen floor.

Nine

Riony counted her regrets as she took her last breaths. One, she wouldn't live long enough to find out whether she was actually still dying of corpsefoot poisoning as she suspected.

Two, she hadn't had a good comeback to throw in Kess's weasel face.

Three, she wouldn't be there for Lyrrin anymore.

That one hurt. That one hurt more than the physical wounds she was dying from.

Her last hope for survival just rode away. On a wolf. *So weird.*

Four, Riony regretted not finding out the story behind *that.*

Riony wasn't surprised Kess didn't help her though. The ashy-haired girl always was cruel.

She probably couldn't have helped anyway. There was only one thing that could revive a body as broken as Riony's, and she'd just used up the one precious available drop to save the broken egg.

Kess didn't look like she did back when she lived like a princess in a castle, when she might have had access to such things. In her early years, Kess had so much access to silvernix that her hair still held a telltale white streak from its use.

Now, she didn't look like she'd seen the ass-end of civilization in years.

Riony could only tell it was her from the unique constellation spray of moles—beauty marks, Kess would have screamed—across one of her cheekbones. That, and the contemptable way she drawled the nickname, *Pony*.

No, this strange, ragged, wolf-riding version of her old master couldn't have had any silvernix.

If she had, she would have used it to save her life, wouldn't she? Even Kess ...

Cold.

The sensation drifted through her in a strange, distant way. Yeah, she was cold. Too cold. Not enough blood left in her system to warm her flesh, too far from the warm spot on the cavern floor.

Cold. Hurt.

Her mind felt muddled, sensations abstract and detached as she faded away.

A throbbing hum built in her ears as her heart squeezed and slowed, and her vision dimmed.

Something snuffled at Riony's ear. She turned her eyes—the only part of her body that she still had some control over—to the side. Something blurry, shimmery, and small moved near her.

The newborn dragon had re-emerged from its hiding spot and snuggled up to her, clinging to even the small remaining warmth that her broken body radiated.

Oh great. There's another regret.

Hey, little one, Riony thought groggily, no longer able to form words aloud. Even thinking hurt. Especially the sinking knowledge that this was the end and that she'd be leaving Lyrrin all alone. She didn't even want to leave the poor, abandoned baby beside her alone.

How could either of them survive without her?

She didn't want to leave at all.

She whimpered and agony shot through her, withering her consciousness away.

The dragonling mewled, tiny mouth opening wide. In the one clear spot between the darkness creeping in around her vision, Riony noticed it was injured too, a razor thin scratch straight across its snout.

Liquid shimmered there, pale and ... silver? Shimmering and opalescent in the same way the drop of unicorn blood had been.

Riony blinked, choking as her throat filled with hot fluid. She couldn't draw another breath.

Bleating again, nuzzling closer, the newborn's snout pressed against her cheek. The wetness of its blood tingled against Riony's frosty skin.

A wave of nausea consumed her, rippling through her body in an unsettling sensation that caused her very thoughts to falter and fail. Her heart clenched and stopped, her lungs unable to hold air, and her mind seemed to rush toward oblivion like a pebble tossed into a well.

Stars wriggled across her darkened vision and it felt as though she was tumbling, falling up into them to never return.

Then the sensations of death transformed. Pain shifted, still overwhelming, but now it swirled within her like a high and low tide meeting at the edge of the sea.

Riony's back arched off the frozen ground, and she threw her mouth open in a silent scream.

The shattered insides of her being, crushed and torn, mended and regrew beneath her bruised and ripped flesh. Bones straightened and stitched themselves together, lungs were patched of holes and cleared of blood, then even the tears and welts in her skin closed, repairing themselves.

The crimson rivers that flowed through her veins surged and felt replenished of what they had spilled.

The cave lit up, some light source brightening all around, and Riony distantly realized it was she who glowed, as though the stars in her eyes had flooded into her flesh.

The light faded, and Riony gasped back into herself, back to a body that felt whole, numbed of the pain that had moments ago been all-consuming.

Breath came easily. Her vision cleared. Even her broken and swollen arm felt whole. She held her right hand in front of her face, testing each finger one by one. Fresh and pink and perfectly functional.

A hysterical giggle burbled through Riony. She gave one quick look behind her, to make sure she hadn't actually died and was now only a spirit. That she didn't see her dead body there separated from her was a relief.

She had been saved. Saved by the tiny creature beside her.

Turning onto her side, she stared at the little being. The baby's horn, the shape of its body ... Unicorns had been extinct since before Riony was born, but the newborn had similarities to drawings, tapestries, and Alderkin carvings depicting them.

She saw it so clearly now but couldn't understand how. Had the drop of healing blood changed the still forming

baby in its egg? Made it somehow more unicorn than dragon?

It seemed impossible, but Riony couldn't deny that the blood *had* just healed her. Brought her back from the precipice of death.

Nothing else could have.

Whatever it was that made Lyrrin the way she was hadn't had the same effect. There wasn't anything unicorn-like about her as far as Riony could tell, beyond her strange hair color. She bled red like everyone else.

But this ... This strange half-dragon, half-unicorn thing that pawed at her, limply trying to crawl into her lap, it had healing blood.

She helped the newborn up, scooping its shivering body into her arms and hugging it for warmth—hers and its. Brushing a thumb over its snout, it came away with the barest hint of shimmer that faded instantly. The baby's own wound that had bled the silver fluid had also closed, healed by its own blood.

Riony's head shook in awestruck denial. A baby dragon. With the blood of a unicorn.

And it looked at her with wide, innocent eyes as though she were its mother.

Oh no. Is this really happening again? Taking Lyrrin as a newborn was a rash decision that had led to a lifetime responsibility Riony hadn't wanted to repeat. But there she was, considering taking another baby into her care.

She'd originally thought she'd heal the egg and leave the dragonling to the mother, but if Kess was to be believed, the mother dragon wasn't coming back. The way she'd reacted to it, Riony feared she wouldn't let the dragonling live even if she did. The vulnerable newborn had nobody else. Nobody but Riony.

And this baby, this one came with even more potential consequences than Lyrrin had.

"By all the stars," Riony said in a hushed voice. The implications settled onto her like the weight of the ocean.

The single drop of unicorn blood she'd carried had been the most secret, most precious treasure she could have conceived of. And here was a creature the size of a small cat, filled with that miraculous blood.

Wars had been fought and races had been annihilated over such blood.

Even before unicorns had become extinct, what she had before her would have been a king's ransom of wealth. Now, with the last unicorn slaughtered more than thirty years ago, this bundle of velvety scales and floppy iridescent wings was unique in the world. Priceless.

Riony dropped her head forward with a deep sigh. "What in all the sparking stars are we going to do?"

TEN

R iony couldn't sit on the frozen cave floor, staring at the extraordinary critter forever. She had to get back to Lyrrin. She had to deal with this thing. This ... part-dragon, part-unicorn ... Dragicorn? Unidragon?

Riony wasn't sure what it really was. Or how she was going to keep it alive. Or keep it secret and safe or what should be done with it. The pressure of stress rose through her chest and she exhaled it in a long, low curse.

Cold. The thought came to her again.

Such a strange feeling, to notice her sensations in that odd, detached way. It was easy to blame those floaty, demanding thoughts before on a confused, dying brain.

Riony wasn't sure it was a good sign that they were

still happening. She *was* freezing though, in just two thin layers of clothing, substantially ripped and soaked in blood, and no cloak.

Now that the rushing heat of fevers and adrenaline were leaving her system, she'd have to move fast to get back home, or have the immense pleasure of another brush with death before she knew it.

In Riony's arms, the unidragon had closed its eyes and seemed to be sleeping. It's shivery, sleepy sniffles melted Riony toward it. It was cute, in an awkward sort of way. Which Riony thought was the best way.

In slow, careful motions so as not to disturb the unidragon—assuming it would be easier to smuggle home asleep rather than awake—Riony lifted the bottom of her long-sleeved top and scooped the baby in close to her stomach.

There were holes in the fabric where the mother dragon's talons had pierced right through, and Riony wrung blood out of the hem. It wasn't a clean or dry place for a newborn, but there weren't any other options right now.

She belted the hem of the shirt underneath the unidragon, tucking it in so the baby was curled in there like a hammock. There, close to her skin, each of them warmed the other. Its small heart fluttering and the shiver of its breath tickled Riony's skin.

It was lighter than she expected. More skin than bone,

and it folded up small, but would still be a noticeable lump on Riony's stomach.

Wary of her freshly healed body, Riony took her time bringing herself into a standing position, but there was no dizziness, no aches or twinges. She felt better than she ever had.

Oh sparks! I'm going to have to hide that my arm's better.

Yoskar, Aishena, and the other delvers knew it was broken. There was no way she could explain how her arm had returned to normal so quickly. She was going to have to feign injury for some time, on top of keeping the unidragon secret.

Between all of that and keeping Lyrrin safe, it felt like too much.

For a split second, Riony considered abandoning the unidragon. Leaving it there in the snow where it would expire naturally and no one would know it had ever existed. No more burdens, no complications. No risks.

She placed her hands over the fabric that held the newborn close to her belly.

She couldn't. It had saved her life—whether it had intended to or not, she owed it. She had to at least make an attempt at keeping the little thing alive.

Plus, it was awfully cute.

Glancing around the cave to take stock of all that

had occurred, Riony noticed a dark patch on the ground, farther down the slope. The way she'd come through after breaking in from the crevasse.

Stepping closer, Riony cheered. *My cloak!* She must have dropped it there in her blind stumble to get home, after using it to hold on to her sword.

She snatched it up, shook it free of chipped ice, and threw it around her shoulders. It made her feel colder at first but would be worth it when she stepped out into the blustery mountain air outside the cave.

It would also mean she wouldn't have to walk all the way through the undercity showing off her blood-soaked clothing.

The march home was filled with internal debates and wary glances.

As soon as Riony reached parts of the undercity tunnels where others moved around, she felt as though somehow she would be caught out instantly, as though everyone would somehow know she had the most precious thing in the world tucked under her shirt.

Even if it were a simple, standard dragonling, trying to smuggle it into the undercity would be the folly of a lifetime. She kept her cloak hanging down all around her, to conceal her lumpy, reddened clothing.

She picked up her pace as much as she dared without jostling the newborn too much, skittering through the

cyan-illuminated pathways until she reached home.

Rolling open the front door, she exhaled deeply in relief, but fears still shook her insides.

"You're back!" Lyrrin squealed.

All nerves, Riony nearly jumped out of her skin. "Hush!"

The door jammed and she pushed it with her shoulder wide enough so she could fit through without squishing her sleepy bundle. Closing it would be more difficult, and Riony looked to her right arm, still in the bandaging Lyrrin had done.

Could she reveal to Lyrrin yet that she'd been healed? And how? Her mind swirled with worries of every potential consequence within an uncertain future.

"W-what happened?" Lyrrin's face was puffy, with angry red splotches across her pale cheeks, accentuating her bright eyes.

"A lot." Riony sighed. "A lot of very bad things."

Lyrrin's lips pulled in and her eyes glistened. "You have blood on your face."

"Bad things, Lyrrin! Very. Bad. Things." Riony scrubbed her cheeks with a handful of her cloak.

"They broke the eggs, didn't they?" Lyrrin part growled, part whimpered.

Riony didn't answer, but her expression answered for her.

"I hate them! I *hate* them! They are horrible, cruel,

sparking monsters!"

"Keep your voice down." Riony glanced back at the still opened door. She dropped her own voice. "They wouldn't have even known about it if you hadn't told them. You have to learn to keep a secret, especially—"

Lyrrin's gloved hands balled into fists, her hood-shadowed face scrunched up, and she squealed a whining roar.

Riony realized her mistake too late. "I'm sorr—"

With tears streaking her cheeks, Lyrrin barged past Riony and bolted out of their rooms.

"Lyrrin, LYRRIN!" Riony yelled.

Tiny, stomping footsteps didn't slow or return.

Riony chased to the front door, but Lyrrin had already disappeared down the long, winding stairway.

The unidragon baby squirmed against Riony's belly. She ran her hands into her hair, tugging at the tangled mess that flopped over her face and screamed at the volume of a whisper, venting every anger she held.

She screamed at the delvers who smashed the eggs, the mother dragon who rejected the baby, Kess who left her to die, and at herself for every stage along the way and for what was yet to come with the new burden she carried.

What am I going to do?

Untying the lacings at the top of her shirt, Riony peeked down at the baby. "Shh, shh. Go back to sleep, please." Then maybe she could go after Lyrrin, bring her back, work something out.

The unidragon mewled at her weakly.

Hungry. The sensation thrummed in Riony's head.

Riony frowned. Hungry? Yeah, she was. But that didn't feel like her. She was hungry like an everyday fact. This was a pleading, pitiable demand. The unidragon blinked lilac eyes up at her from the shadows inside her shirt.

"You? You're hungry?" Of course, it must be. Even newborn humans needed to feed soon after birth.

It trilled a soft whine. ***Hungry.***

"Oh. Wow. Okay. This is weird."

Riony glanced around their mostly bare rooms. Another mouth to feed and they had no food. She had no idea what to feed it either. Where to hide it. How big was it going to grow, and how fast? Was it going to be dangerous? How was it putting its feelings into her *brain*?

One thing at a time.

She couldn't chase after Lyrrin, not still covered in blood and carrying a priceless newborn creature.

Riony swung her cloak off and dropped it on the floor, then carefully extracted the unidragon from under her shirt. Its pale velvety scales were dirtied by rusty smudges of blood.

"Just stay here for a moment, okay?" Riony placed it onto her cloak, then stripped off her two ruined shirts, throwing them into the wastebasket. Maybe she would burn them later to avoid questions.

Her mother's voice told her that one should be clean when handling newborns. Riony decided to assume some of the wisdom around human babies would apply to dragon hatchlings too.

Wetting a washcloth under some warm water, she wiped the drying blood off her face, neck, chest, and arms. Her fingers shook as her cleaning efforts made her confront the bloody mess she was in, the sheer, gory extent of it. Some of the crimson matter she wiped off was chunky in a way she didn't want to think about.

She frantically scrubbed at the sticky, staining red that was the only remaining evidence that she'd been moments from death.

Hungry.

"I know!" she snapped. *Sparks.*

The dirtied washcloth was hurled into the pile with the trashed clothing. Riony threw on a clean shirt and wet a new washcloth. Crouching before the unidragon, she carefully wiped the blood from it too.

Its heavy head wobbled and eyelids drooped every time she ran the warm cloth over its skin. When she brought the rag near its face, wiping its cheeks, it mewled and opened a gummy mouth, suckling at the wet rag.

"Ew, slow down!" Riony balked at the idea that it might take a liking to the taste of her blood. She reached for another clean cloth, but they were all gone, used up during Riony's fever and left in a messy pile across the room.

So she took a clean piece of Lyrrin's clothing from the shelf and dipped the corner in the water, holding the dripping edge to the unidragon's mouth. It turned toward the wet cloth and sucked on it weakly.

All Riony had to offer was water, but it seemed better than nothing. A decent drink of water might settle it down and help it feel full until she found actual food for it. She could scrounge up enough flour to make flatbread. Would it eat that?

Riony filled a bowl with water and placed it in front of the baby, but it made no attempt to lap from it as a cat would. She offered the soaked cloth again, but it seemed to have lost interest.

"What do you eat?" Riony thought out aloud, as though she could magically conjure up the desired food. Her whole world felt turned upside down. She tried to make a plan for the next few steps into the unknown.

Looking over at the bed, she wondered, if she tucked the hatchling into a corner there, wrapped it in blankets, would it stay still? Would it stay quiet? She had no confidence of either.

It wasn't unheard of for some people in the depths

to keep pets, and Lyrrin sure brought home her share of strays over the years, but this was different. She couldn't risk leaving it alone. She would have to wait for Lyrrin to come back on her own.

I hope she isn't out there challenging Yoskar to a fistfight.

Now that the unidragon was cleaned, she scooped it up again. Kneeling, she pushed the baby out onto the bed area and curled the blankets around it, hoping the low, cushiony walls would keep it still and warm there. It rested its chin weakly on the edge of the nest and trilled.

Something else moved beside it, rustling under the blankets. Riony ripped the top layer back to see the same little furry snout that she'd seen Lyrrin feeding before.

"Um ... Sir Butterfur, ah, Spelunk-something?" Riony ventured.

The soft, caramel-furred cave otter twitched its whiskers at her in obvious annoyance and burrowed back under the covers again.

Lyrrin would be thrilled to find out their number of pets had doubled when she got back. Because she was going to have to find out.

Riony wasn't sure where else she could keep the creature other than here with them, and she couldn't do that without Lyrrin knowing about it.

And she would understand the importance of keeping

quiet. Temper aside, she was a good kid and had done well with keeping secrets, at least up until blurting out about the dragon mother, and Riony hadn't been lucid enough to make it clear to Lyrrin at the time that it was something that should be kept quiet.

But Lyrrin had gone eight years without letting people see her hands, so she could be trusted with this new secret.

Once Lyrrin was in on their new charge, she could watch over the unidragon and Riony could get back out to hunt or trade for food. It wasn't too hard to catch a few cave spiders in the darker tunnels. Risky, but they had a decent amount of meat in their armored legs.

And if the unidragon didn't eat meat, she wasn't sure where to turn next. Trade with the compost farm for more mushrooms, or the root farmers for flour or baked goods, or maybe even a breacher for something scavenged aboveground, fruit or green vegetables, depending on the cost.

It had been eight years since her family had fled their previous dragonlord masters, and before that, Riony had never dealt with dragons directly, beyond hearing about them from Kess. She knew the big ones ate meat, but what about the younglings?

What about a dragonling that was part unicorn?

The unidragon's eyelids closed heavily, as though unable to keep them open any longer. Riony rubbed a finger gently across its snout where it had bled and it thrummed a soft purr.

The small vial of dragon glass she'd kept hidden within the acorn for so long had been lost in the dragon's den. Unicorn blood only kept in dragonglass—in anything else it spoiled within moments, but in dragonglass it seemed to keep indefinitely.

They had a few dragonglass bottles in their room, larger than anything silvernix was generally kept in, but they'd probably work ...

If she could bleed this small creature, even a drop could win her any trade she could want within the depths. She'd be richer than the delvers, richer than her wildest dreams.

Tired. Riony felt it again, more shared sensation than language. The unidragon's snout scrunched as it yawned and settled its cheek against her hand.

"Yeah, little one. I bet you are." Riony scritched its neck.

The thought of putting a knife to that soft, pearly skin made her stomach turn.

But could she, if it meant earning what they needed to stay safe? To keep it hidden? To get the unidragon itself the food it needed to live?

Would even attempting to sell unicorn blood out of the blue lead to this creature's existence being revealed? Or would people simply avoid her like that shady woman trying to sell fake silvernix that she saw recently? Riony didn't know. Everything was too uncertain, and she couldn't even take her next steps until Lyrrin returned.

Where was she?

She'd been gone for some time now. Even in her worst tantrums, she'd often cool off and come back quicker than this. Riony's stomach turned again and stress ached between her temples.

The unidragon had fallen asleep and the blankets wriggled beside it as the cave otter burrowed in close, seeking to share its warmth.

Staring at them, Riony questioned if she was having her best or worst idea in recent history. And that was comparing it to poisoning herself.

"Won't know until I try it." Riony grabbed her leather backpack off the floor and gathered up the top blanket from the bed around the unidragon.

Lifting them both, she lowered the newborn into the bag with the blanket tucked all around. It curled neatly into the bottom, just one claw sticking up askew over its head. A wriggle and snuffle, and it settled back to sleep again.

Turning to the bed, Riony chased the moving lump with her eyes.

She tried reaching around under the covers, but the cave otter was too fast, and she got no closer than brushing her grasping fingers against its silky coat. It skittered out, running up the wall with its grabby hands, chittering at her angrily.

Checking her belt pouches, she found the tiniest sliver of mushroom jerky. She held it on display in the palm of her hand, nice and still, until the caramel nose twitched, catching the smell.

"Yeah, that's right, it's a treat for you. You like treats?"

When the otter approached, Riony drew her hand closer and closer to the opening of her backpack, then tossed the crumb in.

Sir Butterfur pounced inside. Riony shut and tied the flap.

Lifting the animal-filled pack onto her back, she felt the otter test the exit a couple of times before it seemed to calm and curl up with the unidragon. At least it might help keep the baby warm, too.

Even though it was still marked with blood, Riony swept her cloak on over the backpack too, hoping to add an extra layer of obscurement.

Then she picked up her sword from where Lyrrin had left it beside the bed and slipped it into its scabbard, made a wish that she wasn't going to have to use it soon, and headed out into the tunnels.

Her first place to look was Delver's Circuit, the richer section of the undercity upslope where Aishena and her brothers lived. She could imagine Lyrrin had marched directly there to make trouble.

Riony passed through the Grand Arch and had barely finished climbing the flowstone steps when she turned an unlit corner and walked straight into Aishena.

Bouncing back, Riony stilled her once-broken arm quickly, reminding herself it wasn't to be used.

Aishena and her brother didn't seem to notice either way. The delver looked back at Riony fiercely as though the collision was an intended insult.

They didn't have Lyrrin in tow, so Riony ducked her head and tried to keep going, but Aishena blocked her path.

Her expression shifted slightly, still angry, but also concerned. "Hey, you seen Benjin?"

"We can't find him anywhere," Yoskar added more aggressively. "Checked the markets, orphans' den, usual places."

Riony stilled, taking a step away and looking back with matching concern. "No. Have you seen Lyrrin?"

Both heads shook.

Not at the markets. Not at the orphans' den. Not here punching Yoskar in the shins. More than one child missing.

Riony swallowed hard. If she'd lost her sister while trying to care for the strange creature in her backpack, Riony didn't know what she would do.

ELEVEN

"You think it's kid snatchers?" Riony asked with a shaking breath. She cast her gaze around them at the other cave dwellers passing by, heading through the archways in the nearby Curtain, the long wall of draping limestone that walled off the upper slope area.

Nobody else showed signs that it wasn't any normal day, that they knew or cared that children were missing.

"No. No way. Not even kid snatchers would be dumb enough to mess with delver families," Aishena growled. "With *us.*"

Yoskar removed his glasses, wiped at them, and returned them in a motion that seemed to be more based in habit than their need to be cleaned. "Although, Zade wasn't at the orphans' den, and it looked less crowded in there than usual. It's not just Benjin and Lyrrin that are gone. Looks like they hit bigger than usual."

"When was the last time you saw Benjin?"

"Not since we left him behind when we went ... you know." Aishena seemed almost ashamed, eyelashes lowered onto her cheeks.

"Smashing up dragon babies for funsies?" Riony asked.

Yoskar jabbed a finger toward her. "It had to be done."

Riony sniffed and took a step closer to him, looking right down her nose into his eyes. "Lyrrin was still in my room when I got back, but then she ran off. She was real upset about something. What was it again? Oh yeah, dragon babies being smashed up for funsies."

Yoskar rolled his eyes. "You want to stand here and fight over it until the kid snatchers are long gone? Or are you going to come with us and do something about it?"

"Come with ... you?" Riony stared, dumbstruck.

The delver siblings had already begun moving, Yoskar in the lead.

All the tension of pain and death and loss had built inside Riony and she was itching for a fight, as though punching something, anything, hard enough could bring Lyrrin back. But Yoskar made a good point. Annoyingly.

They needed to move.

With a stifled groan, Riony hurried after them. "Where are we going?"

Yoskar kept up the swift march. "Back to the orphans' den. Somebody has to know something."

Aishena scowled from behind her steely hair. "Maybe we'll be lucky and Zade's just taken them all for a day trip and he's the only person we will need to string up in the lowest cavern depths while we stuff him full of burning athames."

Riony widened her eyes. "Okay, but I'd normally save that sort of thing for the third date ..."

Aishena either didn't hear or pretended not to. Her hands clenched and unclenched into fists. "If we can't find Benjin, I'm going to kill Brishan and the others. I can't believe they wouldn't help us look. If all us delvers had been out right away ..."

Riony bit her lip. Aishena had really expected her fellow delvers to help out? Without some form of payment in return? Riony eyed the backs of them, their custom-fitted leathers, stuffed packs, and belts carrying more wealth than anyone other than fellow delvers.

Long coils of rope hung by each of their hips with slim, sharp grappling hooks at the end. Aishena had a thick belt with a whole line of athames sheathed, like a row of teeth. Riony wondered whether they still held charges, and what they were charged with.

Yoskar had a long staff, made of real wood, strapped to his back. Along its length were different-colored crystal shards embedded into the timber. Riony had never seen anything like it.

Nobody had that much wealth without it coming at the cost of someone else. They were rich because they controlled access to the depths, charged a premium for what they scavenged, and left others to remain without. Delvers did nothing selflessly.

As much as Riony wanted to be part of those ranks, she wouldn't be like that once she was. Would she? She dreamed of being rich, of not worrying about where their next meal came from. But where did she draw the line as to how rich she could be while others still suffered?

Riony shook off the thought. She had enough to worry about right now.

They reached the tunnel leading to the orphans' den, and Zade was there, approaching from the other direction. He stumbled as he walked, mopping at a bleeding nose.

"Zade!" Yoskar barked.

He looked at them, then his legs folded, and he fell forward. His knees cracked on the ground.

Riony sprinted past the two delvers, catching Zade with one arm before his face could join his knees in the dirt.

He squinted at her. His normally smiling mouth was downturned, and his eyes were darkened by a bruise spreading out from the bridge of his nose.

"Are you okay?" Riony asked softly. "What happened?"

Before he could answer, Yoskar reached him and lifted him by the scruff of the neck. "Where are the kids?"

"I'm sorry ... the slavers ..." Zade winced.

"Back off! Let him go!" Riony stepped between them. There wasn't much room, with Yoskar still grasping Zade as though he was about to throttle him. They stood uncomfortably close, but Yoskar didn't budge.

Aishena prowled beside them. "Let him go? You heard him. Slavers. The kid snatchers have been snatching kids, and this piece of shroom-shit let them!"

"From the look of his face, I'm not sure *let* is entirely accurate."

Yoskar growled, "Did they take Benjin?"

Zade closed his eyes for a moment before looking right into Yoskar's. "Yes, they have him."

With an audible exhalation, Yoskar released his grip and stepped back, chest heaving.

Out of his grasp, Zade slumped forward again and Riony put the arm she wasn't pretending was broken around him.

He offered her a sad, half smile.

"And Lyrrin?" Riony's voice cracked.

Zade's lips twitched and he wiped at his bloody nose. "Yeah ... they got her too. I tried to stop them, the slavers. I noticed them luring the kids out, rounding them up. They moved so fast. One of them knocked me down when I tried to call for help."

He gestured at his swelling face.

Riony worked hard to keep the appearance of calm, speaking through clenched teeth. Her right hand, despite the ruse of being broken, wrapped tight around the hilt of her sword. "Where are they?"

"Already gone. They'll be aboveground by now—"

"Aboveground?" Riony stepped back from him, needing space to breathe. They took Lyrrin, the kid snatchers really took her, and they had her aboveground.

"Which exit?" Yoskar snapped.

"They headed toward Unicorn Gate," Zade said, leaning back on the wall since he no longer had Riony's support.

"It is the closest," Yoskar stared that direction as though he could see through stone and witness the slavers' retreat.

Riony leaned beside Zade, needing the support too, as though she'd been clocked right between the eyes as well. *Aboveground.*

Sure, she went aboveground herself. Rarely, and only where the risks felt lesser, and even then, her estimate of risk had recently proved to be outrageously wrong.

But Unicorn Gate led out into ashy wastes where revs and dragonlords clashed. It was the aboveground they had left behind to hide here in the dark. It was the aboveground where her parents had died.

Aishena was saying something, and when Riony stared, not following, Aishena slapped her cheek. "Get with it! You loaded up? Ready to move?"

"What? Now?"

"No, in four sparking days' time when my brother is dead, and your sister has been sold off to be a dragonlord's footstool. Yes, *now*."

Riony turned cold all over. They were leaving now. She had every belonging worth taking on her already—her sword, her cloak, and her pack. A pack which held an impossible creature, newborn and vulnerable.

"I ... I have no food."

"Get to it then," Yoskar hissed, checking through his own packs and gear.

"And no coin. Or trade."

"By all things mighty ..." Aishena scowled as she reached into a pouch and handed Riony a fistful of sovs. It was more money than Riony had ever held. It would be enough for any food she wanted.

"Really?" Riony took the coins as though they were a

trap about to spring and snap her hand off.

Aishena rebuckled her bag and hauled it onto her shoulders. "You can repay me by making yourself useful in getting our brother back."

"Lyrrin too."

"Whatever."

Zade cleared his throat, straightening up away from the wall. "I'm coming as well."

Riony threw him a look that was a lot more skeptical than intended.

Zade shrugged and turned his face down so that his golden curls flopped over it. "It's like they said. The kids got taken, and I let it happen. And it's not the first time. I wasn't able to do anything before. But if you're going out there, if you're going after them, I'm in too. I have to do something."

Aishena spoke to her brother as though nobody else was there. "No, I don't want that foppish creep coming along."

"Hey!" Zade protested.

Riony stepped in to defend him again. "Foppish, sure, but you know, in a harmless and not creepy way."

He wiped his red nose again. "Wow. Thanks, I guess?"

Yoskar eyed Zade. "The more hands the better. It makes sense to take along as much help as we can for what we may face aboveground. He can come if he wants."

"I do."

Riony reached out and put a hand on Zade's shoulder. Then she asked their small group, "Is there anyone else we should ask that can help too? Other delvers?"

Aishena turned away, growling at a wall. "They ... won't go aboveground."

Zade added, "The other kids that got taken, they have no one else."

Yoskar grunted, then said, "Get what you need. Be fast. We'll meet you at the exit."

Great. A team of dragon-baby smashers and a pretty-boy who faints at a bloodied nose. Still, Riony figured it had to be better than trying to get Lyrrin back alone. Which she would have tried, regardless.

With a nod to the others, she took her fistful of sovs and ran as fast as she dared to the Grand Arch markets. She held her arms behind her back, supporting the backpack as she moved so it didn't bounce too much.

Sheets of milky-clear stone hung like curtains beside towering stalagmites that ringed the cavernous market space. Some pillars were marked with Alderkin carvings, but no one knew if they were purely decorative markings or if they once held magic like other artifacts found in the depths.

Alderkin tools, scrounged from uninhabited lower levels by delvers, were on display at the first stall, a few activated ones glimmering in a rainbow of light.

Ducking to avoid a woman nursing a large shopping basket on one hip, Riony crashed against one seller's table and had to quickly steady a wide crystal box with a chill rune on it. It would have been worth her life if that thing broke. She propped it back up, gave a speedy apology, then dashed onward.

Behind the stalls that had light stones, crucibles, athames, and even rarer treasures, were others selling general groceries. The ones Riony needed.

Mushrooms and shroom-jerky from the compost farms, alcohol and flour from the root farms, loaves, cakes, flatbreads, and hardtack from bakers using the root flour.

The scent of bread made Riony's stomach growl, and she worried again about what to feed the unidragon, and how long it could survive if she couldn't feed it.

As though wakened by her thoughts of hunger, Riony felt it stir against her back.

Hungry.

There were too many people around to speak back to it out loud. Riony had no idea whether the little unidragon could hear her thoughts too but thought as loud as she could anyway.

Hush, hush now. Try to sleep.

Softly, she hummed the tune to the lullaby her mother

once sang for her and Lyrrin. And in her head she sang.

Rest small one, rest ye in peace,
The dragons sleep, the dragons sleep.

There was no time to ponder what Alderkin treasures Riony could buy with the riches she held. She raced straight to the food stalls.

She hit a bakery first, breaking the coin there with one of everything they offered plus a stack of hardtack. The stallholder was surprised to see her buying with so much coin, but Riony didn't stop to answer questions or engage in small talk.

They'll dream of fire, food, and flight,
And won't wake until the morning light.
And lest they wake with fearsome roar,
Safe ye'll be behind closed door.

She bought a netted bag for her new supplies and added in filled waterskins, fresh and dried mushrooms, and even went to the dairy stalls.

Goats in the depths were fed on a diet of root off-cuttings, and their milk had a distinctive burned butter flavor Riony had never taken to. Lyrrin loved it, though. Riony hoped the unidragon would take some, or if not, she would find Lyrrin soon enough and it could be for her.

The stall also sold some goat meat, from stock that was too old to milk. A tough, leathery jerky, barely palatable compared to the mushroom version. She spent the very last of the coin on a few strips of it and a large round of stiff, dried cheese.

So close your eyes, and dream so deep,
While dragons sleep, while dragons sleep.
And in slumber, I'll guard you too,
As all the stars watch over you.

The unidragon's feeling-thoughts quieted in Riony's mind, and it seemed to have settled back to sleep.

Feeling as though she'd bought a year's supply of food in bare moments, Riony made for the Unicorn Gate exit.

The tunnel to the exit wasn't well used. A few guards were stationed there, mostly to fight off any undead creatures that tried to break in.

They didn't have any rules about letting people *out*, though. Not many people were that bold. Riony's passing warranted only a slight raise of eyebrows from the guards.

Were they in on it? They received only a meager salary from the community for this station, but they seemed far better off than that income would suggest. Taking bribes to let slavers pass by with a catch of children?

Riony gave them a sharp glare and silent promise to deal with them when she got back.

Yoskar and Zade were there at the exit already. Riony frowned, wondering why Aishena wasn't there yet too, when she emerged out of the shadows beside Riony.

Aishena glared at the netted bag Riony had hung from a loop on her pack's side. "Why are you hauling your gear like that?"

"Other pack's full," Riony murmured, averting her eyes.

"With *what*?" Aishena hissed.

"With all my unread love letters to you."

Aishena pulled a bitter face as though she regretted every moment of Riony's presence and stepped back.

"Enough. We're moving." Yoskar signaled the guards.

In front of them, two massive stone doors blocked the way. Each was made from limestone with streaks of calcite crystal sparkles, carved into a beautiful vision. Tall trees reached the full height of the doors, intertwining at the top, and between the trunks, unicorns frolicked.

Riony hadn't seen those doors since she came into the depths the first time.

There was a soft grinding sound, and the doors smoothly rolled open.

Staring out over the vast, open world before her, Riony actually felt glad to have the delvers and Zade by her side. The tortured landscape sent a shiver of fear up her spine as they stepped out together.

They were beneath the snow line here, and a river of ice runoff flowed nearby, down the barren, rocky slope until it was lost in a forest below, dark and mangled from repeated burnings.

There may have been some green there, but a steady, light fall of ash from the skies and ever-present smoke made everything seem orange and gray. The air was acrid and tangy on Riony's tongue.

In the far distance, the jagged remains of a destroyed village sat on a low hill, and even farther, the imposing silhouette of a dragonkeep was just visible in the sooty haze.

It was a land of fire and death. Slavers and marauders. Dragons and destruction.

And somewhere, out there, was Lyrrin.

Twelve

Like colossal tombstones, the doors to the undercity slid closed behind Riony. The thundering boom as they slammed shut felt like an ominous toll of a death bell. Separated from the sanctuary of their underground home, Riony's breath caught in her throat.

She sniffed away that feeling of rising panic. Lyrrin needed her, and nothing this blasted landscape could throw at her was going to get in her way.

"They definitely came this way." Zade pointed to where a clear trail of large and small footprints marked a path downhill.

The ground was barren and muddy, over-scavenged of anything worth feeding to humans or livestock that grew within sight and running distance of the safety of the Alderkin tunnels, making the footprints easy to spot.

"If we make haste, we can catch up to them." Yoskar didn't even glance back as he broke into a run. He moved at a blistering, nimble pace, despite all his bulky muscles.

Aishena followed without a word or hesitation, an angular, gray slip in comparison.

"Okay, we're hoofing it." Riony took a moment to adjust the straps of her pack, tightening it as much as she could so it didn't flop around behind her. The speed they would need to move at was already going to be a rough ride for a newborn.

Was shaking bad for baby dragons, too? Riony's head hurt with worry.

The delvers slid down the rocky hillside, taking steep shortcuts that cut straight down across the slower, zig-zagging trail.

Having little respect for the effects of gravity was part of their job, and Riony would have happily joined in the reckless human landslide had she not been carrying a precious newborn in her backpack.

She followed their path more carefully, sliding uncomfortably on her backside down the steeper sections to avoid falling and landing on her back. Loose rocks slipped and tumbled down in front of her and she locked her ankles, found her balance, and skated down with them.

Zade was neither delver nor aspiring delver. He was already breathing hard and scrambling to keep up with even Riony's cautious pace. He kept casting concerned looks between her and the increasingly distant delver siblings.

"Can't we just take the path? It's not much slower," he gasped between breaths as they hit another flat section of passing trail, then ignored it to go straight down the rubbly mountainside again.

"Not much slower is too much slower," Riony shot back.

"Going to be much slower again if we break our necks before we catch up to the kids. Hey! Hey, slow down! We have to stick together!" He yelled out to the delvers who increased the distance between them. He called out a couple more times, but they didn't ease their pace.

"Come on, hurry up. You're not going to let those delvers get to the kids first and steal the big heroic moment from us, are you?" Riony smirked at him.

"You know, I always have wanted to be a hero." Pushing the tumbling hair out of his face, he smirked back and burst into a faster sprint.

As the ground flattened, the trail of slaver and child footprints became clear again, heading toward the ragged remains of the forest.

Riony stretched her long legs into a smooth, loping

run, keeping her chest bent forward and pack supported. The netted bag of supplies banged by her hips, and she grabbed it in one arm to still it. Zade matched her pace, a grim look of determination around his bruised eyes.

A low, faint howl drifted from somewhere far above.

A quick glance back up the mountain didn't show any sign of wolves. Or one wolf in particular.

Kess.

Despite being fully healed by the unidragon, there was a piece of Riony's insides that still stung. Hurt by the abandonment of someone she should have expected that or even greater cruelty from. Why was she even surprised?

There probably wasn't anything Kess could have done for her anyway. Did she actually expect Kess Heithorn to sit by her side and hold her hand as she died?

Probably lucky that she didn't, or I might actually be dead now, and that raging psychopath would have ended up with the baby dragon-thing.

In all that had happened since then, it had been easy for Riony to forget that Kess had ridden into that cave on a wolf and told her to hurry up and die. Riony could have been forgiven if she'd decided to believe the whole experience was some kind of pre-death hallucination.

How in the world is she out here? Riding around on a wolf?

Riony expected the girl to remain cloistered and safe

and hidden away at Heithorn Castle, doted on by unwilling servants and protected by the dragonriders she obsessed over.

Although the Heithorns weren't royalty, they were high enough ranking dragonlords that Kess would have been assured a long and comfortable life. But instead, she was out here, back in Riony's life again, as wanted as an iron spike to the brain.

What caused Riony's teeth to clench was that Kess wouldn't even call her by her name, even now, so many years later, as she lay bloodied and near death.

Pony, Pony, Riony Pony.

There was nothing cute about the nickname. The wolf wasn't the only thing Kess had liked to ride around on.

Riony wondered if she whipped it, too.

The old scars on her back tingled, jostled and scraped by the heavy backpack and thoughts of the past.

Puffs of ash rose with each beat of Riony's footsteps.

"How are you holding up?" she asked Zade.

He huffed out his words. "Still breathing. Not used to running."

"Not my favorite thing either." She eyed the delvers, up ahead and showing no sign of slowing down. They talked tough, but it was another thing to see in action. She was begrudgingly impressed. "But we're going to keep running until the kids are in our sights. Then maybe take a quick breather before beating the spleens clear out of the slavers."

Zade smiled wryly and nodded.

A rough path wound into the charred forest, clear of obstacles besides the odd fallen trunk, blackened and cracked. Riony wanted to keep her mind on that path, on her destination, on saving Lyrrin, but Kess's presence stung at her mind like a poison.

There wasn't a lot Riony remembered about her younger years, before her time at the Heithorns, when her parents had been bondsmen to the Gyrsteins. She and her parents had been Uf'Gyrsteins until she was six.

She did remember when those dragonlords died though. The plague that swept through, the smell of burning bodies. They had once been rich lords, but obviously had exhausted any supplies of silvernix by then.

It was only Riony's amma's special treatment as a prized midwife, housed separately from their lords and other servants, that had spared them the same plague-born end.

After their masters' deaths, Riony's family was sold on, changing from Uf'Gyrsteins to Uf'Heithorns. Moved out of a dragonkeep to a rural estate where the lords lived richly, guarded by their own stable of dragons that the Heithorns themselves were proud riders of.

Lady Heithorn was the one who had the idea that, being as Riony was much the same age as her daughter, she would make the perfect playmate for her isolated child. She gave Riony to her like a gift.

And Riony had known just enough kindness in her life before then to be completely, naively blind to the suffering that Kess would inflict upon her.

Riony saw an instant friend, a pretend sister.

Kess had seen a new pet. Some loyal livestock. A living target to take out every spite and misery on with words and teeth and fists and whips.

Riony cracked her neck, rolling the muscles in her shoulders and feeling the strength in her legs as they pounded the ground beneath her.

She hated that Kess was the beginning of forging her into steel.

Riony's parents, Eylin and Farrad, always talked about the Uf'Gyrsteins as being good masters. Kind masters. But Riony didn't want to be Uf' anybody ever again.

When she and Lyrrin made it alone to the undercity, they decided to make their own new last name. Taken from the names of their lost parents. Eyfarr. Riony felt stronger, freer, having her own family name with no prefix of ownership attached.

Lyrrin had never known a life as a slave, and Riony intended on keeping it that way.

The woods Riony ran through were sparse, with most of

the canopy burned away a while ago. Some trees, although blackened, had new life. Green leaves poked from tangled limbs, and fresh shoots of grasses and shrubs were scattered around the ashen ground.

If they weren't in a hurry, Riony would have loved to stop and browse the varieties of flora growing there. Maybe she would, on the way back, with Lyrrin.

As the plant life grew thicker, the trail disappeared. Zade and Riony caught up to Aishena and Yoskar who stood amongst the brushy regrowth, arguing.

"Tjollaskeep is the closest city. They would take the kids there. It should be due east from here." Aishena had her face turned to the sky, angling toward the brightest spot where the sun was obscured behind the haze.

Yoskar crouched down and studied the ground. "Not necessarily. There are other estates and factories within a few days march in other directions. A fresh batch of young workers could be sold off in many locations, not just the keep."

Catching her breath, a wave of dizziness washed over Riony. She hoped it wasn't a sensation coming from a faltering newborn, and instead considered that it could have been the stress of her recent brush with death, Lyrrin's kidnapping, or the fact she hadn't kept any food down since before she'd broken her arm.

Despite being magically healed, she probably still

needed to eat.

Riony reached with her unbroken arm and pulled a waterskin from the net bag, taking a long drink. She had just taken a bite of flatbread when Aishena turned on her.

"Well?" she demanded, as though Riony could break the argument.

"I just need a moment," Riony puffed around her mouthful.

"She's so weak. She's going to hold us up," Aishena told Yoskar as though Riony wasn't even there.

"You didn't even think she'd still be alive a couple of days ago. She seems to be much better," he replied.

Riony pulled her bandaged arm closer to her chest. "Spite is like a fuel for my healing process."

"Still not sure we should have brought her along. She's a liability, with her arm broken and no brains to spare." Aishena reached out and jabbed her finger into what she believed was Riony's broken forearm.

Riony winced away, but the fact she didn't cry out seemed to win her some approval.

It felt like playtime with Kess all over again.

"Having another sword on our side could make the difference ahead." Yoskar stood back up, squinting into the distance.

Riony finished her bread and put her hand on the hilt

of her sword, grasping it for comfort as she often did. She would have reached for her acorn if it hadn't been lost in the ice cave. Sure, she brought a sword into the mix, but she'd hate to have to admit she didn't really know how to use it.

She could swing it hard at an unmoving target, but that's about all the training she'd been able to do on her own. She wasn't so naïve as to think her opponent in a real battle would stand still for her to chop down like a tree. She only got that lucky once.

"There are some broken twigs that way." Zade pointed off to their left. "They must have passed through there."

"Dubious," Yoskar muttered. "There are broken twigs everywhere. What makes you think those broken twigs are any different to those over there?"

"Also, that's north. We're going east." Aishena pointed, clearly having managed to get her bearings. She muttered to herself about tamebrain creeps they shouldn't have brought along.

Riony had a go at squinting at the bright sky but didn't know how to turn that view into a direction, and as a slave, she never had a chance to study geography growing up. She was lucky her parents taught her to read.

So she looked back at the ground, to see if she could somehow tell the difference between twigs that had been snapped by marching children or some other force.

They all looked about the same to her. Although one thing stood out as she glanced around. Scratches in the burnt bark of a thick trunk, close to where Zade had pointed.

Stepping closer, it was clear the deep grooves weren't some random animal claw marks. They had been quickly and messily carved with the Alderkin rune for Return. A split diamond shape, layered over with an arrow and a cross.

Riony slumped into a crouch before the symbol, pressing her hand beside it.

Lyrrin.

"Over here! We have a marker," she called.

The three others gathered around her, staring at the deep gouges in the trunk.

"It's a rune, see?" Riony traced over it, although she didn't know the right sequence, and based on the way Aishena rolled her eyes she was way off.

Yoskar knelt next to Riony and touched the ground beneath the mark. He rubbed fragments of charcoal between his fingers. "Fresh. But this could mean anything. It could be from anyone."

"No, Lyrrin did this. I know it."

"How? Does she have a knife on her?" Aishena sounded hopeful, as though the eight-year-old could have contrived an ambush and slashed the throats of her captors by now.

"Not exactly," Riony mumbled. "But she loves runes.

She's a clever kid. She did this."

Standing again, Riony turned on the spot and looked sharply through the nearby trees. "There's got to be another one. She'll mark a trail." *She knew I'd come after her.* "Over there!"

The direction of the second carved return rune led them north.

"I told you it was that way," Zade said, offering a lopsided smile. "Broken twigs."

"East," Aishena spat, practically hissing like a cornered cat, slim shoulders raised and pointy. "It's the clearest direction. North has no destination within a week's march that isn't ruined or burnt, and beyond that another week to reach Hjelzahnkeep." She shared a look with her brother. "We head for Tjollaskeep."

Yoskar rubbed the soot between his fingers again, staring between the two options.

"I'm following the runes whether you come with me or not," Riony stated.

Zade took a step closer to her, offering a nod of support. "The longer we keep arguing about this, the farther ahead they get. I want to catch up to the slavers sooner rather than later, and I'm sure you do too."

"Evidence suggests north," Yoskar said with a commanding finality.

Aishena's face paled and her lips puckered in as he moved over beside Riony and Zade. When he straightened up and stared back at her, she scampered over beside him like an obedient pup.

Yoskar and Zade stepped off ahead, as Riony took a moment to adjust her pack again, feeling a squirm of movement against her back.

When she looked up to move forward again, Aishena stepped in front of her, blocking the way.

She snarled and whipped her long sheets of silvery hair away from her face. "If you're wrong about this ..."

Aishena ran her hands along the row of athames at her belt and did her trick of looming over Riony despite being a head shorter.

"If you lead us in the wrong direction, away from Benjin, forget ever becoming a delver. If you stop us getting our brother back, we'll make sure you're never even allowed back into the undercity again."

THIRTEEN

Riony and the others took a slower pace now. Each of them was on high alert, casting their gaze wide in all directions as they pressed on. They had a rough heading, but if the slavers turned off a different direction and they missed Lyrrin's mark, they could go on too far the wrong way, get lost, lose precious moments backtracking.

But each time Riony fretted that the gap had been too large since the last sighting, another rune came into view.

Good work, Lyrrin. Keep it up. We're coming for you.

They moved with an intense purpose along the trail, rune after rune. The first time one was carved into a rock rather than ashy trunk, Yoskar had raised his eyebrows.

"Wow. Soft rock," Riony said.

The delver didn't say anything as he kept up the lead.

Yoskar and Aishena remained ahead of Riony and Zade, still acting like self-designated leaders, but not as far ahead as before.

Their path wound through the wooded descent of the mountain. The land felt twisted, cursed. Ancient trees loomed over them, blackened and tortured from being burned, attempts at regrowth, being burned again.

The ground was littered with the ashy branches and fallen trunks of those that couldn't cling to life.

Faster growing plants like vines took the opportunity to spring through the charcoal, shooting lines of vibrant green up black trees and draping across the thin canopy. The only birdsong was the shrill cry of an eagle, somewhere far above in the clouds.

Riony kept her ears pricked for the sound of a wolf's howl but didn't hear it again.

The air had a crisp chill, blown from the snowy peaks above them, and the two critters snuggled together in Riony's pack helped keep her warm.

Hungry. The feeling reached her again.

The initial run down from the Alderkin depths entrance had stirred the newborn creature awake. It wasn't moving much, only a few weak wriggles. Riony hoped that as it had only just left the egg, that it felt at home in the enclosed space.

She also hoped the otter wasn't crowding it too much. But it didn't fuss or cry out.

Only the twanging intrusions into Riony's mind of its hunger kept her aware of its presence. Intrusions which felt more desperate and sad as they continued to march the trail downhill.

Riony would have pulled the pack open to try to feed or comfort the animal, but Zade remained close by her side.

"When was the last time you were aboveground?" he asked conversationally, as though small talk was the thing Riony needed most right now. Maybe he was making an attempt to distract her from their troubles, which was sweet in theory, but not even the best conversationalist could lessen Riony's weight of concern right now.

"I haven't been this far out since Lyrrin and I made it to the undercity a couple of years back." Truthful, technically. Riony didn't want him prying into her recent adventures.

Zade turned his face upward. "I do so miss the sky when I'm underground. How about you?"

"Yeah. I miss it lots." *I miss it, and a whole lot more.*

With a kind smile, Zade said, "The slavers can't be much farther ahead. And your sister is a tough one, clever too. Things are going to work out."

There was a pressure against Riony's back as the cave otter tried to force the bindings on the pack. She covered its movements by shrugging her shoulders and adjusting the cloak that hung over the bag.

Riony was worried its struggles might hurt the newborn. If she could just slip some food in through the top, at least it would be happy. But after a second brief escape attempt, it calmed again. It seemed content to curl up and share warmth with the unidragon, as Riony had hoped.

"More footprints here," Yoskar called from ahead.

The few sightings of the slavers' trail they'd had between rune markers seemed to have calmed Aishena down. But she still walked in a jangle of twitchy anxiety, as though itching to break into a sprint again.

Riony just hoped that their slowed pace was still gaining on the slavers. They couldn't be moving too fast while herding a clutch of children along with them. Riony couldn't get Lyrrin moving fast at the best of times.

Hungry.

Riony winced as the feeling ached through her mind, the demand growing more powerful.

Zade reached out and put a hand on her shoulder. He looked at her with concerned eyes, shaded by a cloud of warm blond curls. "Don't worry. We'll get you to your sister. I promise."

Riony swallowed awkwardly. "Uh. Thanks."

His intense expression was softened by a smile that

tugged just one side of his lips.

Riony shook her head. Even now, as they chased slavers over a burned and blighted land, he managed to find a genuine smile. It warmed her with hope. "How do you stay so positive?"

"I just know that good things happen to people who deserve it."

Riony bristled and the warmth she felt a moment earlier fled her skin. "Sounds like a very Taen sort of philosophy. Does that also mean if something bad happens the person deserved it? Did the kids deserve to be kidnapped?"

Zade squeezed his grip on her shoulder. "Of course not. But I do think things happen for a reason. Things will work out, for everyone. Trust me."

His grin grew, and Riony found herself smiling back.

"What reason? The kids getting kidnapped doesn't make any sense." Aishena appeared like a wraith on Riony's other side.

Zade's expression soured, and he let go of Riony. "Kids have been taken before."

Aishena scoffed. "Loner kids. Orphans without anyone to care if they are gone."

Zade fixed her with a glare. "I cared."

"And what did you do about it? Nothing. And I bet you still wouldn't have if the slavers didn't slip up and take a couple of children that do have people who care enough to go after them." Tossing her silver hair over one shoulder, Aishena then rested a palm beside her collection of athames strapped at her belt.

Zade held the delver's stare but didn't reply.

Riony swallowed. "The way you two are sandwiching me right now is making me feel uncomfortable."

"Uncomfortable?" Aishena tsked. "I was expecting you to end that statement with one of your lewd comments."

"You're the one who went there, not me. Maybe you're projecting your own desire for a three-way sandwich. And I'll tell you right now, I'm honored and I'm in. If we leave Zade out of it. Sorry, Zade."

"This isn't the time!" Aishena growled.

"I don't mean *right now*. I'm okay with setting time aside after our perilous rescue mission is a success." Riony thumbed the straps of her backpack, trying to feel the optimism in her words. Trying to stay positive like Zade.

Aishena just shook her head. "I still can't believe the slavers took our brother."

"They probably just took advantage of us not being around at the time they were doing their snatch and grab." Riony's tone grew cold. "Maybe if you didn't decide to go and kill a bunch of—"

Aishena's hand shot out and grabbed Riony by the

front of the shirt. Riony stumbled as Aishena yanked her in until she felt her hot breath snarling over her face.

"Stop messing around!" Yoskar snapped from ahead. "Get back up here, Aish. We need more eyes on the trail."

With a soft growl, Aishena snatched her hand back and stalked away to catch up with her brother.

Zade raised his eyebrows. "Kill a bunch of what?"

"Never mind."

With a shrug, Zade turned his gaze away to the woods around them. "She's just on edge from being aboveground."

"Yeah. I think we all are." Riony sighed and leaned into her forward march.

"Is that why you're excluding me from end of mission celebration plans?" He smirked, but almost sounded hurt.

"Oh. I was just joking around. Mostly."

Zade watched her with friendly eyes for a long moment. "Or maybe I just haven't charmed you enough yet."

Riony chuckled and gave him a warm smile in return. "I really don't think that's going to change my preferences but I'm always open to being treated with anything above pure contempt."

Zade gave a hearty chuckle. "And as for being aboveground, it's not all that bad."

"Yeah, right up until a rev pops out of the ground and bites your neck out."

Yoskar, clearly keeping his ears and eyes on everything, called back from ahead. "This area has been burned very recently. Unlikely we need to worry about revenants. Once burned, they stay dead."

Riony crushed some charcoal under her boot and it disintegrated in a puff. Yoskar was right, they had moved into an area where nothing had been given a chance to regrow again.

Pale ash powdered the ground, not yet washed into the soil by rain. Over beside a low cliff, the ground still smoldered, ghostly sheets of smoke gusting into the sky.

But Riony wasn't sure Yoskar was right about not having to worry about shadow revenants. Riony *always* worried about revs.

The charred forest continued to thin out as the slope grew steeper again, trees replaced by sharp outcrops of stone that formed a crumbling maze. A soft crunching sound startled the four of them, freezing them like deer.

A bovin pawed at the sooty ground, working to unearth anything edible beneath the burned surface that it could munch on. It was massive, the large hump on its shaggy back easily twice Riony's height. But it wouldn't be any threat to them.

The cud-chewing creature gave them a lazy glance from its hooded eyes before continuing its attempts at grazing.

Riony's parents told her how bovin used to travel the plains of Elundrae in huge herds, in numbers so great that the odd member being taken by a wild dragon hardly mattered.

Now the herds had all been rounded up into farms to feed the ever-growing numbers of city dragons, riding dragons, and factory dragons.

The single, solitary bovin seemed so sad. Riony wondered where its family was.

The color of light changed as they continued on, a warmer glow washing through the smoky skies. Riony tried to get her bearings on what time of day it was. So much had happened since she'd woken from her fever, and she didn't even know when that was or how long she'd been out beforehand.

Had Yoskar said a couple of days?

Squinting at the sky, Riony pleaded with the sun not to set before she'd found Lyrrin again.

HUNGRY!

Riony stumbled, clutching her head.

"Are you all right?" Zade reached for her, then called to the others, "Hold up, something's wrong."

Riony brushed him off and straightened up, offering an awkward chuckle. "No, I'm fine. Don't worry. Just stubbed my toe."

Zade frowned at where she rubbed her temple. "Um ..."

"Because ... I was dizzy. Because I'm hungry. I just need a moment. Alone. Don't worry, you can keep going."

Forehead twisting further, Zade turned from her to the others, who continued walking. "Can you just wait?"

They made no sign of even listening.

"We've got to stick together," Zade grumbled. With an exasperated look, he chased after the siblings, calling them back.

The moment he stepped away, Riony pulled the backpack straps from her shoulders and placed it carefully on the ground. She hunched over the opening, both to block any view of what was inside and stop anything inside getting out.

The first thing she saw when loosening the ties was a furry caramel snout pocking out. "Go on, get back in there!"

Riony held the otter at bay with one hand as she fished around for food with the other. She hoped with her back turned the others wouldn't see her using her 'broken' arm. She thrust a piece of mushroom jerky at the bag opening.

The snout twitched, then vanished, replaced with a grabby paw that reached out blindly until it latched on to the food, then pulled that food back into the bag with it.

"What's going on?" Aishena yelled from ahead.

Riony cast a look over her shoulder. Zade had caught up to them, and the three had stopped, waiting just ahead of a large rocky outcrop. The trail they were on now was a clear goat track that ran through a narrow crack between the massive, jutting stones.

HUNGRY.

"Nothing, just taking a short break. I'll catch up," Riony yelled back. She could hear Zade and Yoskar arguing in low voices.

Riony quickly opened the bag wider, and drooping, weak eyes of the unidragon blinked at her. Riony waved a piece of goat jerky near its nose, but it didn't take it. She quickly tried again with a piece of cheese.

Hungry. The unidragon whinnied a pitiful whimper, but didn't take the hard lump from Riony's fingers.

"I'm trying," Riony whispered back.

The stomp of footsteps behind her made her heart rush as Aishena marched back her way.

Riony lashed her bag closed again, lifting it onto her back, but before she could turn around, the footsteps had stilled.

"Do you hear that?" Aishena had stopped mid-stride, head cocked at an angle.

Shifting the weight of her pack to hide any movement within it, Riony shrugged. "Nope, can't hear a—"

A gurgling scream interrupted her, punctuated by two more shouts.

"Oh, *that*," Riony said.

"Watch out!" Yoskar yelled, as a figure emerged from

the narrow pathway between the rocks ahead.

The man tumbled in a shambling run, slipping and gasping. His dirty brown tunic was slick with blood, and he clutched at the oozing mess of his stomach.

Riony dashed forward, good hand on her sword.

The man landed face-first on the shaley ground in a clatter before she reached him.

"Rev?" Riony asked. She stepped back in shock as Yoskar approached the body and checked.

"No. Still warm. He was alive a moment ago."

Aishena reached them too, glaring at the path ahead, where more screams emerged.

Zade's face had paled and he shook his head at the recently dead before him.

"I'm going to see what's happening," Riony said, tightening her grip on the hilt of her sword.

"This man wasn't a rev, but *something* killed him. Something through there," Yoskar warned.

"And that man might have been one of the slavers," Riony snapped back. She pulled her sword free with her left hand, pointing at the rocks. "We might have caught up. That could be the kids on the other side."

Aishena was moving first, and Riony had to put on a burst of speed to meet her pace. The crevice was shaded and cool, cutting a crooked line that blocked their view of what was ahead until they rushed out the other side.

There, in a clearing of rock shards between massive boulders, three men brawled in a brutal fight. Riony tracked the figures as they tumbled and clawed at each other. Not three men. Two men, and a rev.

The shadow revenant had once been human, not reborn from the corpse of some other animal. It must have been a fresh corpse, too, as it still had flesh on its bones.

That set it apart from the ones who had killed Riony's parents. Riony would never forget their sickening yellow skeletons, the grasp of their rough, boney hands. The crackling sounds they made as they moved. The snap of their jaws.

Her stomach bottomed out and her grasp on her sword shook.

Yoskar and Zade caught up to her and Aishena.

Their movement drew the attention of one man, who had blood dripping down his face. He locked eyes with Zade. "Help us!"

"Where are the kids?" Aishena ignored the battle before her, scanning around as though the children were hidden behind the scattered rocks.

"We should help them," Riony whispered.

Yoskar pointed across to the continuing pathway. "The kids aren't here; this isn't them. We should get out of here before that thing turns on us."

Another man dropped limply to the ground before Riony could argue.

The rev launched itself at the remaining one who'd called for their help. A furious flurry of limbs and teeth, wrenching and gnashing at the man's face.

Riony found herself marching forward.

She knew Yoskar was right. They should get away, keep moving as fast as they could to find Lyrrin and the other children.

But her lips curled in anger and her knuckles turned white around her sword and her feet kept moving.

She was only halted by the man she intended to save collapsing into a bloody pile.

And the rev turned its attention to her.

Oh sparks.

Riony lifted her sword just in time as the revenant flung itself at her. A puff of ash burst off the creature as it collided with the metal. Riony coughed and swung blindly. She put all her strength into the swing, dragging the undead body along with the blade, pushing it away from her.

The clamor of movement caused the creatures in her backpack to buck and scamper about.

There was a spattering of curse words and arguments from the others behind her as she blinked her eyes clear. The rev charged again.

It moved faster than a living human, its sinewy arms and gnarled hands grasping stronger. One latched around Riony's upper arm, the sharp-nailed fingertips sliding into her flesh like a skewer through a rope worm.

Gritting her teeth against an emerging scream, Riony leaned away from the toothy jaw that snapped at her neck.

The unidragon and otter stopped moving, lying perfectly still again. Not in rest this time, but frozen in fear. The wave of terrified sensations from the newborn overwhelmed Riony.

She shook it off and tugged her arm to the side, readjusting as much as she could within the monster's grasp to bring her sword between them. She held her sword in her left hand, which she wasn't used to, and it was slowing her down. Making her clumsy.

But she wasn't sure yet if it was worth giving up the ruse that her right arm was still broken. As long as she could swing her sword, she wouldn't give up.

With a cry of effort, she sliced, then thrust, cutting into the chest of the rev, then trying to run it through. Her aim failed, unsteady, and she slipped to the right.

But the rev let go, forced back for a blink of a moment. Riony wasted no time, slashing again. Another puff of ash escaped from the strange, flaky flesh of the rev. It writhed under her blow but didn't stop, trying to straighten up and attack again.

Riony didn't give it a chance. She hacked at it another time. She had no fancy footwork, no special names for her movements; she didn't even know if she was holding the sword right. But the one thing she could do was keep chopping, landing blow after blow until her muscles burned and long after.

Blood dripped down her right arm, and she kept the already bandaged limb still and close to her chest.

She had the creature at bay, but it showed no sign of letting go of its twisted semblance of life. The cuts from Riony's sword sliced into the ashy skin, leaving huge gashes, but revenants didn't feel pain.

"Um, a little help?" she called out, keeping her eyes on the monster.

More swearing, and the gloom of the day seemed to brighten with warmth behind Riony.

"Get out of the way," Aishena hissed.

Riony dared a glance over her shoulder. Aishena strode forward, a burning athame in each hand. She clutched the hilts fearlessly as the crystal blades radiated scarlet light and licks of flame.

The rev's claw swiped right past Riony's nose. She dodged away, stumbling back.

With the path clear, Aishena vaulted in. With an elegant spin that put all of Riony's basic slashing to shame, she

stabbed a flaming blade deep into the chest of the revenant.

It jerked like a puppet shaken by its strings as the heat spread through its body, glowing through the ashy flesh, then it collapsed at her feet.

Riony opened her mouth to thank the delver but was silenced by a withering look.

"You have to burn them, tamebrain. That or completely smash them to bits. But burning is the only way to be sure."

"I mean, I do know that. I just wasn't given my free burn athame as a special welcome gift to the wasteland of the undead."

Rolling her eyes, Aishena deactivated her remaining athame, then stepped close to the corpse to retrieve her other one.

Placing a foot on its chest, she yanked the burning dagger free.

And the revenant surged back into life. Teeth snapping, limb flailing life.

But it couldn't be. Riony gaped, horror crawling through her veins. *It was burned. It should stay dead.*

Riony blinked hard, hoping the nightmarish vision would fade, that the rev would lie still again.

The undead monster still moved. It lashed out, wrapping a clawed hand around Aishena's ankle, trapping her in its grip.

FOURTEEN

The revenant growled, deep and guttural. It lashed a second hand around Aishena's ankle, twisting until a cry was forced from her throat.

For a moment, Riony could only stare in shock at the still-moving undead.

How? How was it still moving?

It was even ashier than before, still glowing and smoking from within its burned and hollow rib cage. It hissed and snarled like a wild creature as it tried to claw itself up Aishena's leg.

Yoskar ran in first, grabbing his sister from behind and wrenching her backward. The rev didn't let go. It dragged along the ground after them and Aishena kicked at its grasping hands with her free leg.

"Get off! Get it off me!"

Riony's petrified body snapped back under her control, and she shook herself, inhaled deeply, and prepared to fight the undead thing again.

Zade circled in, a sharp hunting blade in one hand and the pallid tint of worry on his face, but he must have known as well as the rest of them there wasn't much he could do with that small steel blade. He hung back, cursing.

With an aching left arm, Riony lifted her sword high and brought it smashing down with a roar. She hit true, right across the rev's forearms, and thankfully not Aishena's struggling legs.

The blade cracked straight through one arm, severing the rotting flesh, breaking through bone. The clasping hand, removed from its body, released Aishena, and its second arm recoiled too.

With the tug-of-war with the creature ended, Aishena and Yoskar stumbled backward from unburdened momentum. When Aishena put her foot down to steady herself, she cried out again, hopping and limping.

The rev was already back on its feet. It shook its dismembered arm at them as though in anger, a shimmer of ashes raining from it.

"Run," Yoskar yelled. "We have to get out of here!"

Riony nodded, her gaze shooting desperately around the area surrounded between towering boulders. There were a few paths leading out. She couldn't see any runes from here. "Which way?"

"That way!" Zade yelled, pointing to a narrow path at the back of the clearing.

But the rev rushed toward them, blocking that option. Aishena's injured leg collapsed under her as she broke into a run away from it.

Yoskar scooped her up and over one shoulder. "Away from the rev!"

"Yeah. Yeah, smart idea." Riony took the lead, sheathing her sword and moving at a frantic pace down a pebbly slope, away from the rev.

Zade puffed beside her, and Yoskar kept pace easily, even with the additional weight of his sister. Everybody's expressions were paled and grim.

Glancing over her shoulder, Riony flinched to see the rev still close behind, close enough to hear its bared teeth clattering. The clearing vanished over the crest as they part ran, part tumbled down the hill, and Riony's heart clenched painfully at the thought they were going the wrong way.

"We should stop and fight it," she gasped out. "We could—"

"It didn't die," Aishena snapped, bouncing over Yoskar's

shoulder, her arms dangled down his back, still clutching her extinguished athames. Her hair hung all around her face like a shroud. "It should have died. If the burn didn't kill it, I don't know how ..."

They skidded on a landslide of loose shale, then the ground flattened out again. Massive trees loomed ahead, and they ran for them. The snarl and clatter of the rev remained close behind, never slowing, never tiring. Breath burned in Riony's lungs like dragonfire.

Breaking into the cover of the forest, Riony widened her eyes, trying to spot anywhere to take shelter—a hollow trunk, a climbable tree, an abandoned hut. Anything they could block off or defend.

They couldn't keep running forever, but the rev could.

The forest was dark and claustrophobic, thick with new growth, unburned for much longer than the path they'd been on before. A thin fog clouded the woods, obscuring the trees and vines that writhed and twisted around them, heavy with the scent of decay.

The ground was slick with moss and the remnants of old ash and littered with fallen logs and jagged twigs, forcing Riony and the others to dodge and leap between them, sliding and stumbling.

Only a few thin streams of orange light broke through the canopy, and placed in the center of a larger beam were some blocky, unmoving silhouettes.

"This way," Riony gasped out.

The others veered along with her, flocking as though in formation. Growing closer, the silhouettes manifested into clearer forms. Immense crystalline standing stones, laid out in a circle between the trees.

In the middle was an additional stone structure, ancient and crumbling, but still walled on at least two sides, as far as Riony could tell.

The structure was familiar, and even one wall to put their back to was better than nothing.

Riony pointed. "Over there!"

Zade and Yoskar—still carrying Aishena—crashed ahead toward the standing stones. Riony forced another burst of speed into failing legs. The first stone passed by her side, then she snapped backward, caught by a hand on her backpack.

She grunted and bent forward, trying to tug free. The rev held tight. The straps of the pack strained against her shoulders. A couple of stitches popped.

"Let go!" She kicked out behind her with one leg.

Her boot made contact and the rev was knocked away, rattling back over twisted vines and fallen branches.

Off-balance, Riony fell hard on her side. She flipped around quickly, crawling backward like a crab across a ground

slick with slimy, rotting leaves. The rev scrambled along the ground toward her, slithering forward in a disturbing, uneven motion on three limbs.

It watched her, locked on to her with hollow, blackened eye sockets.

A strange frisson of energy shivered up Riony's back, and just as the rev's remaining hand reached for her foot, it stopped. Twitching and snarling, it moved in strange juddering motions, backing away, almost as though in pain.

It lunged forward again, hissing and lashing its arm out, but some invisible boundary in line with the standing stones held it back.

Riony continued away from the revenant anyway, struggling back onto her feet.

"What's happening?" Zade asked as she caught up to him.

They both slowed then, eyes locked on the rev, who stalked the perimeter of the stone circle, grinding its teeth and hissing and throwing its whole body at the apparently solid air.

"I have absolutely no idea," Riony replied.

Yoskar also turned to see why the chase had ended. Frowning, he put Aishena down.

She hopped over to the wall of the central building, leaning there with a scowl as she stared at the revenant. "Why did it stop?"

"Again, I don't know." Riony turned to take in the ruined shrine. She'd seen Alderkin ruins like these before. They were scattered all over Elundrae. There had been one practically in the backyard of Heithorn Castle.

Whatever the shrine had once been to that magical race, the crystalline building was now mostly shattered, ornately decorated chunks spread among the overgrowth. Vines and lichens clung to its remaining weathered walls.

Intricate engravings and runes could still be seen etched beneath the plant life taking over, faded and worn away by time. Only the large standing stones, that could have been there thousands of years and probably last another thousand years, stood tall and strong.

Alderkin temples like this held no magic anymore, lost with the extermination of that race, but something was keeping the revenant from crossing the border.

Zade flinched as Riony took a step toward the prowling revenant. "Keep away from that thing!"

Riony nodded, but she still took another step closer.

The revenant howled and thrashed at the air, trying to claw at her, but unable to move close enough to fulfil its bloodlust.

Riony reached out and placed her palm against the standing stone closest to the revenant. The hairs on the back of her neck all jumped to attention, a shiver zinging up her scalp. Her forehead wrinkled.

What was that?

"There's something. Something about this place ..." Riony had touched Alderkin standing stones in the past, but they'd never felt like anything other than cold, lifeless rock before. And never heard even the whiff of rumor about them being safe from revs. That would be the kind of info people would talk about.

Yoskar moved beside her, right in front of the feral undead creature. He pushed his glasses back up his nose and eyed it warily. "It really can't get in?"

Over at the wall, Aishena grunted and slid down onto her backside. She brought her ankle up onto her other knee to inspect it and grunted again. "Whatever the reason, it seems stuck out there. And *I'm* stuck here."

Riony looked up, trying to catch a glimpse of sky. The canopy of tall trees growing inside and outside of the stone circle shadowed them, and no brightness could be seen through the rustling leaves.

The sun must have set. Riony's heart raced. "We can't be stuck here. We have to keep going, catch up with the kids."

"Did I say *we*?" Aishena asked.

Riony's hands clenched into fists. She'd never been apart from Lyrrin overnight. The thought that Lyrrin would spend a night without her, aboveground, under slavers' control, sent her into a blind panic. "I'm not waiting."

Aishena rotated her foot with her hands and inhaled sharply. Then nodding to herself, she stood back up. "Agreed. I'll distract the rev, keep it over to this side, while you all head out the other side and try to pick up the trail again."

Riony stopped mid-protest, mouth gaping, unprepared for that offer.

"No!" Zade snapped. "What haven't you understood yet about having to stick together? It's suicidal to split up."

Aishena just shrugged.

Zade threw his hands into the air, huffing a frustrated laugh. "Yoskar, you wouldn't leave your sister behind, would you?"

Yoskar's expression remained impassive. He cast a scrutinizing gaze around the ruins. "If she still can't keep pace in the morning, then yes."

Aishena didn't seem concerned by this statement at all. She nodded in firm agreement.

Zade shook his head, aghast. "She's your sister!"

"She is. And that's why I trust her to manage herself while I continue on for Benjin, who must be prioritized in this instance."

"Wait, what do you mean, in the morning?" Riony asked.

"We make camp here." Yoskar moved away from the

prowling revenant, back closer to the shrine wall where Aishena and Zade had remained.

Riony stalked over beside him. "But—"

"The sun is down, and the slavers will have to make camp too. They probably already have, earlier than us, taking the stamina of young children into account. We will catch up tomorrow." He removed his pack, putting it carefully down onto the uneven, broken paving.

"We could be catching up now, get the kids out while the slavers sleep," Riony said, shifting from foot to foot. Her arm still bled and stung, and her whole body screamed for rest, but her mind, ever stubbornly deaf to her body's woes, wouldn't listen.

"You can do what you want," Yoskar said. Kneeling beside his bag, he unstrapped the crystal studded staff off the pack, then began digging through the contents. "Good luck lasting till morning alone out there."

Zade threw Riony a long, pleading look. "Please, can we stick together? I don't want you to end up like those slavers back there."

"Ugh. Fine. We stay. But the moment Aishena can hobble along again, we move on." Riony frowned at the delver, who stood with her back against the wall with a defiant look upon her face.

Riony was in possession of a remedy that could make

Aishena be healed and moving again right now. Her pulse hammered in her ears and her head spun, unable to form clear decisions. Could she do that? Could she reveal what she carried to these three? She didn't trust them, that was for sure, but was she risking Lyrrin by not?

A faint, desperately pitiful cry of *hungry* washed over her thoughts.

The truth couldn't be fought any longer. They had to stop. Riony had to stop.

She hoped Yoskar was right about the slavers stopping too.

Aishena pulled her pack off and dropped it beside her but remained standing. Her athames were back in her hands, and she grasped them with white knuckles. "Brother, this place feels strange. I don't like it."

Riony raised an eyebrow, wondering if the spooky delver had felt the strange shiver of energy she had.

"We stay. If whatever is keeping the rev out holds, this is our safest option to rest. If it doesn't, we move on again regardless." Yoskar kicked at the ground, clearing an area on the smoothest section of ancient paving. Roots and tendrils wound their way around the broken stones, growing out of the cracks.

Riony paced around, still unable to settle. She glared back at the revenant that had chased them so far off their path, still growling at them from across the ruins.

"Who were those guys back there? The ones the rev made spare parts from. Just some random overworld crazies?" she asked.

"No. They were with the slavers. I recognized them from earlier when they took the kids," Zade said, a dark expression shadowing his face.

Aishena asked, "But why were they there? Do you think the rev attacked their group and they stayed behind while the others got away?"

Riony shuddered. If so, they must have been so close to catching up. The kids could have been just ahead of them. And now they were offtrack.

Yoskar shook his head. "The positioning of the event was the ideal location for an ambush."

Riony just stared at him.

"You didn't notice? Of course not. Just rushed right in without a clue."

"I noticed," Aishena muttered.

"Shut up. No, you didn't," Riony muttered back.

Yoskar sighed in a deliberate display of unsurprised disappointment. "I expect those three slavers were waiting there for us."

"An ambush? Why?" Zade asked.

Yoskar shrugged. "Probably a tail guard, left to take out anyone trailing them, just in case. That would be a clever tactic. Then they just got unlucky when the rev found them first."

The mention of the creature had them all turning to watch as it continued to tirelessly test the boundaries. It hadn't slowed its thrashing, ravenous attack at all.

"Did you see how strange it was?" Aishena asked softly. "Charred and ashy, even before I struck it with a burn athame."

The abnormal revenant growled at them from the growing shadows, its remaining arm beating and clawing at the air.

Riony remembered the puffs of soot that flew from it each time she struck with her sword. She'd assumed back then that it had just gotten dirty, rolling about in the charcoal-covered forests. Sparks, she didn't know what revs did in their spare time. She was pretty sure they didn't bathe though.

If it had been covered in that flaking soot for another reason though, a reason like maybe it had been burned already ... Riony shuddered at the implications, a brisk chill blowing through her that seemed to come from within.

FIFTEEN

There was something strange about this place. A zing of energy was building and thrumming under Riony's skin. She blew it off as caused by the stress of their mission to retrieve the children and the fear of the revenant still patrolling the invisible border between the standing stones that kept it from its human prey.

No matter what she felt about this place, it was where they had to rest.

Nocturnal birds chorused the fall of night, cooing eerily through the woods around the Alderkin ruins. Twisted and gnarled branches seemed to move of their own accord, as if alive and watching the intruders closely. The forest felt old and primal, a place where the shadows and the spirits of the dead still roamed. At least one still did.

Within the ruins, the once-grand entrance to the building beside them was now a gaping hole, covered in vines that obscured the way in. Riony poked her head through for a look.

The temple's interior was dark and silent. One standing stone stood within it, formed from a thick slice of an immense sparkling geode. Alderkin runes that Riony had never seen before marked around the edges. Elegantly carved reliefs of unicorns on the walls were obscured by lichen and moss, making the depicted creatures look ill and mangy.

The ceiling had caved in at the far end, taking part of the wall with it. Otherwise, the temple interior was bare, looted long ago.

It would be warmer and more sheltered in there than camping beside the exterior wall. But through some unspoken agreement, everyone settled for the night outside.

Yoskar quickly got to work on a campfire, breaking dead sticks into a pile on the uneven paving. Aishena remained leaning on the wall, hands still tight around her athames and eyes on the revenant.

Zade put his hands on his hips, taking in their campsite as flames licked to life, brightening everything with an orange glow. "No way. No way! Do you all see what I'm seeing?"

Riony had just begun unloading her bags and quickly reached for her sword again.

But Zade's face cracked into a wide grin, and he jogged over to a small tree tucked in beside the wall of the shrine. "Apples!" he shouted, far too loud for common sense.

"Apples?" Riony froze, dumfounded.

She didn't believe it as Zade reached into the foliage and plucked a round red fruit into his hand, holding it up for them to see.

"No way," Riony echoed. Her mouth flooded with saliva at the memory of their taste. She rushed over, and Zade tossed the apple to her. Bringing it to her nose, she breathed the sweet perfume in deeply.

"I can't even remember the last time I had fresh fruit of any kind!" Dried fruit was the main trade from aboveground that irregularly made it into the undercity, and even then, Riony couldn't often afford it.

She cast her eyes over the branches, counting quickly. Most of the apples were ripe, or ripe enough she'd eat them anyway, and there had to be at least a dozen. She almost snatched at them with both hands at once, but quickly stilled her right arm.

It's broken, remember? As far as everyone else knows, anyway.

Zade laughed as he raced to pick the rest himself,

gathering apples into the scooped-up hem of his shirt. Riony smirked back at him, leveraging her height to snap up a bigger harvest.

"I don't see what all the fuss is about," Aishena scoffed, glaring hard at Zade. "I had apples only a few months ago."

Riony cradled her bounty as she went back where she had left her netted bag next to the now roaring fire. "You don't want any of these, then?"

Pouting, Aishena limped from her position at the wall over to the fire as well, taking a seat on a chunk of toppled pillar. "I didn't say that."

Riony sat cross-legged on the ground, rolling the apples from her arms into her lap. She longingly stared at her treasure of ruby delights.

As much as she wanted to, she couldn't withhold them from the delver. Aishena hadn't hesitated to give her that much wealth and more to buy supplies with before they left. Even if it was probably pocket change to the delver.

She picked two apples and lobbed them over to Aishena, who caught them deftly as though snatching arrows from the air. Aishena nodded a stoic thanks. Zade, still grinning, handed a couple of his collection to Yoskar, then the two of them took seats around the fire as well.

Riony slipped out of her backpack straps and let it down gently onto the ground behind her, keeping it obscured

by her body and cloak in case of movement from within. Then she picked the ripest of the apples and brought it to her lips.

The rush of tart juice and sweet crunch of flesh brought tears to Riony's eyes. It had been years. Her whole body sang with delight at the flavors dancing over her tongue.

As she savored each bite, she thought of Lyrrin. It seemed wrong to be experiencing something so blissful while Lyrrin was in danger.

Aishena must have felt a similar way, as she nibbled on the fruit with a dull expression, punctuated by soft, gruff sighs.

"We're going to get the kids back." A steel-hard determination settled over Riony. She knew what she was saying had to be true, because she knew she wouldn't stop until it was.

She picked up her remaining few apples, holding them in front of her. "And we can share the rest of the fruit with them when we do."

So they didn't get bruised in amongst her other supplies in the netted bag, Riony put the fruit away into a pouch on her belt. She couldn't put them in her backpack; the cave otter would surely demolish them. The backpack was just for animals now.

Riony remembered the out-of-charge athame she'd

picked up on her trip out to the mountains. She never had a chance to show it to Lyrrin before. It must still be tucked away in her backpack, under the blanket cushioning the unidragon.

Another present for Lyrrin when I get her back, she thought, and returned to finishing the apple.

Nobody replied to her proclamation, but she noticed Aishena stash away one of her apples as well.

Zade smiled softly, his tumbling hair glowing in the light of the flames. "I used to live right beside a whole apple orchard once, just outside Tjollaskeep."

"Not far from here then. How long have you been underground?" Yoskar asked.

Zade shrugged. "A couple of years? I haven't really counted. It's not the sort of anniversary I like to celebrate."

Riony grunted an agreement around her full mouth.

"But my family, we were farmers before that. Hard work, but not as hard as it's been since. Not as hard as the kids in the orphans' den have it."

Riony paused her chewing and tilted her head toward him. "It's good of you, how you look after them."

She felt bad that she hadn't done more herself but found raising even one child to meet her capacity.

Zade beamed, and he looked back at Riony in a way that would probably have melted the right girl's heart.

"Thanks. I'm proud of how I've been able to help the kids. I'm glad you can see how important what I do is."

"Real savior, aren't you?" Aishena rolled her eyes. "You don't know hard work until you've been a delver."

"Is that an invitation?" Riony replied. "Because I accept."

With a huff, Aishena threw the core of her apple at the roaming revenant. It snarled from the shadows beyond the glow of the fire.

"Wasteful." Riony clung to the remains of her apple, nibbling away until she'd eaten everything but the seeds. She shuffled around, stretching her legs out in front of her with her legs splayed out wide, letting the worn muscles rest and enjoying the coolness of the stone beneath her.

Zade stared at the revenant warily, as though the lobbed food scraps would be the thing that taunted it into breaking through the invisible barrier. When it still didn't approach, he turned his attention to Riony again.

"How about you? Been underground long?"

"Not long enough to forget what being a slave feels like," Riony replied and spat her final apple seed into the dirt.

"I'm sorry."

Riony sniffed, then smirked the pity away. "Weren't you a slave too, just on a farm?"

"I suppose. I guess it never felt like that though. I mean, the farm was owned by dragonlord masters, but we had a

decent life. Hard work but satisfying. And they protected us from the revs."

A bitter, vicious edge twisted Riony's smile. "Of course, they protected you. Have to keep their livestock alive, after all, or who else will do all the hard work for them?"

Zade stiffened, and Riony knew she was going too far. But the threat of Lyrrin falling to that fate of slavery riled up her every nerve.

What if she ended up owned by a family like the Heithorns?

She stared at the dragonlord sword that lay beside her. "Protecting the land is one fine excuse to keep the rest of the population enslaved. To take what they want and kill who they want."

Riony expected Yoskar and Aishena to defend the dragonlord way. She was sure there was dragonlord blood in them. People didn't end up with that silvernix tinted hair from a peasant ancestry. Hair that pale was found most in families who had been exploiting unicorn blood for generations.

They remained quiet, though, staring into the fire with only cursory glances toward the others or between themselves.

It unsettled Riony that Aishena, at least, hadn't bitten back.

"You don't disagree?" she taunted the delver directly.

Aishena caught her eye for a moment before looking back into the fire. She readjusted her sitting position, wincing as she moved her swelling ankle. "We've lost family to dragonlords, too."

Riony drew quiet. Yoskar didn't add any further explanation, just glared at his sister over the flames which lit the glass of his spectacles.

"Your parents?" Riony asked tentatively.

Aishena's lips twitched. "Yeah."

Zade shook his head, turning away to stare at the ground.

Riony kept her eyes on Aishena. The harsh lines of her angular body and sneaky ghoulishness held a deep grief that Riony had never noticed before, beneath the bravado and venom.

"Hey," she called out. "See that purplish-leaved ground cover beside you there?"

Aishena's eyebrows twisted at the odd question.

"A poultice of it will help ease the inflammation on your ankle," Riony finished.

The delver's face remained confused for a moment before it softened. With a sharp nod, she plucked at some leaves and rubbed them softly onto her skin around the top of her boot.

"No, a poultice, a—for the love of stars. Let me show

you." Getting to her feet, Riony strode over and knelt in front of Aishena.

The delver balked as Riony took the injured foot onto her lap and worked the boot off, but she didn't pull away or object.

The whole process was slow and clumsy, as Riony had to work with her left hand only. Aishena just stared at her with wide black eyes and darkening cheeks.

Pulling up a big handful of the wine-tinted foliage, Riony worked it between her palm and a stone paver beside her until the membranes broke down and it mashed into a soggy pulp.

"Like this," she said and gently applied it in a thick layer all around the ankle. "We just need something to keep it in place."

Still kneeling, Riony straightened up and ripped at the lower hem of her shirt, pulling a strip off right around the bottom. The removed length left more than a little of her stomach showing.

As she bent to tie the makeshift bandages, Aishena muttered, "You did that on purpose to show off your abs, didn't you? Just like you wander around the undercity in that ridiculous sleeveless tunic all the time. Can't resist showing off your muscles."

"Aw, you noticed!"

"That's not ... I ..." Aishena punctuated her stuttering with a grunt.

Behind Riony, the other two had begun laying out blankets for their bedding.

Then Zade called out, "Um, Riony? What's in your backpack?"

Oh sparks.

Riony spun around. Her abandoned pack wriggled on the ground where she'd left it.

Closing her eyes for a second, Riony took a deep breath, then strolled over to the bag. She knew she couldn't keep her secret for long.

"It's just one of Lyrrin's pets." Untying the pack, she reached in and grabbed the wriggling cave otter firmly from the scruff of its neck. She pulled it just close enough to the bag opening for the others to see.

There was no way she could keep a live animal hidden in her bag for long. That's why she brought along two. Sir Butterfur made the perfect decoy.

"That's what you had in there all along?" Yoskar raised his eyebrows.

"Why," Aishena said, more a mocking statement than question.

"Because I wanted at least one thing around here who appreciates me." Riony pushed the wriggling sausage of fur back into the bag and closed it up again.

Aishena's eyes turned to the poultice on her ankle. "You aren't … unappreciated."

"Oh really?" Riony perked up. She held out her arm, displaying the mess of coagulating blood around the rev's claw marks. "Don't suppose you want to return the favor, then? You could come over and tenderly tend to my wound. Maybe we could even go and tenderly tend a bit more of each other over in a dark corner of the shrine there."

Riony jiggled her eyebrows up and down and tipped her head toward the empty structure.

Aishena's face scrunched. "Why are you *like this*?"

Riony shrugged. "Why are you *not* like this?"

Yoskar pinched the bridge of his nose and turned away.

"So, that's a no, then?" Riony asked. Without waiting for a reply, she picked up her backpack and netted bag in the same hand.

"Where are you going?" Zade asked, looking to get up from his blanket and follow.

Riony offered a wicked smirk. "I'm not going far. Just going to find a bit of privacy to go and tenderly tend to myself. Unless there are any takers? No? No? No? Okay, good night."

Swaggering away, Riony breathed out a sigh when nobody attempted to follow her through the entrance of the shrine. Her heart was racing.

She hadn't felt anything from the unidragon for a while now. No sensations of hunger. Even pulling the otter in and out of the bag hadn't disturbed it. *Please still be alive, little one.*

The interior of the shrine wasn't very large, and most of the rear end of the room had collapsed in, leaving a gaping hole to the night sky above and mess of crystal and stone piled on the ground.

Riony was happy not to venture any farther and tucked herself into the corner right near the doorway.

Activating her light crystal, Riony quickly dug through her supplies to retrieve a large piece of shroom jerky. Opening the pack again, she thrust it into the face of the ready-to-escape otter.

The silky-furred critter took a moment to rethink its plan, then grabbed the food and burrowed deep into the backpack. It pushed around the body of the dragonling, and Riony peered in, desperate for signs of life.

Jostled by the otter, the newborn weakly opened its eyes.

"Hey, hey there, little one," Riony whispered soft as a breath. She scooted down onto her side, holding the pack open close to her face. "I'm so sorry. I'm sorry I've been shaking you all about and haven't had a chance to feed you. We've got time now."

Sorting through her netted bag, Riony retrieved the skin of goatmilk first. The unidragon had drunk some liquid before, so she hoped this might sustain it.

But when presented with a corner of cloth soaked in the milk, the baby turned its snout away.

"No? You don't do milk?"

She tried goat jerky again. Surely it must eat meat. She took a big bite herself, chewing as she waved the remainder in front of the dragonling's nose.

Hungry. It looked at her with a pitiful sniffle.

Riony's heart twanged like a plucked bowstring. She tried some of everything she had to offer.

It took nothing more than a few suckles of water, dripped from a flask over her fingers.

In between trying to get the unidragon to eat, Riony gave her arm a swift wipe down and tied one strip of cloth around the deep scratches, tightening the knot with her teeth. In desperation, she even offered the rag with her blood on it to the hungry critter, but it didn't take it.

The otter poked its snout back out, trying to snatch at the tiny banquet laid out on the ground.

"Quit it, Sir Furrybutt Whatever-your-name-is." Riony tossed it some more food to keep it out of the way. "How does a rodent like you get knighted anyway?"

How was Lyrrin so good at this? She'd managed to

bring in and keep alive all sorts of creatures, and there Riony was, failing at feeding the one most precious creature of all.

Heat burned in the back of Riony's eyes. She only knew one thing Lyrrin would do.

"Hey, little one. We're going to name you, okay?"

It blinked milky, translucent eyelids over its large lilac eyes.

"Little bit dragon, little bit unicorn. Okay, then. How about Dracuni?"

She reached out a hand, and the newborn nuzzled against it.

"Yeah. That's it. You're Dracuni. You know what that means right?" Riony settled down, curling protectively around the backpack and the delicate life inside.

"I've named you now. That means you aren't allowed to die on me."

SIXTEEN

The ground was hard and cold and Riony's restless mind swirled with worry.

She worried that Dracuni was fading from starvation before her eyes.

She worried that a lack of sleep would make her falter tomorrow and fail to save Lyrrin.

She worried that the revenant who continued to growl and pace too close for comfort would suddenly burst through into the shrine and devour them all.

How could anyone sleep through that?

She hoped Lyrrin was able to get some rest. That she and the other children were at least being kept safe and alive by their captors. She figured they would be, for the most part. The children were a valuable commodity for the slavers.

But Riony also had enough experience with people who treated other humans as a commodity to know that they didn't mind a little wastage.

Keep your head down, Lyrrin. Don't let them see you marking the trail. And try to sleep. You get super cranky when you don't sleep.

Riony sent her thoughts out into the dark night, as though she could connect with Lyrrin's mind the way Dracuni seemed to connect with her own.

That was unlikely. Riony had to console herself in the knowledge that Lyrrin was a tough kid. Lyrrin's mother had been strong, too. Riony knew that from being at the birth.

Riony had been Riony Uf'Heithorn, slave and whipping-girl to Kess, for years when Lyrrin's mother came to the Heithorn estate.

She and Kess had watched through a high window as the elegant, determined young woman arrived by dragon, along with her mother and a dragonguard big enough that he could have been a dragon himself.

The woman had the whitest hair she'd ever seen, a slight bulge to her stomach, and a steely look of defiance that glared down on every command she was given by her mother even as she followed them. Riony had never crushed so hard and fast on anyone before the way she did on that bold young woman.

She projected an instant kinship with her from that feeling, that rebellion in the face of obedience. She tried out mimicking the young woman's insolent expression that afternoon and got an extra-long whipping in return.

That evening, Riony had returned to the servants' quarters, to the small room her family shared, as she did each day after her duties with Kess. And she begged her parents to take her and run away from that place, as she did each day after her time with Kess.

And just like each day, her amma and pabba said no. The Heithorns weren't kind masters, but the world outside their protection would be even crueler.

"It couldn't be worse than this," Riony moaned as her mother applied an herbal ointment to the fresh wounds on her back.

Pabba had only just returned from his work in the fields and kicked his dirty boots off at the door. "You only say that because you've only ever lived under the protection of dragonlords."

Amma tsked. "I'm so sorry that spoiled child treats you this way. I know she has troubles of her own, but she's a right monster. We will get you out from under her control, one day. Your midwife training will continue, and soon our masters will see you are more valuable used elsewhere."

A scowl and pout were the politest things Riony could offer in reply.

"Did you see the young woman that came in today?" Pabba asked. He pulled up a simple, wobbly wooden stool beside where Riony leaned over the table.

Riony blushed. "Yeah?"

"She's come all the way from Draekhanhelm—"

"The capitol?" Riony perked up.

"Yup. All the way here to give birth because the Heithorns have such an excellent midwife on staff."

Amma smirked. "That's me, by the way."

"She's pregnant?" Riony sat up, mind taken off the stinging welts on her back. She pulled her shirt back down, feeling it stick to the wet ointment.

"A few months off the birth still. But I've already asked if they will allow you to be my assistant when the time comes." Amma wiped her hands clean, working the rag over the four plain steel rings she wore across her fingers.

"You think I'm ready to be at a birth?" Riony wasn't so sure, already cringing away from the idea based on just the knowledge and theory she'd been taught about the process. Plus, she was only ten, younger than others her amma had trained when they had started assisting in births.

Amma ruffled her hair. "We'll make sure you're ready, and

we'll show them that's the place you deserve to be. A respected midwife, not a plaything to a monster in girl's clothing."

It was that hope alone that got Riony through the coming months. She was always on the lookout for the beautiful moonlight-haired woman. The mother-to-be roamed around the estate often, shadowed by her mother and mountainous dragonrider bodyguard. Riony kept her eyes on the woman's growing belly, counting the days.

Nobody seemed to know who the young woman was or spoke of her by name. She was simply referred to by all as "the guest." There was an air of secrecy around her entire existence that thrilled Riony, as though most of the estate pretended she wasn't even there.

The birth came early. And went long.

Riony wasn't sure she helped very much, but she followed all her mother's orders with all the speed and precision a ten-year-old in a highly stressful environment could.

The guest's mother paced around the birthing chamber the entire time, wringing her hands. The beast of a bodyguard had been left in the adjoining entry room just outside.

Hours and hours passed, intermittent with bursts of frantic efforts and periods of waiting with nothing to be done but listen to the guest's wailing screams.

Every time the young mother seemed to have been pushed beyond her limits, every time she seemed to wane and faint, she would come back, drawing again on some unknown reservoir of power. Riony was shaken with awe at her strength.

All through one long night the labor continued.

With one final push, Amma announced the babe born.

"Her color. I'm not sure she's breathing," she said softly to Riony as they worked together to cut the cord.

"What is it? What's happening?" the guest asked feebly.

"Let me see," the guest's mother barged in between them as Amma briskly rubbed the newborn down.

Riony gasped. "Look, she breathes!"

Amma lifted the infant, preparing to hand her to the sobbing mother, when the older woman snapped. "Bring it in here!"

Confused for a moment, Amma watched as the older woman headed over to the entrance chamber. With a frown, she quickly swaddled the newborn and carried her along as she followed, beckoning Riony after her.

They stepped out into the small adjoining chamber that led into the birthing room. The burly guard waiting there eyed their appearance, but his only acknowledgement was the twitch of his nose.

Riony hadn't been this close to him before. He looked like he crushed tree trunks between his thighs for fun. Like he could barely fit through a doorway without grazing his

biceps. Riony glanced down at the small bumps of muscle on her own arms, aspiring to be that strong one day.

A small table stood in the center of the space, meant to hold gifts to mothers and their newborns, laid out as the woman was in labor. As the guest didn't seem to know anybody at the estate, there was only one small flower decorating the table surface.

The old woman tossed it aside. "Show me the baby."

Amma laid the swaddled newborn on the table. "Oh, she's still a bit blue. But I'm sure she'll be all right soon."

Amma frowned as she wiped at the infant's scalp. White mucus cleared away, but the blue coloring remained.

With very little care, the older woman unwrapped the newborn, leaving her cold and bare on the table. The baby squinted at her with the brightest blue eyes Riony had ever seen. Her tiny mouth opened, but she didn't cry.

"It's her hair," Riony said in amazement. "The blue color is hair."

The older woman sucked in a sharp breath and grabbed the baby's arms, inspecting the hands. Fingers so small that Riony could barely believe they were real were closed in tight fists. There was a blue tinge to the skin there too, and when the older woman forced the hands open, she gasped.

"Was silvernix used?" Amma asked softly. "Any time during the pregnancy?"

The older woman said nothing. She backed away from the table, her chin lifted and a hard expression growing.

Riony reached out, touching the newborn's strange hand. The baby wrapped her fingers in a strong grip around her finger. "Still, she's healthy. Especially for an early birth, right, Amma?"

The older woman shook her head and turned from them, speaking to the guard. "Dispose of the newborn. It can't be allowed to live."

Riony's eyes shot wide-open and she stepped in front of the table. "No! You can't kill a baby!"

Amma moved beside her, clutching her arm and trying to pull her away, hissing under her breath.

The older woman threw a disdainful look back toward them. "The witnesses too. Get rid of all of them."

The guard gave a rough grunt of agreement and drew his sword.

The older woman left, returning to the birthing chamber.

Riony could hear the young mother inside, questioning in a weak voice.

"Your child didn't make it. And I'm cleaning up the other loose ends of this mess for you."

A wail and weeping followed that clawed into Riony's soul, only distracted by the glint of the sword that approached, ready to end her life and her mother's and that of the tiny,

special little being that had only just taken her first breaths.

"Please, please just let us go. We won't tell anybody anything," Amma pleaded with the massive man. She still clung to Riony, trying to drag her away from the protective position she'd taken in front of the newborn.

A deep animal snarl built in Riony's throat. She set her stance, refusing to move. It wasn't fair! They couldn't just kill the baby. She didn't want to die either, but she wasn't going to try to trade her life for another.

From the lazy smile and sickening look of pleasure in the man's eyes, Riony doubted he'd take any trade anyway. He seemed excited by the very concept of hacking down three defenseless victims.

A fire of defiance flared over Riony. She snatched her arm free from her mother and launched herself in a flurry of fists and teeth at the man. She wrapped her whole body around one of his arms, flailing and fighting as hard as she could.

Like a drowning kitten, she was grasped by the scruff of the neck and lifted away. The guard rumbled a harsh laugh as she continued to kick and thrash, futile against limbs that were as thick around as her whole body.

That laugh drove Riony mad. She contorted like a wild animal, and a foot finally connected. The clang of steel followed, the sword knocked free from the man's other meaty hand.

With a grunt of annoyance, he dropped Riony as well, as though discarding a soiled washcloth. She landed hard on her knees and collapsed face down on the smooth marble tiles. And right in front of her eyes lay the sword.

She snatched it with the speed of zinging adrenaline and unsteadily jumped back to her feet. Her hands grasped tight around the pre-warmed hilt and the tip of the blade dragged heavily along the floor.

"What are you going to do with that, little girl?" The guard snuffled and snorted at his own humor as he smirked at her. "As if you're even strong enough to lift—"

The sword tip piercing through his chest left his words unfinished.

Riony had lifted the sword. She had been strong enough. Her hard-worked arms moved fast and she'd thrust the blade deep into the thick bulk of the man before either of them could think any longer on the likelihood of that action.

Riony put *everything* she had into that thrust. Every bit of strength Kess had worked into her, every shred of anger at the scars on her back, every tear shed on hopeless pleas to flee, to try for something more than *this*, every hope and desire that burned in her that she and her amma and the baby would live.

She and the guard stood like that, connected by the sharp line of steel, for a long moment, as though neither

of them could believe what had happened. Then the man gurgled. Blood dripped from his lips. His hands shot out weakly, grabbing wildly at the air around the sword as though he couldn't see despite his wide eyes still staring down.

He stilled, then slowly toppled backward. Riony kept hold of the sword, tugging as the suction of his body fought against her. Her hands had locked around the hilt as though nothing could pry them open ever again.

She remained holding that bloodied sword as her amma tried to drag her away. As she was scolded for what she'd done, in a voice that held pride and fear in equal measure. As she refused to run without taking the newborn with them.

She held that sword as her amma wrapped the baby back up and they all fled together, out through a window and across the fields. As they scurried along the stone walls of paddocks until they found Riony's pabba tilling the earth as the sun rose.

He took the hoe in his hands and the sack that held his lunch and nothing more. Riony still grasped the dragonguard's sword as they left Heithorn estate behind for the undead wastelands beyond.

"That's how I ended up with a sister," Riony whispered to Dracuni, who whimpered soft sleepy sounds from within the backpack.

And now I have you, too.

Taking Lyrrin had been easier than taking Dracuni, in some ways. Riony still had her parents back then. They knew how to care for a newborn, and Lyrrin was a good baby, a quiet baby, who didn't cry once as their family hid under trees from the hunt of dragonguards sent out to retrieve them.

Amma knew how to feed Lyrrin, clean her, settle her to sleep. Riony learned over time, too, and helped as much as she could. She did, after all, feel somewhat as though Lyrrin were *hers*. Her decision to take. Her responsibility.

Now Riony was alone, and none of her midwife training could have prepared her for this.

Another newborn taken. Another responsibility so immense it felt like it could crush her.

Now two lives depended upon Riony, and all she could think was that she was failing them both.

SEVENTEEN

Riony groaned and shifted, her body bruised by the hard ground beneath her. She opened her eyes and blinked. A dim light filtered in through the gaping hole across the shrine.

The night had been spent not so much in sleep, as in simply waiting for morning to arrive. Riony decided that anemic glow was morning enough. She stretched out her whole body, then rolled over onto her stomach, pressing into a quick set of push-ups, as she normally started her days.

Once her body had built up a warm flush, she stopped and checked on Dracuni and Butterfur, offering them both some food—taken greedily by the otter and ignored by the dragonling.

Riony chewed ravenously on some dry cheese herself as she stepped out from the ruined shrine to see the other three already awake as well. They all looked like they had about as much sleep as she had.

Yoskar kicked out the remains of last night's fire, and Zade sat off to the side, a troubled expression in his gaze as he stared out into the forest.

"Morning," he said when he noticed Riony join them. The bruise the slavers had given him had settled in, dark purple around the bridge of his nose and yellow along his bottom eyelids, making his blue eyes seem a sickly gray.

"Where's our new friend?" Riony asked, scanning around the perimeter of the standing stones.

"We lost track of the rev sometime during the night. One minute it was there, then it was gone." Aishena stalked around the campsite like a cornered beast, collecting scattered supplies and checking her weapons. Her gait was uneven but steady. Her injured ankle was taking weight.

That was good news, at least. Riony wasn't sure about the rev though.

"Does anyone find it creepier that it left than if it had stayed?" she asked. "What is a rev leaving to do? What pressing business did it have that was better than waiting to chew on our tasty flesh?"

"Doesn't matter," Yoskar said. He strapped his pack

closed, then hoisted it onto his back. "We should move on before it decides to come back."

Riony nodded, her nerves all sharp and jangly within from worry and lack of sleep. She ducked back into the shrine for her netted bag and pack and threw her cloak over the top. Stepping back out again, the others were all similarly loaded up and ready to go.

"What's the plan? Which way do we take from here?" she asked. They could go back the way they came and try to pick up the trail again from there, but that was a long way up a steep and slippery slope.

Riony looked to Aishena for an answer, but she only stood at attention and waited for Yoskar to speak.

Yoskar held out both arms at a right angle. "That direction"—he pointed with his left hand—"is where the rev ambushed the slavers and we went offtrack. If we extrapolate that path farther north, we'd end up crossing the low peaks that were in this direction." He pointed with his right hand.

Riony put her hands on her hips. "Extrapolate my ass. Your best plan is to aim yourself at a whole mountain range and hope for the best? How are we going to actually find them if we don't find any markers again?"

Zade squinted at where Yoskar pointed, as though he could see the mountains through the dense forest.

"Stonewing Crest is that way. It's a bit of a climb, but there's a good view over the rest of the area from up there. We'll be able to get our bearings and hopefully even see some sign of the slavers."

"Aboveground expert all of a sudden, are we?" Aishena scowled.

"At least he's helping. And that sounds promising." Riony flexed her feet, ready to move. She liked the idea of being able to look down on the land and spot her sister. She longed for any way to see her again.

Riony gave Aishena and her ankle an evaluating look. "Are we all ready?"

With an awkward twitch of her lips, Aishena said, "I'll keep up. The poultice helped."

A smile broke on Zade's face. "Wonderful! Look at us, sticking together. We're going to make it."

His optimism did little to scratch the surface of fatigue and worry amongst the others.

All four of them were on high alert as they stepped out from the ring of crystalline standing stones. Nothing burst out from the tangle of trees at them, so they picked up the pace, eying the surrounding woods warily as they alternated between a swift march and a jog as the terrain allowed.

As the tree trunks thinned, the ground sloped upward again, and soon they broke out from the forest and onto

an incline of wind-battered grasses and rubbly stones.

Still, there was no sign of the revenant. That left a cold jellylike feeling in Riony's stomach, as though the odd, ashy creature might jump out at them again at any moment. *Why hadn't it died when it was burned?* None of them seemed to want to mention it, discuss it, or even think about it.

It was probably just a fluke anyway. Aishena's burn athame might have been faulty or something. Too low on charge. Riony didn't know, but she knew revs died when you burned them so something else must have gone wrong this one time.

Larger outcrops of rock jutted out from the earth like teeth, and their path soon became a trial of finding their way around the large stones and climbing the low cliffs and overhangs they formed.

Riony's legs burned and sweat dripped down between her shoulders and her pack. She chewed on her lip as they walked, but Zade kept by her side, offering her reassurance whenever a frown overcame her face. Somehow, he seemed so certain they would find the kids again, and that sure hope kept Riony going.

He kept them on track, pointing upward to a high peak ahead. The ground grew treacherous as they went higher. Sheer drops and gaping crevasses shot through the

steep mountain, causing the group to zigzag around them.

A shadow passed over Riony, making her flinch. A carrion hawk circled overhead on vast wings. Not quite as big as a dragon, but a healthy size, grown large from plenty of options to scavenge in this land of death. Riony chased away thoughts of the creature picking at her bones. She never liked birds.

As they edged along a narrow path, Riony looked over the drop and gulped. It had not been nearly long enough since the last time she'd fallen down into a deep hole and wasn't nearly prepared to do so again.

Not to suggest I would ever be prepared to do that again. It would take wild and impossible conditions to even consider it, like if throwing myself into a pit would get Aishena to date me.

The delvers didn't appear to care about the risk of falling or the strain on their muscles, setting a fast pace that Riony matched. Zade had more obvious signs of struggling but didn't slow them down. A couple of times Riony reached her hand to him to help drag him up a steeper bluff, and he'd offer a beaming smile in return.

Once, she reached her good hand to Aishena and was surprised when the delver took it. Riony quickly ruined the moment by winking and jiggling her eyebrows at her, making Aishena scowl and storm ahead.

After what felt like hours, they finally reached a large,

flat outcrop that jutted out into the air. Surrounded by gorges on most sides, it looked out over lower peaks and a valley beyond. The view was clear right out to the east and north horizons.

Riony stepped up to the sheer drop and took in the view, scanning the landscape hungrily for any sign of their target. Aishena moved beside her, shading her eyes against the sun and peering out as well. Zade remained a few steps behind them, catching his breath, drinking from a waterskin and rummaging around in his pack.

The forest stretched out beneath Riony like a green carpet, and in the distance, she could see the glimmer of a river. Beside that river, a line of smoke slithered like a silver serpent up into the sky.

"There," she gasped out the word, her lungs still heaving from the climb.

Yoskar reached behind himself, pulling free the crystal-studded staff he carried. Holding it before him, he traced a rune on a smoky stone near the top. With a soft crackle of magic, the crystal cleared to a shimmering transparent glass. He held it to his eye and looked toward the smoke.

Riony stepped closer, hoping to work out what he was seeing. She didn't even know quite what he was doing, angling the staff around and staring through that cleared stone. Light glinted in the corner of her eye.

She hadn't seen an Alderkin artifact like that before but wasn't surprised the delvers were keeping all the best stuff to themselves.

"It's them," Yoskar said.

"Can I have a look?" Riony asked.

"No." Yoskar set the staff back down, holding it like a walking stick as he deactivated the rune. "Seems like a more permanent camp, defensive palisades, larger tents. And cages. Cages with kids in them."

Riony shivered, the sweat on her skin chilling as her body cooled and a wind blew over her. "Even if the new lot of kids they took isn't there yet, that's probably where they are going, right? But how many slavers are there? How are we going to go up against them?"

"We can work that out when we get a closer look. If we hurry, maybe we'll catch up to Benjin still along the way. And Lyrrin," Aishena added.

"Move now, think later. Easy. My usual plan, honestly," Riony said.

They turned back as Zade was packing his waterskin away, face still flushed from the hike.

"You okay?" Riony asked.

"Yeah. You all are so fast though. I'll do my best to keep up. We're close now, we can do this."

Riony found herself smiling in return.

There was a clearer path leading north, as though sometime in the past this had been a passage regularly taken by travelers, until people stopped traveling overland as much. It led them from the lookout toward a gaping gorge, strung across by a ratty-looking rope bridge.

Riony poked her toes at the first plank. "That looks like a whole bunch of *nope*, held together by dust and cobwebs."

"It's the fastest route," Yoskar said.

Aishena pushed Riony out of the way. "We can secure it with our ropes if you're too scared of something delvers deal with all the time. Feels sturdy enough to me."

Spurred by a surge of competitive spite, Riony was about to fight Aishena back for the chance to be the first to plunge into oblivion, when movement across the gorge caught her attention.

From behind a boulder, a large charcoal-colored wolf emerged. It strode on silent paws to the other side of the bridge, Kess perched on its back like a mangy gargoyle.

Riony's whole body went rigid.

"Is that …?" Aishena peered with confused eyes across the gap.

Riony muttered, "One of the world's cruelest and most vicious creatures, riding on a wolf? Yup."

"Little Kessara Heithorn?" Yoksar finished his sister's sentence loud enough to echo across the gorge.

Even from a distance, the snarl on Kess's lips was clear. The midafternoon sun glinted off her bared teeth.

"You guys know each other?" Riony stepped back, eying the delver siblings. She'd never seen them on Heithorn estate, but there had been the odd occasion that Kess was taken away to a dragonkeep for some purpose or another.

But only very rarely. Her parents generally avoided revealing her to their noble peers unless forced to.

"Look who we've found," she drawled.

"Sorry, who is this?" Zade asked.

There was something decidedly more feral about this Kess than the one Riony had once known, and it wasn't just the fact that she was riding on a wolf.

Kess had always been on the smaller side, but now she was both small and sharp, all wiry arms and razor cheekbones and pointy chin. Her storm-gray hair was half-bundled on her head in a matted mess of unkempt braids and half-draping down in tangled locks, wilder than the creature she rode.

Just one streak of white marked the front of her tresses, evidence of the wealth of silvernix that had once been spent on her.

Back at Heithorn Castle, braiding Kess's hair had been one of Riony's duties. It looked like she didn't have anyone to do that for her anymore.

"What are you doing out here?" Yoskar called across the bridge, ignoring Riony's question. "What are you doing *on a wolf*?"

"Could ask you two the same thing." Kess and her wolf approached the other end of the bridge but didn't step onto it.

Riony cupped her hands around her mouth and yelled back, "They aren't on wolves, you unfortunate accident of meat and emotions!"

Zade snorted.

Riony had been lying in a rapidly chilling pool of her own blood the last time Kess crossed her path. That had made it hard to get some appropriately scathing digs in at an abusive master that wasn't her master anymore. She fully intended on catching up.

She moved to the front of her group, standing right at the edge of the bridge, hoping Kess would cross it so she could catch the wolf-rider's face with her fist a few times too.

Kess leaned forward and patted the wolf on its jowls. "Griskin here caught wind of a familiar scent, something interesting he wouldn't let me ignore. Didn't think it would be you. Not since your organs were more outside than in when I saw you last in that ice cave. You were as good as dead."

"Wait, wait. You're not suggesting your wolf can talk,

are you?" Riony hollered back. "Is it a language only other dogs can understand?"

Kess stared back dully. "With your lack of functioning brain matter, I wouldn't expect you to understand anything."

"I understood your mother's body pretty well last time I saw her!"

Yoskar grabbed Riony's shoulder and turned her toward him. "When were you dying?"

Riony winced and tried replying with just an innocent grin and shrug.

Kess said, "That dragon mother she messed around with ripped her all to shreds. You can imagine my surprise that she's up and walking around."

Zade held up his hands. "Hang on, dragon mother? Ice cave? Internal organs on the outside? What has been going on?"

"After ..." Aishena's face paled. She turned to Yoskar. "We must have missed it by moments. That dragon could have gotten us, too."

"Ah, you were the other two intolerable wastes who were there as well. Pony's keeping secrets from you too? Something let her walk out of that ice cave. Something that left her without a scratch."

"Your arm?" Aishena stared at the bandaged right arm that Riony still had up near her face.

"Um, whoops?" Riony said, waving back with wriggling fingers and swinging the supposedly broken arm back to her side. *Guess that ruse is over.*

"You've been pretending *this whole time*?" Aishena spluttered the start of a few more words, as though calculating out the running and climbing and fighting Riony had all done with her left arm only.

"Enough!" Kess cried. She pulled a dagger the length of her forearm and held it threateningly above the rope holding up the bridge. "How did you get out of that cave alive?"

Riony froze. That bridge was her shortest path to reaching Lyrrin. She held her hands up in surrender. But there was no way she was going to surrender the creature in her backpack.

"Kess, don't," Yoskar said. "We need to go that way. Our brother is in trouble. Slavers have him. Her sister, too."

Riony shot him a dark look. She didn't want Kess knowing a thing about Lyrrin.

"Since when do you have a sister?"

"Since I last banged your amma," Riony threw back.

"Would you stop?" Yoskar stepped in front of her and addressed Kess again. "Ignore this oaf and her half-witted insults—"

"Kess is a half-witted insult," Riony said.

Yoskar spoke over her, giving Kess a more reasonable

tone than she ever deserved. "You seem to have been aboveground for a while. Help us out. You must know this area better than us. Help us get our brother back, and we'll make it worth your while."

Kess lowered her blade a barely perceptible amount. "You can make it worth my while, by making her answer my question. I want to know how she was healed. A runaway slave like her wouldn't have silvernix. I want to know what it was that helped her walk out of that cave. Then I'll help get you where you need to go."

Riony shot a pleading look at Yoskar. "You can't trust her."

A closemouthed grin grew on Kess's face, and she lowered her dagger entirely.

Yoskar folded his arms. "Tell us. Tell us all how you survived."

"Survived what? Maybe she's the one lying about the whole dragon ripping me up incident."

Aishena stood beside her brother, creating a wall of interrogation. "Even without additional injuries, you've been remarkably healed compared to how you were before."

"Go on, Pony," Kess called.

Riony fingered the hilt of her sword, judging if she could throw it across the gap and skewer Kess to the cliffside instead of being forced to answer. She doubted her aim was that good, though, and didn't want to risk losing her sword into the gorge.

"Fine!" She flung her hands up. "I did have some unicorn blood."

Aishena pouted skeptically.

"*You* had silvernix?" she said, heavy on the *you*.

"Just one little drop. It was a gift to my grandmother for saving her master's wife during childbirth, ages back when silvernix wasn't as scarce. I've just been carrying it around since then, you know, waiting for the right time when all our insides were on the outside."

Everyone stared at her silently, as though trying to judge the likelihood of her statement.

Riony pulled her cloak away to show her bare neck to the delvers. "It was kept hidden in the acorn. That's why it's gone now. I used it."

Exactly *how* she used it, she didn't need to say.

Aishena and Yoskar looked at each other and shrugged.

Riony turned to Kess, who seemed entirely unsatisfied with the answer. "You saw how the dragon left me. How else would I still possibly be alive other than using silvernix? Think I put on a poultice, you abominable, ill-nurtured fart-face?"

"Careful, you'll use up all your big words, Uf'Heithorn."

"I'm not Uf'Heithorn anymore, and never will be again!"

"You two clearly have some history." Yoskar took a step

forward onto the bridge. "But we made a deal. Riony gave you an answer. Let's move on, and you can help us find the stolen children."

Kess lifted her dagger. "You think we made a deal? You're almost as tamebrained as Pony."

She brought the blade down, lightning fast over the rope. It sliced straight through. The slackened tension of the bridge creaked and twanged, an explosion of ripples running from Kess's side to theirs.

Then in a sickening slow motion, the whole bridge swung free. Riony lunged forward, grabbing Yoskar and dragging him back onto solid ground as the planks gave way beneath him. They fell in a tangle together in the dust.

Scrambling to her feet, Riony considered again throwing her sword. The bridge clattered against the cliff wall beside her, dust rising and obscuring her view for a moment.

She screamed across the ravine, "There are two things I hate about you, Kess, and it's your face!"

Panic worked her lungs. That bridge was her path to Lyrrin. She growled in frustration as Kess casually rode away.

EIGHTEEN

Aishena knelt beside Yoskar, fussing over him before he brushed her aside.

"This is your fault!" she snapped at Riony.

"Saving your brother's life? You're welcome." Riony stalked up and down the edge of the gorge, glaring at the other side.

Aishena grabbed her shoulder, forcing her to stop and look at her sour face. "Why did you have to keep goading her? If you'd kept your big mouth shut—"

"She would have done it anyway! That's what Kess does. Given any two choices, she'll always find a third that's even crueler. She was *never* going to help you. Even if there was something in it for her."

Riony turned her face to the gray sky, her neck muscles straining as she wanted to scream and curse with all her might. Only the knowledge that Kess could probably still hear her and take satisfaction from her misery blocked her throat.

Leaving me to die alone was one thing, but if this stunt of Kess's stops me from getting Lyrrin back, I'm going to make it my life's ambition to carve every bit of misery out of that wolf-riding snot-licker as I can.

"If Riony used to be Uf'Heithorn, she probably knows what she's talking about," Zade said gently.

Riony backed that up with a dark glower. "I've got more than enough scars to prove it, if any of you want me to strip off so you can take a look. It might turn into a special moment. I'll see the concern on your lips as you try to stay strong at the pain I must have suffered."

Aishena closed her mouth and stepped back, turning her eyes away.

Yoskar got to his feet and moved to where the bridge had fallen. "Regardless, that was our way forward." He fidgeted with the delicate but strong cave-silk rope coiled at his belt. "It's too far across. Maybe we can tie our ropes together, Aish, but even if we could get a strong hold on the other side, it wouldn't be easy getting across."

"I could climb down, tie a rope to the end of the bridge, then—"

"We'd need both to span the distance. We'd have to get you over to the other side first, then maybe we could try to bring the bridge back up for us."

Yoskar and Aishena huddled together, tossing ideas back and forth.

Riony bounced on her toes, desperate to break into a run. Lyrrin was probably just there, in the valley below. There was no way she could make the jump, but her legs tensed as though they wanted to give it their best shot.

Zade looked up and down the length of the gorge before them with a pained look on his face. "There's another way."

Everyone turned to him, waiting.

"I think I know another path. I used to live near here—"

"Tjollaskeep? It's farther to the east," Yoskar said.

"But I've been through here before, on my way to the undercity the first time. I came in at the bottom of the gorge and had to find a way up. There's a path, farther along that way. It's steep, but it will get us down into the valley in the right direction."

"And you think you can remember the right way?" Aishena's tone suggested she was skeptical about his answer already.

"Yes." Zade's voice was firm and he straightened up to stare her in the eye. "I want to catch up with the kids as much as you do."

"I doubt it," she hissed.

"We all want to get to the kids as fast as we can," Riony said. "You really think you can get us there?"

There was a steely determination in Zade's eyes. "I do."

"Lead the way," Yoskar commanded.

Aishena opened her mouth, but a look from Yoskar silenced her.

Riony gave Zade an encouraging nod, and he turned, moving at a swift jog along the side of the gorge.

They all followed behind, clumped together at first, but soon trailing one at a time as the path narrowed between a cliff on one side and the sheer drop into the canyon on the other. They had to slow down, placing their feet carefully on the unstable stones.

What looked like a dead end approached, but before Riony could question it, Zade took what seemed to be a step off the edge into open air.

He dropped about knee-deep, then stopped and began heading back toward them. Riony leaned over and saw the narrow path, switching back their way, then zigzagging down the cliff face.

Yoskar and Aishena reached out to each other and connected a link between them with a rope. They didn't offer to do so with the others, nor did Riony or Zade have the right connections to hook onto anyway.

Riony would have felt better with something tethering her from slipping down the rough, rocky slope, but she also didn't want to stop long enough to fashion some kind of harness like the delvers had built into their leather armor.

Progress was difficult, with the ledge sometimes becoming so narrow that they had to turn face-first toward the cliff and cling to it as they tiptoed along.

Riony worried they were going too slowly. Too slow to reach Lyrrin in time to save her. Too slow to reach Lyrrin in time so Lyrrin could help save Dracuni. There had been so few pleas of hunger in her mind that morning, and they grew weaker and weaker.

Each time she tried to speed up, the path narrowed again.

Sweat ran down her forehead into her eyes and her heart hammered. And then Zade dropped off the edge in front of her, disappearing from sight.

"Zade!" she cried out.

"Down here," he replied. "We've made it."

Wiping her eyes clear, Riony looked over the end of the ledge, at the ground just a body-length below.

With a huff of relief, she almost leaped the rest of the way as well, but instead turned and lowered herself carefully so as not to jostle Dracuni. The more the newborn could sleep, the more it could conserve its energy until it ate. She didn't worry so much about the cave otter. It had eaten itself into a stupor the night before and would probably sleep through anything.

Landing beside Zade, Riony punched him lightly on the arm. "Don't scare me like that."

He smirked in return. "Didn't think you scared easily."

"Aw, it's like you really know me."

Zade quirked his lips in a half smile at Riony. "Wouldn't mind getting to know you a bit more. Maybe you can tell me all about dragons and ice caves and almost dying once we get where we need to be."

Aishena and Yoskar dropped lightly beside them as one, then unclipped from each other.

Aishena gave Riony an appraising look. "You climb well. You might make a decent delver after all."

That sort of admission from Aishena was as rare as horn ivory. Riony wanted to say something cocky like, *I'd make as good of a delver as I would a lover*, but found instead that she flushed hot from head to toe and had to clear her throat and look away.

"Me too, right?" Zade asked with a wide grin.

Aishena recoiled and shut her mouth tight.

A shallow rocky creek ran along beside them, just a thin trickle of water.

Zade pointed up the length of the gorge the way the water ran. "If we head that way, it should curve around

and come out not too far from where we would have been if we took the higher path. Then it's just up the river to the slavers' camp."

Riony's heart kicked up a notch. They were close. So close.

Aishena and Yoskar also seemed to buzz with nervous energy, and nobody said anything else as they broke into a run again.

Hungry. The voice was tiny, fading, barely edging through the pulse beating in Riony's ears.

But she couldn't stop now. Couldn't slow down. Not when the slavers were within sight. Each breath pelted Riony's lungs, and her legs still burned from the climb, but she couldn't—she wouldn't—slow down.

They followed the meager creek until another branched into it, then another. The walls of the gorge shortened from an imposing, claustrophobic height looming over them on both sides, down to a lower ledge, then again to just a pile of boulders and rubble.

Then the land opened out before them in a burned-out meadow. The river ran along their side, and the ground was marshy as they sprinted for the cover of a blackened copse ahead.

The smell of smoke was in the air, but not just normal smoke. Cooking. The char of roasting meat. Riony's stomach clenched, and she felt Dracuni plead with her again.

The proximity to the slaver camp kept them quiet, and they moved through the burnt trunks and rough brush in slow and careful movements. The odd sound of a cracking twig or shift of dirt set Riony on edge, and she shot warning glares to the others to be more careful. Only Aishena managed to remain entirely silent as she treaded the path.

Yoskar took the lead, and as the ramshackle palisades of the camp came into view, he snuck up a low rise around to one side. He motioned to them all to keep down, and they crouched and scurried between scratchy bushes.

They lined up behind a fallen log, and Yoskar put his finger to his lips and pointed over it.

They were high enough there that they could see down into the camp.

Riony popped her head up to look, and Aishena slapped her down.

"You're like a signal fire with that hair!" she whispered and grabbed Riony's hood, pulling it over her head for her.

Sneaking around was more Aishena's thing than Riony's, and she did have a point. Riony muttered a thanks, then looked again.

The palisades barricading the camp were more charcoal than wood. Within them were large tents made of crude leather and thin metal posts. Cheap, scrounged-up materials. Since the dragonforges burned day in and day out, and the

dragonriders burned the land, timber was scarcer than steel.

More metal caught Riony's eye, and she spotted two large cages, not far from where a carcass was being turned on a spit over a smoldering fire.

The simple barred cages were packed with children, at least thirty or more crammed into the small space.

Some slavers were bringing a couple of final kids up and loading them in. They must have only just arrived. Riony scanned over the faces.

"Benj," Aishena gasped, pointing to the back corner of the closest cage.

Riony squinted and spotted him too. The ashy-haired boy stood there, his back to another child who was crouched low by the bars and shadowed by a large hood. *Lyrrin!*

Riony's heart was ready to fly out of her throat. Her sister was there, within sight. She just had to get her out, somehow.

Lyrrin seemed to already be working on that. Riony could see the pale ungloved skin of one of her hands, working against the corner bar.

Is she trying to cut through? Riony knew that Lyrrin's nails were sharp. They were sharper and stronger than they had any right to be. But would they be enough to cut through steel?

Riony felt a surge of pride in her sister either way. *Good girl for trying. I'm almost with you. Once I get through those slavers…*

Each tent was big enough to sleep at least five men, and as the sun lowered over the mountains, Riony counted ten milling about, seeing to cooking and chores. Over by the palisade entrance, another seven stood in a group, having some kind of meeting with ...

"Sparking *Kess*!" Riony growled.

"What's she doing there?" Yoskar whispered.

"Selling our fine asses out to the enemy, what do you think?"

Zade popped up over the log to look too, silent counting on his lips as he scanned over the number of slavers.

"If she's warning them of our approach, we have to get in there right now before they have any chance to prepare or move on," Yoskar huffed. "It's not ideal, but if we hurry, they may still be distracted by dealing with her. We could head around the back, over there, and—"

A shrill, piercingly loud whistle cut him off.

Riony whipped around to see Zade with two fingers in his mouth. "What in this razed earth are you doing?"

He stood up and took a few steps back from her and the delvers as the bushes around them erupted.

Grizzled, armored men surrounded them, swords and crossbows targeted.

Slavers, all around, and Zade stood beside them.

Nineteen

"Zade." The word was a low, warning drawl from Riony's mouth. She scrabbled around from where she crouched and reached for her sword, but the closest crossbow shifted her way and she stilled, remaining on her knees. "What have you done?"

Zade offered a gentle smile, tilting his head. "I told you I'd get you to the slavers."

"You ..." Riony couldn't speak around the anger, as though it swelled in her mouth, thickening her tongue. He had. He'd led them all the way. Always helpful, always staying positive. Because he'd always known exactly where he was going the whole time.

A swell of disgust made bile rise up Riony's throat. She couldn't believe she had started to like the traitor, that she'd trusted him. Any fondness was gone now, replaced with seething vengeance.

Yoskar had his head bowed, shaking it as though his own hindsight was catching up to him too.

Aishena growled through gritted teeth. "You creep! You're dead, Zade. Dead."

"Aishena, you had me worried a couple of times. Thought you were onto me. But then I realized you're just naturally unpleasant to everyone." Zade smirked as he looked down at her. "This is for the best. Don't fight. There's no point in getting yourselves hurt."

Riony snarled, "Oh, I could think of a few good points. I can help drive them through your skull if you like."

Zade dared to flash one of his brightest smiles her way, as though they were still friends, joking around.

"All right, all right. Enough of all that." A tall and imposing slaver stepped forward. The man wore ragged hides but moved with the bearing and confidence of royalty. He swaggered up beside Zade and smiled at him, turning his face to reveal a large burn scar around his left eye.

A twinge of recollection shook Riony. She'd seen him before.

Zade's shoulders slumped as though a great tension

had been relieved, and he grinned at the man. "Thank the stars you got my signal! Things might have gotten messy if they'd made it into camp."

"Yep, saw you flash us from up on the lookout cliff. Was a little surprised you weren't coming in with Hamric and the others." The slaver looked around, as though the men he mentioned might still be on their way.

"They didn't make it. Rev attack," Zade replied solemnly.

"The ambush?" Riony hissed. Not just a tail guard, after all, but men Zade was supposed to meet with. If it wasn't for that revenant, the slavers might have had her and the delvers captured much sooner.

Riony's body shook. She felt used, tricked, by the revelation she'd walked right along willingly into the slavers' trap.

"Shame. Quite liked that guy. Still, you made it here anyway." The scarred man moved closer to examine the delver brother and sister. He bent down, scratching his stubbly chin as he eyed them. "Yep. I suppose it does look like the ones we're after. Good job."

Zade beamed. "I told you if you took their little brother that would lure the other Hjelzahn siblings out from underground."

Hjelzahn? As in Hjelzahnkeep? If so, they weren't just dragonlords; they were direct descendants of the Dragonking.

Well, that explained their steel-bright hair. No doubt fourth or even fifth generation, but still with their own stars-damned dragonkeep. Riony stared at Aishena with questioning eyes, but Aishena didn't meet her gaze.

"Yeah, it was a good plan, kid." The man slapped Zade on the shoulder.

"You took Benjin on purpose? To get to us?" Aishena's words were thick with venom.

Zade's eyes brightened, as though he was proud of how everything had unfolded so neatly for him. "Your mother has a big bounty out to get her children back. I had wondered whether the missing kids were you lot. I mean, you sort of fit the descriptions and bounty portraits, but I wasn't sure until Benjin went and bragged about it."

"Our mother ...?" Yoskar's voice was shaky and timid. Riony had never seen him like that, normally so stoic and bland. Now, he looked downright terrified.

Zade brushed a bounce of curls away from his face. "I'm just trying to reunite a broken family. I don't know why you two were hiding out, but it wasn't right, taking Benjin with you. He's young and deserves to be with his parents."

Aishena moved in a flash, lunging a couple of steps toward Zade before she was brought to a halt by a wall of sword points.

A bounty set by their mother? Somehow hurt by the

revelation of the lie, Riony whispered across to Yoskar. "You said you lost your parents."

He didn't look at her. "We did. We didn't say they were both dead."

Riony muttered in a low tone, "Sure, but you knew that was clearly a misleading use of words—"

"Is this really the time?" Yoskar turned and snapped.

Riony shrugged and rolled her eyes. "I have the capacity to be mad at all of you all at once."

The scarred man grinned at Zade around a mouthful of yellowed teeth. "This is excellent work, kid. Between double the number of kids as usual, and the bounty from the three Hjelzahns, you can buy your way into whatever dragonkeep you want."

Riony jolted at the man's words. "*As usual*? You've done this before? Selling children's lives away?"

She suddenly remembered where she'd seen the scarred man before. In the undercity, begging near the orphans' den. Or pretending to beg.

She'd seen him there, the same day she'd broken her arm and found the dragon eggs.

Looking around the rest of the group that had them surrounded, Riony's skin crawled. They were a weathered lot, etched with the scars of countless battles, expressions hardened by the merciless tasks of their trade.

The one with the grizzled red beard and piercing ice-blue eyes, wearing the dinted chest plate. And the woman at the back, with a motherly face and missing front teeth, brown hair hanging in a thick, heavy braid. A scrawny man with frizzy yellow hair that fluffed out around his ruddy copper skin.

Riony had seen them, too. She'd seen those faces before in the undercity.

The slavers had been right there under their noses the whole time.

And Zade, working for them.

"You don't know what you're talking about," Zade shot back. "I'm saving the kids' lives. You know what the conditions in the orphans' den are like. That's no kind of life for children, alone and abandoned. I've been helping smuggle them out to the safety of the cities where they should be."

Riony raised her eyebrows and cooed. "Oh, I'm sorry. I get it now. It's all been done from the goodness of your heart! Not at all for the sweet cut that you're getting on the price of their lives as you sell them off to become slaves."

"Why'd you bring this loudmouth along?" the scarred man grunted.

Zade chuckled wryly. "Hadn't meant to, but her little sister caused a fuss so she got rounded up with the rest of them, and then this one insisted on coming along."

Riony snorted out a puff of anger.

Zade stepped closer to her, and the skin around his eyes wrinkled in concern. "I'm sorry you got caught up in this, Riony. We don't have to be enemies. We could use someone strong like you on our side. I thought we were getting along really well."

"Yeah, that was before I found out you were the disgusting creep Aishena said you were."

"We can work this out. I can help make sure you end up somewhere good, maybe even somewhere together."

Riony squinted at the sky, shaking her head. "Yeah, that'd be real nice. It would give me the opportunity to remove your head from your shoulders."

Zade smirked, still for some reason thinking she was joking. He reached out to her where she knelt. "Come on, this is your chance to do something more than hide like a rat underground. We'd make a great team."

Riony cringed back from his offered hand. "Yuck."

Zade's face twisted, finally catching up that she wasn't being flirty with her threats. "You're really going to turn down the chance for you and your sister to live comfortably in the safety of a dragonkeep? The bounty on the Hjelzahn children is enough to make all of us rich."

Riony stared at the sky again and sniffed. "Well, good

luck spending your bounty, because we're all going to be dead when that shadowdragon comes down to rest here."

A few of the slavers jerked their eyes upward.

Riony scooped up a handful of ashy dirt and threw it in the face of the men closest to her, then threw herself at them right afterward.

She didn't even take the time to draw her sword. She just launched herself bodily at the nearest man, bowling him over and taking the slaver beside him with them. She crashed down on all fours on top of them. A crossbow bolt sliced through the air in front of her nose.

Aishena took Riony's cue and didn't hesitate to join the fight. Silver hair flew as she ducked and spun away from the swords pointed at her chest.

With the twitch of a wrist, an athame was activated and flung into the neck of a crossbow wielder. It whistled through, swinging around in a shining blue arc, returning to her waiting hand.

Return rune, Riony thought in awe. Just how many active athames does that delver carry?

In the initial burst of surprise, Yoskar stepped forward with his staff, already ablaze from a red burn crystal at the end. He swung it with his thick, powerful arms in a wide arc at the line of swords before them.

Men dodged back, crying out in alarm. Some weren't

fast enough. Their swords clattered from their grasps as the tattered fabric of their sleeves lit up in flames.

Aishena fought like a creature possessed. Her arms flashed at a blistering speed, one throwing and catching, then throwing and catching the return athame. In her other hand was another crystal blade, lit up pale green, clashing blocking blows against any weapon swung her way. Two more men had dropped at her feet.

Riony reached for her own sword, hoping to knock down a few slavers herself. Before she could pull it free, a bone-shaking jolt cracked over the back of her head. She fell face down, landing on the squirming man beneath her again.

"In the back? Rude." Grunting in pain, she tried to right herself and face the cowardly attacker. She twisted to the side, wary of landing on her back and the creatures held there, and a foot came down hard on her wrist, knocking her hand off her hilt.

Bodies moved all around her, kicking and grasping at her. She tried to swat them away and stand up, but her wrist was held down firmly by the heavy boot.

"There's too many," Yoskar cried.

Aishena bellowed a guttural growl in reply. There was the sound of a falling body.

Riony roared at the man pinning her wrist down. "Come

on, let me draw my sword. Don't you want a fair fight?"

The large scarred man loomed over her. He sucked air through his teeth and his foot shifted. Riony struggled her hand free, but the man's boot came up to kick her swiftly in the face before she could touch her sword. Her neck sprung backward, and dark spots filled her stinging eyes.

She shook her head and spat blood, scrambling to get back to her feet. Her arms were clasped by multiple hands on both sides, and she wrenched and struggled, throwing one man into the dirt.

But her wrists were drawn ever inward, and the harsh scratch of rope wrapped around them.

Her vision was still clearing as she was relieved of her sword. To her side, Aishena stood with a blade held to her throat as another man plucked at her belt, relieving her of athame after athame. Yoskar was on his knees next to her, blood running down one temple.

More ropes came out, and the delver siblings were bound too. With some more not so gentle kicks, the three of them were roused back to their feet and into movement, flanked on all sides by the slavers.

"Well, that was a bit of excitement for the afternoon," the scarred man grumbled. "Let's avoid any more. Get this lot back to camp and into chains."

Into chains. Riony's heart contracted in her chest,

hollow, raw, and rattly against her rib cage. She tensed her wrists in front of her, trying to wriggle free from the rope. It held tight. She kept trying anyway, rubbing her skin raw.

Depths damn it all. This couldn't end like this. She wouldn't be a slave again.

"I told you not to fight it." Zade appeared next to her with a look of concern as he took in the blood gushing from her stinging nose.

Riony sucked that blood in and spat it in his face.

His expression twisted and he wiped at the mess with his sleeve.

"You're more savage than that brat sister of yours. You had your chance. You deserve what you get from here on out." He moved away from her side, blending in with the other slavers who surrounded them.

And Riony, Aishena, and Yoskar were marched, bound and bleeding, into the slavers' camp.

TWENTY

It wasn't the scratchy, tightly wound ropes tying her wrists in front of her that hurt Riony the most. Or the split lip and aching nose from where the boot had met her face. Or the throbbing lump on the back of her head.

It wasn't even how from her cage, Lyrrin watched her and the delver siblings being brought in through the palisade gate, and how her sister's bright expression of hope had dropped away. It wasn't even the feeling of a ticking clock, counting down until someone took her backpack and discovered what was inside it.

Riony was massively displeased to discover that the thing that stung her deepest, was that Kess was there, watching from her perch atop that large wolf, with hooded eyes and a satisfied smirk as Riony lost her freedom once more.

But if anything was going to give Riony the fire needed to put a halt to that outcome from occurring, to spite Kess was high on the list.

"I will not serve a master again," Riony grumbled to herself under her breath. "Not one like the Heithorns. Not *any*."

Aishena and Yoskar said nothing as they were herded along in front of Riony. Their expressions were shut down and locked tight, as though preparing for the worst.

Riony had no idea what the three siblings had been hiding from. Whatever secret made life in their dragonkeep home so unbearable they had run to the underground, Riony couldn't guess, and from the looks of the delvers, they were holding that secret close.

Aishena looked to her older brother for guidance a couple of times, and although his expression was racked with the wrinkles of thought, he shared no great plot for their escape. His glasses sat askew on his bleeding face, but he didn't raise his bound hands to straighten them.

Riony hoped he hadn't already given up. She could see in Aishena's tensed movements that every part of her still yearned to fight, so at least Riony would have someone on her side when there was a chance to make a move.

She cast furtive glances around the area, trying to gauge their chances.

The slavers' camp was a hive of activity, with scores of men and women in ratty clothing moving about their end-of-day tasks with the rowdy energy of triumph.

A lot of them wore beaten-up metal armor in mismatched pieces. Cheap and easy to find remnants from the past war, and the weapons hanging from belts and stacked beside tents seemed the same.

The slavers marching Riony and the delvers in were arguing about how to divvy up Aishena's haul of athames and how they worked. Riony's precious sword hung on the belt of the scrawny man with frizzy yellow hair. She yearned to have it back in her grasp. If only she'd had it ready to swing earlier, maybe they could have avoided capture. But she wasn't ready at all for Zade's betrayal.

A few slavers cheered as they saw the new batch of valuable older captives being marched in. Must be a great day for them. They'll probably have a party.

Sucks being one of those captives, though.

Riony scanned the faces of the slavers, her nerves rattled. Nobody chose to live aboveground, outside of dragonkeeps, for good, happy reasons.

Sometimes, they had no other option and survived by running some immoral grift—like kidnapping and slave

trading—out of desperation. Sometimes they remained aboveground by choice. Those were the ones to be wary of.

It was a brutal life that attracted those with brutal desires.

The scarred leader who headed their little parade had that ruthless glint in his eyes.

A new man with a limp and body as withered as the revenant they'd fought yesterday came over to join the leader, walking with him through the camp.

Kess had followed them in too, her wolf padding silently alongside. Riony did her very best to ignore her.

"Got what we were waiting on, then?" the withered man asked.

The leader raised one eyebrow over the flame-scarred side of his face, stretching the wrinkled skin with it, as though the answer was obviously right before them.

"We ought to pull up stakes and get moving. Been here in one place too long."

The leader slapped a hand onto the slim man's shoulder. "Relax, Colber. We scored big today. Let the team celebrate. We'll move on in the morning."

Colber did not relax. He jittered disturbingly, eyes twitching. "Last watch from farther north reported what they thought was the shadowdragon passing over."

"Last watch from northern lookout drinks more than what's good for her."

Another man with a tuft of orange hair like a struck match tucked his chin toward Kess. "Wasn't this one asking about seeing a seasong dragon flying north? Was probably just that."

The leader gave Kess an assessing look. "Didn't you get what you were after? Why you still creeping about our camp? Get outta here before we put you and your pet in one of these cages too, girl."

Kess narrowed her eyes slightly and dropped back, but like the bad smell she was, she stuck around. Riony's shoulders tensed. What had she wanted, and gotten, from these slavers?

Colber stepped closer to get the leader's attention again. "Iarl, please—"

"We only just got the kids in the pens, and it's getting dark. We rest, we imbibe, we move on before bird's fart tomorrow." Iarl released his grip on the man with a rough shove, pushing him away and leaving him behind.

Iarl brought them over to a large firepit, which cast flickering light across the faces of those around it in the dimming twilight. A dripping spit roast crackled, letting off a fatty, savory scent.

Hungry.

Riony's eyes popped wide. *No, not now you aren't. Please, Dracuni, back to sleep.*

They were close to the cages, and Riony kept her eyes on Lyrrin, trying to reassure her. Sure, Riony was outnumbered and outmatched, but she was still standing, still breathing. So she would keep fighting, however she could.

Aishena seemed to have the same idea and made a break for it when she saw Benjin there too. She only made it two steps before she was tripped over by Iarl's extended foot.

With her hands bound, she smacked face-first into the dust. Heaving, she wriggled until she got her knees under her. She sat up and glared daggers at the man.

When he backhanded her, it set off a ripple of whimpers through the children in the cages. No doubt they all looked up to her. She was a delver, paragon of the undercity, and there she was, beaten down into the dirt. A few children began sobbing.

We're not done yet, Riony whispered silently to Lyrrin.

Riony doubted Lyrrin understood the words, but she must have understood her determined expression, because she nodded once, then ducked into the corner again, working her sharp nails against the bars. Without a word, Benjin shifted to stand in front of her.

A brusque female slaver with impressively wide shoulders gave Riony a shove, pushing her toward a cart that had manacles attached all along each side. The cart was simple and bulky, constructed from thick timber beams, chipped and gray in a way that suggested it could have predated the taming of dragons.

Some sections were patched with metal to reinforce the weathered frame. Worn by time and use, it bore the scars of countless journeys along rough terrain and smelled of old hay and older beer. Riony wondered how many slaves had been chained to those sides over the years, delivered to their fates.

"What are we going to do with this one?" the slaver woman asked, her voice deep and husky.

Riony felt movement in her backpack. She had to get out of there, and fast. She whispered desperately to the woman, "You could slip me out of this rope and back to your tent. Claim me for yourself and I'll make it worth your while."

"Right you will. Before or after you try and knock my brains in and run? I wasn't born yesterday, and it takes something far prettier than you to make me consider the risk." The older woman barked a laugh and clamped the heavy manacle around one of Riony's forearms. Beside her, Yoskar and Aishena were chained as well.

"You don't have to be hurtful about it," Riony muttered.

Iarl stepped closer and gave Riony an appraising look. "Not sure what we'll do with her. Much older than is worth bringing on as a slave. Much harder to break. Not impossible though, just takes a lot more work."

His eyes glinted at the final word.

"That one's no good as a slave." Kess, still lingering, decided to put her dumb opinion in. "I can tell you that from experience. Better to put her down here and now before she stabs you all in the back."

"Oh, baby, don't be jealous. You know you're the only one I want to stab in the back," Riony crooned.

"See how she treats her master?"

Riony opened her mouth to make Kess regret using the term master when a desperate plea of **Hungry** caught her off guard. Riony winced at the sheer anguish coming from the newborn as it squirmed again.

Riony turned her head down and softly hummed the lullaby she'd sung to Dracuni before, hoping to lull it back to sleep.

Iarl leaned away from her and gave her a worried look, as though she'd gone mad. Eying her arms, he said, "She'd probably only sell cheap for hard labor anyhow. Might be easier to waste her to the worms now."

"Tsk, you would be missing out by not keeping me around," Riony said. She needed to stay alive beyond the next few minutes if she was going to hit upon a chance to get herself and her loved ones out of there. "I've got skills. Midwife, herbalism. Plus, I'm superhot—despite what *some* people with bad taste might think. You'll get a great price for me. Promise."

"Hey, boy?" Iarl called over his shoulder. "Is this true?"

Zade appeared again from the crowd that had formed around to take in the new acquisitions. He didn't look at Riony, just kept his eyes downturned, shadowed under a flop of golden hair. "Well, she knows herbs at least. Got a nasty streak though."

"Only to traitorous foppish creeps who deserve it," Riony butted in.

Zade continued. "So she could be valuable, if you can break her."

Iarl's weathered lips lifted in a grim smile. "Oh, I can break her."

Kess scoffed. "Good luck with that. Better than you have tried and failed."

Shaking her head, the ghastly gremlin leaned forward, and her wolf turned away.

Zade looked up to Riony then, making eye contact. He still had a smear on his cheek from where she'd spat her blood at him. His expression was dark and cold. "Just do me a favor, Iarl. Wherever she ends up, keep her separate from that little one with the blue eyes over there."

Riony growled and lunged for him, held back as the chain between her arm and the cart snapped straight.

"You've got a very special death coming your way, Zade."

He stepped closer to her, nose to nose, with Riony straining at the end of her tether. He grinned his bright grin. "Maybe I'll take your sister with me."

She dug her heels into the ground and roared, tensing every part of her body, and the heavy cart behind her shifted. It barely moved at all, but it was enough of a jolt forward that Zade jumped back and had to wipe the terrified look off his face.

Yoskar snarled at her under his breath, "You're going to get your neck wrung if you don't quit it."

Iarl took a step forward, wide-eyed and frowning. "What in the stars has she got wriggling around in her pack?"

A few paces away on her wolf, Kess's head snapped around, shadowed eyes pinning Riony in their gaze.

Riony swore as her backpack jumped as at least one of the creatures within it bucked at the closure.

"... Sir Butterfur Spelunkychunks?" Riony said.

Iarl stared blankly at her reply.

Zade waved a hand dismissively. "Just some pet she's all protective of. Cave otter. Been carrying it all the way since before we left the undercity. We can add it to the dinner menu tonight."

Over at the cages, Lyrrin's head popped up again amongst the other watching children, horror stretching her features.

A keening bleat whimpered from behind Riony. *Shh, shh, please, Dracuni!*

Kess's back straightened, and she turned her wolf around again, prowling toward Riony.

Iarl folded his arms in front of him and glared. "Is that what cave otters normally sound like?"

"Yes, absolutely," Riony answered.

Kess turned her attention to Iarl, moving close to him. "You know, I think maybe I'd like to take that one off your hands for you."

Iarl didn't flinch at the proximity to the huge wolf and met Kess's calculating stare. "*You know*, I reckon we'll keep her. Seems you misjudged her value."

"I know what I'm talking about with that red-haired monster. If you don't believe me, that's your loss. But I've got a good few gold sovs to offer and that's far more than she's worth."

Iarl unfolded his arms and casually picked at his fingernails. "Why you so interested in taking her, then? I think maybe you've been trying to bargain us down from the beginning. Knew something we didn't and thought you'd bluff us out of our catch."

Kess's sudden interest in her drew a cold sweat out of Riony's skin. She couldn't let Kess take her, not with the way Kess was angling around, trying to get a clearer view of her backpack. She could not let that dragon-obsessed goblin get her hands on Dracuni.

Riony said, "She just hates the idea of anyone inflicting suffering on me other than her. She's definitely underbidding the value of the satisfaction she'll take in that."

"Quiet, Pony!"

"Look, she's acting like she owns me already, ordering me around. Don't let her get away with it."

Iarl stepped in between them. "Listen, girl. If the catch here really has got midwife training, knows herbs, and can pull a cart like a bovin, I reckon we're going to get some decent bids for her at market. Thanks to Zade, we also know pretty well how we're going to keep her in line."

He nodded over to the cage where Lyrrin watched with wide eyes under her hood. Turning from Kess to Riony, he tilted his head and his eyes sparkled. "We keep you and your sister together, you'll behave as you're told, won't you?"

Riony swallowed. "Yes. Anything."

"There we have it." Iarl smirked.

With a grunting huff, Kess plunged one hand deep into a pouch strapped beside her on the saddle. Metal clattered all around as slavers reached for swords, but she quickly withdrew her hand and held something tiny up into the air.

The glass glinted and shimmered, an opalescent silver.

The slavers went quiet.

"I'll trade. Silvernix for the slave," Kess hissed.

Iarl narrowed his eyes at Kess and sucked air through his teeth.

Riony blinked, trying to understand what she was seeing. Her breath came heavy. "How ... how long have you *had that*?"

Kess ignored her. "You won't get a better deal anywhere in Elundrae."

"Right you are about that," Iarl said. He reached out a hand, and Kess snatched the tiny vial back.

"The slave first."

Iarl looked from Kess to the crowd of slavers surrounding them. "Could just take it from you if we want."

"Not before I smash it on the ground and we all lose. Just be a good little scumlord and make the deal."

Iarl spent a moment thinking it over, then shrugged and signaled for the husky woman to unlock Riony's manacle. Riony's mind swirled and her body felt shivery and wrong for all the anger running through it.

The manacle released, but Riony's hands were still tied in front by rope, and the slaver woman lashed another rope around that and handed the end over to Kess like a lead on a dog.

Kess dangled the vial between her fingers, and Iarl snatched it up. He held it close to his eye, turning it side to side and inspecting the contents. Then a grin broke across his face.

"We really have had a good day, friends!" he called out over the crowd, holding the silvernix high. A cheer went up and they banged on metal in applause. "First good sale of many to come!"

Kess rolled her eyes at them and gave a tug of the rope. Riony refused the first, but moved slowly on the second. Looking back, she nodded to Lyrrin, trying to reassure her. Tears shined off Lyrrin's cheeks from under the shadow of her hood.

Riony had hope though. She was probably in the best position to escape as she could get, now. The moment Kess took her out of sight of the slavers, it wouldn't be hard to overpower the little goblin and get away.

The wolf might be an issue. But still better than being manacled to a cart in the middle of scores of crazed overworlders.

Riony cast her eyes over the slavers and a warning chill of danger ran over her. She didn't like the way they continued to eye her and Kess, how Iarl and Colber whispered to each other. How Yoskar and Aishena slumped and looked away.

But yet again, what she found she didn't like the most, was the satisfaction on Kess's sly weasel face at taking ownership over her once again.

TWENTY-ONE

Kess felt close, so close to having what she always wanted. That redheaded menace was carrying it, and now she had them both.

She steadied her breathing and cultivated an air of extreme apathy as she turned Griskin away from the slavers and led Pony from their camp. But inside, her nerves stretched taut, twanging with both anticipation and the fear that her dreams could again be crushed.

You can't fool me, Pony. I know you've got more in that backpack than you're letting on. The creature that wriggled and mewled in there sounded much like the dragonlings she used to watch back on her family's estate, newborns just hatched but not yet gone through their taming ceremony.

It made her remember the time her older brother, in a rare moment of sibling affection, took her down to the hatchery to see a new batch of etherdarts, bred for him to choose the dragon that would grow to be his steed.

Her jealousy that he got to own one of those beasts had been high, but the excitement at seeing the fresh hatchlings overrode that emotion. Born from etherflame and treedart parents, they were already large, fresh from their eggs, and glittered in deep reds, earthy browns, and dusky purples.

Kess beamed, reaching her hand to touch the still-soft newborn scales.

Her brother sat with her on the low stone edge of the hatchling pen. The hatchery air was stifling, warmed beyond comfort by an etherflame chained on the level below that had been broken in battle and was only good for heating now.

"Which would you choose, if you became a dragonrider?" he asked.

"I *will* become a dragonrider," she replied.

"Whatever. But which one?"

She answered without hesitation. "The purple one."

Largest of the litter and with a striking array of horn buds around its skull. Its eyes were already open wide, bright and alert in a way tamed dragons' eyes weren't. She could imagine how magnificent it would grow to be. She could imagine soaring in the skies on its back.

"Do you think, after you've chosen—"

"Shh, it's Mami and Fadda!" her brother hissed. He hid Kess in a dark corner behind a pile of hay bales—she was never meant to have left the castle.

When their parents arrived, Kess watched, silent and seething, as her brother selected that very same purple dragon to be *his* steed.

"What about the rest of them?" he asked.

"We only have silvernix to spare on taming one," Fadda said. "The rest are waste."

"Good," her brother had said, staring over his parents' shoulders at the hay bales with a dark smile. "We don't need more than one new riding dragon anyway."

Kess hated how her heart squeezed into a painful lump at the memory.

I'll show him. I'll have my dragon soon.

She wasn't sure how Pony had done it, saved herself and one of the dragonlings from that cave. Maybe she really did have some silvernix on her that she used to heal herself after Kess had left, then took a dragonling—from where? It must have been hidden when Kess was in the cave.

When had she hidden it and why? The sequence of events didn't make sense. The mystery of it all had been bothering Kess since that day in the mountains. She'd gone back into the ice cave to check if Pony was still alive, not long after leaving her to die, and found her entirely gone. Only a frozen pool of blood remained to prove she'd even been there.

The lack of Pony in that cave, dead or alive, confused Kess almost as much as why she'd bothered to go back into the cave herself. She hadn't changed her mind about saving the intolerable woman, not really. She did have the means to save her though, and *if* Pony *had* still been alive, maybe Kess would have considered making a deal of some kind for the silvernix she needed to survive.

Only if Pony had anything of value to offer. Only if there was something in it for her, to salvage the wasted situation.

Kess couldn't imagine what that could have been, but she hadn't really considered using the silvernix on *Pony* without some payoff, had she? The woman had deserved to die, especially after ruining Kess's chance at one of the dragon's hatchlings. And it was a rude shock to find out that she hadn't.

Kess had wondered whether the mother dragon returned, somehow unseen, and swallowed Pony's body whole. Then Kess saw the bloody footprints leading out of the cave. Kess couldn't believe Pony had walked out of there. Even if she had, surely she just walked off to die somewhere else.

When Griskin picked up her scent again down from

the mountains, Kess sought the answer to how Pony had cheated death.

Silvernix was an obvious answer, but for a brief, yearning moment, Kess had hoped there was something else, some other healing magic those cave dwellers had dug from the Alderkin depths. Something miraculous that she could use. That was something she wanted almost as much as her own dragon.

At least now she had one of those things.

Pony walked painfully slowly behind her, a dull, sullen look on her dumb face. Before they were even halfway to the gates, the oaf planted her feet in the ground and yanked back on the rope connecting them, almost pulling Kess off her wolf.

Kess glared back at her and pulled the rope. "Keep moving, Pony."

The oaf tugged back, the rope drawing taut between them. She stared at the ground, her face hot and red, and her voice was low and flat. "How long did you have that silvernix?"

"That's what you want to know?"

"*How long*? Did you have it ... did you have it in the cave?"

Kess sighed dramatically and rolled her eyes. "Of course, I did. What, you thought I might have just stumbled across it in the last couple of days? Silvernix isn't easy to

come by lately. And, of course, I would *never* have wasted it on a life like yours."

Pony breathed roughly. "You ... I was dying! And you ... you could have ..."

"Aw, does that hurt your feelings?"

Stilling, Pony turned her face up and stared Kess down. "I don't even know why I'm surprised."

Kess's face flushed then, and she turned away, tugging on the rope again. "Don't know why you're angry. Clearly, you're fine. Seems to me that if I'd stepped in, I would have ruined your plan to steal a baby dragon for yourself."

Pony stumbled a step forward before renewing their tug-of-war.

Kess's grin grew. Pony's emotions were always as easy to read as a book. "So yes, I'm glad I never wasted silvernix on you. I'm not even going to let those dullard slavers keep what they have now. I'll be back for it soon enough. I'm going to need it to tame my new baby dragon, after all."

"You're wrong. I don't have one. It's just a cave otter. I'm telling the complete truth that I don't have a dragon in my backpack," Pony growled.

She'd never been a good liar either, but for some reason managed it then. Still, it gave Kess pause. She better not have set herself up for stealing silvernix back from slavers just for some cave otter.

No, it sounded like a dragon. It has to be.

"We'll see soon enough." Kess looked the brutish woman up and down, taking stock of what she might be in for once it was just the two of them. Pony had grown a lot since they were kids, and she'd been tall for her age then.

That felt like a lifetime ago. That other life, back when Kess lived in a castle, luxuries all around. She'd had many slaves back then. But when Pony and her parents deserted, it had felt like a very personal abandonment.

Kess knew abandonment well. Friends who would spend time with her, then mock her behind her back. Her own family, too ashamed of her to stay in a dragonkeep where others could see her, cloistering her away to an isolated estate.

Or the time she was taken out into the blighted wilds by her own blood and left alone to perish.

Pony, though, had been one constant of Kess's life for years growing up. Somewhere along the way, the fact that Pony was *forced* to spend time with her was lost. The fact resurfaced like an explosion when Pony had the chance to run and took it.

Kess thought she'd never see Pony again, and never wanted to. Kess knew she was better off alone. Just her and Griskin. The only one she could trust.

Thoughtfully, she mumbled, "Who'd have thought

it would be you who helped me become the dragonrider I was always meant to be?"

Pony lifted her bound hands in front of her in a pleading gesture. "I'll go with you. I'll be your slave again. But please, will you buy my sister too? I won't leave without her."

Kess narrowed her eyes, scanning over the cages back near the fire. The slavers had dispersed, moving around in the dimming shadows of the camp. "Sister? Which one is she?"

Pony tensed, and her face made some ugly shapes before she seemed to make up her mind. "The little one in the hood. Bring her along, or I'll yell out right now that I've got a baby dragon in my backpack and see what the slavers think of that."

"Do that, and I'll kill the girl myself." Kess brushed her fingers along a row of slim bone throwing daggers kept in her bracer. "I have excellent aim, don't you remember?"

Beneath her, Griskin's fur shivered, and he growled a long and low warning. Kess leaned over and petted him, enjoying the wary look on Pony's face as she took in the huge wolf.

"Why do you have to be such an enormous asshole about everything?" Pony grumbled.

"Because nothing, not you, not your sister, *nothing* is getting between me and owning my own dragon as I deserve!"

A growly voice muttered from beside her, "Yeah, I don't know about that, little girl."

The heavy hilt of a sword clocked Kess on the temple before she could turn to see who spoke. Her teeth clattered and skull shook, the world wobbling in her vision as she tipped sideways.

Kess let go of Pony's rope and grasped out desperately for Griskin but had been pushed too far across by the blow. Her feet slipped free of the stirrups and the saddle disappeared from beneath her. She thumped into the ashy dirt, head ringing.

"Get the wolf!" someone commanded.

A dark web flew in the corner of Kess's spotty vision, falling over Griskin. He yelped and growled. She tried to lift herself, crawling forward on her elbows toward his struggling form.

There was more scuffling to her other side. Pony, hands bound, landed face-first like a toppled column, and the four slavers who knocked her down kicked at her where she fell. She rolled on her side, taking the hits to her stomach and face like an idiot.

"Traitors!" Kess shrieked at everyone around her. No matter that she'd intended to go back on their deal too. At least she had the decency to plan on slipping back in at night and taking the silvernix without an audience. Maybe even pop

some of the cage doors while she was there. If she had the time.

The slavers snatched Pony's rope, dragging her along the dirt kicking and cussing back to the cart where the Hjelzahn siblings were still chained.

The man with the scarred face stepped in front of Kess, staring at her as she lay prone on her side.

Lightning fast, Kess reached for her throwing daggers. A boot came down on her hand, kicking it away from her weapons.

The rough, reedy man, Colber, chuckled. "Look, boss, she's real angry at you now."

Kess shook her head, trying to shake off the pain. Griskin was down, trapped under a heavy net of steel rope, the kind used for catching massive livestock or small dragons.

Across at the cart, Pony stood again, the manacle being re-latched around her arm. Pony stared back at where Kess remained sprawled in the dirt, her mouth a thin, flat line.

Don't you dare feel sorry for me. Don't you razing dare!

The leader grinned dangerously. "Real mad, aren't you? Come on, then. Get up and fight me, wild girl."

Kess's whole chest heaved as she panted angry breaths.

"I'll even give you one free shot. What are you waiting for? Get up."

Pony's voice drifted over the camp, piercing Kess like a knife in her back. "She can't."

TWENTY-TWO

"**S**hut your mouth, Pony!" Kess screamed from where she lay on her side in the dirt. If she could have murdered with her eyes alone, Riony would be halfway to rigor mortis.

Everything had turned around again, and Riony was freed from Kess's ownership again—yay—only to be back in chains—boo.

Sparks. I should have just left with Kess, knocked her and her smug face off that stars-damned wolf, then come back for Lyrrin with two arms free and swinging.

The revelation that Kess had unicorn blood with her when Riony was dying had knocked her around though, left her feeling strangely twisted up inside and punch-drunk, and she'd screwed up her chance.

Riony casually tested her newly reattached manacle, latched on one side just above where rope still bound her two wrists together. She slowly strained as though yawning, but neither the rope nor chain budged.

"What do you mean, she can't?" Iarl called back.

A jab of guilt jarred Riony's gut. She'd spat those words in spite, but as the slaver held her with a questioning glare, she felt wrong revealing Kess's condition to them. On the other hand, Kess was a traitorous goblin who had left her to die when she could have been saved.

"I mean she hasn't had the use of her legs since she was born. She's always found some other way to get around." Riony drawled the last sentence out, holding Kess's venomous glare.

A small crowd of slavers had formed around them again now. A couple laughed out loud as Kess pulled herself into a sitting position and reached for her knives again. A sword tip close to her neck stilled her hand.

Iarl tilted his head as he examined Kess. "Why didn't you use your silvernix on yourself? Reckon I would have preferred my legs working than to trade that away for a loud-mouthed and defiant slave."

"You're dumber than you look if you think I haven't tried unicorn blood before."

A grin spread on Iarl's face.

Oh, you idiot, Kess.

"Got a plentiful supply of the stuff then, have you? Thought as much. Nobody offers gold sovs up front for a slave, let alone a vial of silvernix. Not unless they have all that and more." Iarl winked slyly with his burn-wrinkled eye, then lifted his chin to Colber. "Search her. And the wolf."

The scrawny man grabbed Kess's shoulder and flipped her over onto her stomach. She scrambled her arms about, trying to press herself back up, as her legs remained motionless. Colber put a knee on the small of her back and patted her down.

Riony grimaced and looked away. Her teeth were clenched hard together, and every part of her body felt riled up in a way she couldn't quite place.

It seemed fine for Riony to fantasize about knocking Kess off her wolf, because she knew the monster Kess truly was on the inside. Seeing these shart-faced thugs push Kess around and laugh at her fired up something primal inside Riony that she didn't want to examine too closely.

"Aish, please tell me you've got some secret backup athame stashed on your person somewhere," Riony whispered across the cart to the delver chained on the other side.

Aishena turned her palms upward and muttered in heavy disdain, "Where exactly do you think I would be hiding one?"

"I mean, I have some ideas, but you've already turned down my romantic advances before so ..."

"Hey!" Iarl yelled at Riony. "Who are you to this wild girl, that she'd pay so much to get you back?"

Riony's gaze shot over to Kess, still pinned to the ground like a bug, then she quickly looked away. "I'm nobody to her but damned livestock. I told you, she used to own me and thinks she still does and will bring everybody into her stupid grudge against me. She'd trade you the moon itself if it means she can get just one more claw under my skin."

Iarl scratched at his stubbly chin. "Nah. Nah, I think you're both lying. There's something more going on. She's been looking for you, for sure, you're right there. I reckon it's why she showed up here in the first place, with her lame excuse of making trade."

Riony bit her lip and looked back over to where Kess was having her belt unbuckled and pulled off. The pouches' contents were emptied out onto the ground and searched.

She hadn't ratted them out to the slavers? Riony thought for sure that's why Kess was there. Coming through to do some trade while children were being sold under her nose was almost as coldhearted though, Riony had to admit. Just not the full extent of coldheartedness as she expected from the malicious goblin.

"'Course, she didn't hint at what wealth she was carrying then. Not until you showed up and she saw what she really wanted. Now we know the scruffy little thing's a rich bitch

in disguise."

A few brave slavers approached the wolf—Griskin, Kess had called him—and were poking their hands through the netting to search the saddle and its attached bags. Griskin twisted and snapped his teeth at them, but the net held him back from snagging their flesh.

"Come on, there's got to be something!" Iarl yelled at them as they turned out clothing, cookware, and more and more and more bone throwing knives than anyone could have reasonably expected.

"Found those gold sovs she was talking about." A bald slaver with an eyepatch tossed a leather pouch over to his leader.

He opened it and his fingers flicked through the contents. A scowl remained on his face as he watched Colber finish his search with an empty-handed shrug.

Kess had stopped struggling and lay with her forehead pressed to the ground, her face hidden under a fall of her tangled charcoal-toned hair. Her ears had gone a violent shade of red.

A nasty feeling of heat crept up Riony's neck and cheeks too, and she had to look away. *It must be my body's reaction to the sheer joy of seeing Kess humiliated, that's all.*

Beside Riony, Aishena and Yoskar were whispering fast words to each other. Maybe they were coming up with an escape plan, some way to get them all out of this. Riony

hoped they'd share it with her, too.

But Iarl was already wandering toward them. He had his eyes locked on Riony in a way that made her skin crawl. "You know what, search that one too. Maybe little wolf girl is obsessed with something she's carrying, rather than the livestock herself."

Riony's skin flushed cold, and she took a step back from the approaching husky woman who had chained her up before. Her backside bumped against the solid cart behind her, nowhere further to go. She raised her bound hands in surrender.

With a half-hearted smile, she said, "You sure you don't want to take me back to your tent? We could do a full strip search, all alone."

"You really think I have more lust than logic, don't ya, pet? That and you think mighty highly of yourself."

Riony gestured at her body. "I mean ..."

The woman let out a rough chuckle, then shot her hands out faster than Riony expected. Not that there was much she could do.

The woman stabbed her knife into the netted bag at Riony's side, cutting through and spilling the contents on the ground. She kicked at the wheel of cheese and strips of jerky. "Nothing in this lot."

Then the woman grabbed Riony by the front of her

shirt and slid the sharp dagger down her bare arms, slicing right through the straps of her backpack. One side, then the other. Riony couldn't even flinch away without risk of that blade going into her arms.

Other hands grabbed the pack from behind her before it could fall.

Riony turned, and there was Zade, staring her down with a twisted pout as he squatted just beyond the length of Riony's tether. Which she tested aggressively.

"Something in there, for sure," Iarl muttered as he smirked at her futile struggles.

"Zade," Riony's voice broke in its battle between pleading and warning. She tried to speak soft enough that only he could hear. "What you find in there, don't tell them. You don't understand ... Just tell them you can't find anything. It will be worth it, I promise."

Zade laughed as loud as an actor on a stage. "She's still trying to bargain with me! As though a deserting slave's promise means anything. We'll have your precious cave otter for dinner, and we'll have whatever else you are hiding in there for ourselves too."

Across at the nearby cage, Lyrrin had stopped working on the bars and was standing, watching with a wobbly tremble to her bottom lip.

Riony had been terrified of the slavers getting Dracuni.

That imminent outcome still made her stomach churn, but now a new fear unlocked that they might hurt Lyrrin's cave otter right in front of her.

Kess's attention had turned to the bag as well. Not even the dirty tear-smudged cheeks and reddened nose were enough shame to keep her from lifting her face to see what she thought was Riony's secret stolen dragonling being revealed.

Close, Kess, but not quite.

Zade worked the knotted closure free. As he pulled the opening wide enough, a bolt of sleek, caramel fur burst out and upward. The otter made a great, wriggly leap for freedom, launching itself out of the bag and into the air.

Zade toppled over onto his back, crying out an embarrassing yelp.

A ripple of laughter and insults rolled across the watching crowd as he scrambled backward from the skittering otter, batting it away with his hands. Sir Butterfur's snout twitched at the sky, his whole body snapping to stillness for one breath, before zipping away across the ground and vanishing.

Riony bared her teeth at Zade in a vicious smile. "No wonder you had to turn to selling babies as slaves. If you're scared of cave otters, you were never going to survive long in the undercity."

Zade snarled and threw a handful of dirt her way.

A harsh, choking laugh was building slowly, hysterically, from Kess's direction. She had gotten herself upright again, sitting slouched over and shaking her head with each dark chuckle.

"That's really what was in there all along? A razing cave otter?" Her head snapped up so fast it brought a second sword point out from a nearby slaver to warn her back.

Kess howled across the camp, "You cost me *everything*, Pony. You have ruined everything. I've clawed myself up from nothing before and I'll do it again, and then I will turn every part of my attention toward destroying everything of yours!"

A harsh shiver ran up Riony's spine as Kess rolled her gaze over to Lyrrin's cage.

"Wow, she's a bit overdramatic. I see what you mean now," Iarl scoffed.

"Told you," Riony replied, then tried again to bluff herself and her backpack's contents free from scrutiny. "She's just crazy obsessed with hurting me. I don't have anything valuable."

The slave leader's eyes narrowed on her, then he waved a hand at Zade. "Come on, get back to searching that bag. Unless you're scared!"

Zade brushed himself off and moved back to kneel beside the bag.

Dracuni had been very still for a while now, only the occasional pang of fear would thrum from the newborn's mind through to Riony, frightened by the yelling and probably the panicked signals Riony's mind must be sending back to it.

She couldn't break free from her bonds. She couldn't reach Zade and throttle him before he revealed Dracuni to a camp full of slavers. And Kess. She couldn't save Lyrrin or the other children. She was stuck, and her muscles burned with wasted, useless energy.

As Zade moved to peer inside her bag, Riony couldn't watch.

She turned her eyes to the sky, to the last edges of flame red from the fading sunset licking over the heavy clouds. She prayed to Amma Moon, for Dracuni's safety, for Lyrrin's, even for her own. For something, anything, to free them from this moment.

Through the clouds, something moved, darkening the sky.

It swirled, moving in languid gusts. The clouds dispersed around its massive, shadowy form. Two hot coals of red light moved together in the gloom. Eyes. Eyes that held death, destruction, pure evil incarnate.

Riony's whole body turned to ice.

Anything. Anything but *that*.

TWENTY-THREE

"Shadowdragon." The word stuttered out on Riony's breath, as though even it wanted to retreat into her body to hide. She couldn't take her eyes off it, the churning, wicked shadows that flew in the shape of a dragon.

From nearby, Iarl rasped out a laugh. "You're not tricking us twice, tamebrain."

But at least one slaver must have been curious enough to follow her gaze. There was a yelp of fear, and then a sharp curse, and then cries went up all over the camp.

"Oh, mighty moon," Zade gasped from beside her.

Riony dragged her gaze away from the creature of evil that descended upon them to see whether Zade was referring to it or whether he had gotten a good look inside her pack. She exhaled in rough relief when she saw him looking skyward as well.

Everybody had their faces turned upward now. Some were frozen like statues, and others had already begun to scoop up anything they could carry and run. But even in their frantic retreat, all kept their eyes on the shadowdragon.

Maybe it wouldn't land. Maybe it would pass by and curse the ground somewhere else. Riony strained again at her bonds. She cast her gaze over the sharp points of the burned palisade stakes and crude weapons stashed around the camp. Nothing was close enough for her to use to break herself and the delver siblings beside her free.

The dim glow of twilight faded suddenly as the shadowdragon descended from the sky with a ghostly grace. The sinuous coil of shadows and smoke that formed its body twisted and writhed in the air. A deep, mournful rumble emanated from its chest as it touched down onto the ground.

The closest people underneath the shadowdragon's path had run to avoid its touch, but it settled in over the top of the palisades and tents and fires as though they were made of nothing more substantial than air, or as though it was.

The ghostly dragon seemed to shift and warp as it moved, its edges blurring and fading into the surrounding

darkness in licks of curling blackness. Only those burning red eyes gave it a sense of life and intent.

Sobs tore from Riony's throat and tears streamed down her face completely unhindered. Not from her own fear. But from the waves of mourning that seemed to wash from the ocean of shadow before them. Sounds of weeping came from all around, especially in the direction of the cages.

A deep sense of unease already had Riony in its grips, and then the shadowdragon opened its wispy jaws and unleashed a skull-piecing roar.

The ground shook.

The sound was a visceral assault on the senses, like the anguished wail of ten thousand lost souls.

As the roar reverberated through the air, the earth shook again, cracking and splitting open. Small and large eruptions burst across the campsite all around the immense shadowy monster.

Rotten flesh and bleached bones clawed out from those holes. The corpses of animals, from small rodents to large birds of prey, to an enormous bovin, all rose from the dead, drawn inexorably back to a twisted semblance of life by the dragon's mournful cry.

Even grubs and bugs and worms and flies, any that were recently dead, any that hadn't rotted away entirely, made the ground itself writhe as they twitched back into life.

A few human skeletons, ancient and worn, pulled themselves out of their long-lost graves as well. Their movements were slow and awkward, as though still in the grip of death as they shambled out of the earth. But as they turned their eyeless gazes on the humans cowering before them, they drew rigid with terrible purpose.

Riony had only seen the horrifying effect of the shadowdragon's presence in person once before. The day it had come to the secluded village she and her parents had been raising Lyrrin in after fleeing the Heithorns.

The founders of that settlement had said they'd cleared all dead things from the earth before settling there, that it was a safe place. And it was, for years.

But the shadowdragon's call went deep, right into the heart of the earth itself and to the bones of anything that lay sleeping far below the surface for centuries.

And it turned them into revenants, mindless, withered creatures that seemed to want nothing more than to bring more death to the world.

The shadowdragon's nebulous wings flapped, causing no disturbance in the air around it as it lifted itself back toward the sky and left those on the ground to their fate at the hands of its curse.

Riony's tears stopped. She yanked at her chain again, her breath hitching.

Sparks, sparks, sparks, razing sparks!

The slavers also reawakened from their shock and mourning as the shadowdragon grew distant. They scrambled for swords and axes, crossbows and flaming torches, anything to defend themselves as the dead rushed into their attack.

Beside Riony, Aishena and Yoskar's faces were grim as they braced themselves for the onslaught. No weapons, not even their own arms available to defend themselves with.

The first of the undead animals reached them. A dreer, only just as tall as Riony. It must have been a baby when it died, which made it all the more disturbing as it snarled and snapped at them, decaying flesh hanging from its jaws.

Riony kicked out at it with all her strength, her chains clinking. Her foot connected with the dreer's skull, sending it tumbling back with a sickening crack.

But there were more, coming fast. An undead boar raced past, almost knocking Riony off her feet as it charged toward another victim. Its thick hide stretched across its bones like a tough leather, crackling as it ran. Aishena and Yoskar grunted as they fought to kick away their own attackers.

Fear and pain shot through Riony's head like a knife. Not her own.

Scared.

Wide-eyed, Riony cast around and saw her pack,

abandoned where Zade had been moments before, as combatants stomped all around. She lunged for it and Dracuni in desperation.

Brought up short by her chain, she toppled forward, feet slipping out from under her as she overextended. The bag remained out of reach.

Scared!

I know, little one. Riony slipped and stumbled back to her feet, Dracuni's terror overwhelming her. Every nerve in her body screamed to reach the newborn and keep it safe. It was all she could do to keep herself safe as the dreer returned, needing another sharp kick to knock it away again.

"Over here, keep these two safe!" Iarl called out.

A small wall of bodies emerged from the chaos, weapons readied, lining up before the three of them chained to the cart. The two valuable bodies of the Hjelzahn siblings, and the spare.

Zade hurried in beside them, burn athames glowing red in the gloom.

"Those are mine," Aishena growled low, trying to reach out and snatch them back or maybe wrap her tied hands around Zade's throat.

He kept just out of her reach. "Tell it to your amma when she comes to pay for you."

Across the camp, the massive bovin revenant charged straight through one of the tents, tearing through the leather and metal structure and upending slavers as it went.

Screams punctuated the clang of metal against bone and the thunder of pounding feet. Riony took a chance to turn and check on the cages and found herself grateful that Lyrrin and the kids were still inside them.

The children cowered from one side of their enclosure to another, dodging away from the human rev that was trying to grab them through the bars. The strong metal would give them some protection, at least for a while, but Riony had to get over there fast, because this number of revs wasn't going anywhere anytime soon.

And if that stampeding bovin set its course in line with the cages ...

The sound of the shadowdragon's roar still echoed in her mind, the depth of its mourning sadness rippling in her chest, and Riony wondered if they were all going to die there. But she couldn't let herself give up—not now, not ever.

Children were screaming louder now. More revs surrounded their cages, snapping and reaching for them from every side.

There wasn't enough room for them to all huddle out of reach in the middle, and louder shrieks cut through the

din when a child would be grabbed by a clawed hand, the rev trying to pull them through, then being wrenched back away by the other children.

Riony screamed in frustration herself, as she longed to run over to Lyrrin's side and protect her. And then a crackling bolt of **Pain!** withered her knees. From the corner of her eye, she saw the boot that knocked into her pack as a man raced by, kicking it and its precious contents across the ground.

Pain!

Dracuni! Riony almost yelled it aloud. She reached for the bag again, now closer, but still out of reach.

Her voice broke as she cried out, "Zade, free us! Get these depths-damned chains off us so we can help fight properly. You know we can."

Zade plunged one of the burning athames into the empty rib cage of a skeletal fox. "I wouldn't even be here still fighting these things if it weren't for the bounty. Those two are wanted alive, and we're not letting some revs take that from us, and we're not going to risk letting you run."

"Zade, none of us are getting out of this alive at this rate. There are too many revs. You can't protect us here!"

Zade sneered back at her. "I'm not protecting you at all."

A swarm of undead insects flew at Riony's face, clouding her vision, biting and stinging. They couldn't

rend her flesh the way a larger revenant would relish in doing, but they creeped her out even more. She swatted at them with her bound hands and whipped her head side to side, trying to shake them off.

When she could see clearly again, her stomach dropped away and she forgot how to breathe.

The massive bulk of the undead bovin, standing twice as tall as any human, with bones as thick as Riony's biceps, was coming right at her. Its hooves beat like thunder on the ground, churning up dirt and dust in its wake.

As it got closer, the earth shook beneath Riony's feet. It was going to crush them all. She pulled herself as far as she could on the length of her chain, trying to separate herself from being squashed between the beast and the heavy wooden cart behind her.

"Look out!" she cried.

Only Zade seemed to pay attention, turning to the approaching beast. He dove for cover at the last moment, leaving her and the delvers and the other slavers at the mercy of the charging behemoth.

The bovin's solid horns were down and its heavy skull made contact with the cart, right beside Riony, and everything exploded.

TWENTY-FOUR

The force of the impact was like the boom of thunder, and everything wrenched into the air. Timber tore and cracked. Splinters and bodies flew, strewn about in the wake of the massive, rampaging revenant.

Riony was yanked by her bound hands into a barrel roll, tumbling and smashing against the broken cart. For a moment she was upside down, and she curled her body in to brace for the inevitable return to the ground. Yoskar let out a gasping moan, and Aishena yelped as Riony collided with them.

A metal cartwheel flew in an arc past Riony's face and disappeared into the distance.

As the world stopped spinning, what was the cart now lay split in two, cracked right down the middle where the bovin had hit it and charged through. The two sides had folded over, landing on top of each other and bringing Riony through the air to land on top of the delvers.

"Are you okay?" Riony grunted as she rolled herself off Aishena's lap and took her feet off Yoskar's shoulder. She wriggled around to get her feet back underneath her. A hot graze stung all the way up Riony's bare left arm, the skin stripped and red raw. Splinters the size of toothpicks jutted from the edge of the scrape.

The delvers in their protective leather armor may have been battered but seemed to have remained untorn.

"Why are you so depths damned heavy?" Aishena pulled herself from the dirt. Dust clouded around them, kicked up from the bovin's hooves and impact. Screams still sounded all about them as the slavers and revs clashed.

Getting to her feet, Riony gave a tug of her bound hands, still tied in the middle and still chained to the cart. Or what was left of the cart. Her side had come cracking down onto the delvers' side, and when she pulled, it nearly toppled over on top of them.

Yoskar hissed at her efforts. "Don't pull it this way. Push it off, you tamebrain."

Riony snorted at the insult but gave the command a

try anyway. She leaned into the splintered wood and metal wreck, and Yoskar leaned beside her. Her half of the cart was mostly just one slab now, the heavier, sturdy section of its base that had the manacles bolted to it.

With one big heave, it slid off the remaining part that the delvers were attached to.

It had fared less well. The wheel on that side was gone too, and the beam along the side of the base where the chains were attached had cracked, but not quite come free.

"We have to get out of here and over to the kids," Aishena said. She kicked at the splintered beam. "If I just had one single damned athame on me still!"

"You'll know to keep one hidden next time," Riony said. "I'll offer you some suggestions when we get out of this." Frowning at the split wood, Riony nodded to herself. "I can break that. I'm sure I can break that. Move over this way a bit."

She waved at Aishena to create a gap between her and Yoskar, then strained at the end of her chain to drop herself in between them. Crouching with her feet braced against the lower part of the cart, she leaned forward and hooked her fingers into the cracked section.

Bending forward like that, her manacle rasped against her skin, pulled as tight as it would reach. But if Riony pulled upward from there, it would slacken.

Exhaling, she clenched her fingers around the timber and heaved. There was a satisfying crackle of ripping wood, but it didn't come apart.

The growl of a rev grew suddenly loud. A human revenant cut through the dusty haze, backlit by the nearby campfire. Riony ducked as its skeletal fingers snatched at her, its teeth chomping the air at her back.

Aishena and Yoskar lunged forward in unison and kicked the rev, launching it back into the rest of the camp.

"You guys keep the revs off me, I'll get you off this cart. Then you can get me off."

"Do you have to say it like that?" Aishena groaned as she stomped her foot on something small and slithery.

"I didn't even mean it that time!" Riony readjusted her grip, tensed her shoulders, and hauled upward again.

Snap, snap, snap. The splintered timber tore. She released, gasped a few breaths, then pulled again. As she felt the wood lift and break, she kept going, crying out as she strained every muscle in her back.

One final splintery strand broke and Riony jolted as the beam snapped in two, right along the seam that the manacles were bolted into. She tumbled backward, then was caught by her own chain, spun back around toward the cart again.

Metal jangled as the delvers gave a final kick and tug

of their own, and the manacles came free from the cart.

The cuffs were still clamped around the delvers' arms, but the other end of the chains now hung free. Aishena looked at the detached end in awe, then up at Riony.

Riony nodded to her, then turned her gaze back to where her manacle was attached. It wasn't already splintered like their side had been, but with all three of them, and their hands somewhat freer now, she figured they could crack it.

"Aish, come on," Yoskar said softly.

"But ..."

Riony whipped back around to them and found Yoskar was already moving toward the cages.

"No, no, don't you dare!" Riony gasped.

Aishena hovered, her lips pulled closed in a thin line.

"Come on!" Yoskar growled. "Benjin needs us."

He broke into a sprint. With the barest flutter of a glance back at Riony, Aishena ran after him.

Riony wrenched at her chained arm. Her muscles burned in agony all over. She released a long, primal scream into the sky.

With her face turned upward, she breathed though a shaking sob, then opened her eyes again.

A sharp shock of ice shivered through her as she saw the shadowdragon, still there, circling high above.

I have to get to Lyrrin. I have to get to Dracuni. Sparks!

Raze both of those depths-damned delvers!

Glaring at the half-cart she was still attached to, she dug her feet in, wrapped both hands around her chain, and leaned backward. Her muscles shook and twitched from over-exertion. The timber groaned but didn't break, only shifting on the dusty ground.

Riony clenched her teeth and grunted, taking a step backward, and the half-cart came with her.

She could move it. She could move! Slowly, very slowly. Each step felt like a full days' workout, but she could move.

Riony took in her options. The cages were across on the other side of the campfire, which must have been smashed into by something during the fighting. It now lay spread out across the ground in a field of glowing embers.

Her backpack and Dracuni were a few steps away in the other direction.

Silhouetted bodies clashed in the darkness all around against the ghoulish undead. She couldn't see Zade anymore, and Kess seemed to be gone too, despite the wolf still being trapped under the net.

Hopefully some rev with very big teeth had dragged her off somewhere to have a good chew on her gristly bones. And honestly, good riddance.

For some reason, the revs seemed to be ignoring the wolf. Riony had noticed that before, that they seemed to

only have a frenzied desire for human blood. She hoped the same applied to Dracuni. Since the backpack still lay mostly untouched, she assumed it did.

A body lay close to Riony's side, still and surrounded by a dark pool of blood draining into the dirt. The poor man who'd tried to convince the scarred leader to move camp earlier.

Poor fellow was right. A sharp stake of wood jutted from his stomach. And his short sword lay beside an open hand.

It wasn't her sword. Riony wasn't sure where it might be at this point. She'd do anything to get it back, but until then, she'd take any weapon she could. It was only a couple of steps away, and Riony heaved the half-cart toward it. Her back and arms dripped with sweat.

She dropped to the ground beside the fallen slaver and propped the short sword between her knees. Holding it tight, she sawed at the rope binding her wrists. The chipped, serrated blade made short work of the bindings and her hands came free.

Shaking out her sore arms, Riony grabbed the sword into her right hand and rose to her feet with a huff of determination.

With a weapon in her hand, she felt like her chances of survival were no longer zero.

She gave it one good swing against where the manacle

bolted to the half-cart, but it showed no sign of breaking, and she didn't want to break the old sword instead.

Every part of her screamed to go to Lyrrin. She would drag the damned half-cart right across the field of embers and fire to get there if she had to.

But she could still feel the pang of Dracuni's fear, hunger, and pain hanging like a weight over her mind too. And Dracuni was closer.

Squinting through the hazy twilight, Riony sought out Lyrrin in the cages.

There was a flurry of movement in that direction.

The cage Lyrrin hadn't been in was now empty. The door hung askew, twisted open by who knew what.

The children that had been in it were now skittering all around the campsite, screaming and trying to find their way free from both the slavers and the revs preying upon them.

Yoskar was there, lit up with the bright glow of red Alderkin magic. He'd found his staff again and was swinging the flaming end, knocking back attackers as he rounded up children behind him.

Aishena was beside the other cage that Lyrrin and Benjin were in. She had no glow of magic about her but swung her attached chain like the deadliest of weapons as she stood guard before the cage, and the children crawling out of it.

A small gap was broken through in the corner were

Lyrrin had been working with her nails. The bar was cut cleanly in two places, just tall and wide enough for a small child to wriggle out on their belly.

They were sliding out, one at a time, with Lyrrin still on the inside, encouraging them through.

A rush of pride burst into Riony like a deep breath after almost drowning.

Even the damned delvers. Maybe they were right to leave her. The kids needed them. Outside their cages they were easy pickings for the revs.

"You'd better get them all out of here safely," Riony muttered.

Turning away from the cages still felt like the hardest thing she'd ever done, torn between her two responsibilities. But Dracuni was close, only a few steps away.

She had to get the newborn off the ground. Even if the revs weren't interested in the backpack and what it held, one misplaced foot could mean the end for the precious creature.

Especially with that massive bovin rev still charging around the place. It had just gone right through one of the palisades and was coming back into camp on the other side.

Riony tucked the slaver's short sword into her belt and dragged the half-cart toward Dracuni. Her arms shook and ached. One step there, and she had to stop and draw the sword again, swiping it at an approaching hawk-rev that swooped at her.

She knocked it out of the air with her first strike, and it took three more before the mindless thing stopped moving.

One more step and she was near her pack.

Crouching beside it, Riony placed her fingers at the opening. She held her breath as she looked in at the completely still body of the unidragon baby. Only a quick blink of its wide lilac eyes showed it was still alive. Only the slight shiver of fear rippling over its soft, scaled skin.

Riony's heart broke at the terror and sadness washing from Dracuni. The poor thing must have thought she'd abandoned it.

"It's okay. I'm here."

Dracuni's heavy head turned upward and made a weak mewling sound.

"Hang in there. You can do it."

The din of combat seemed to be slowing, but the growling of revs and cries of pain continued. The slavers had fought hard, but there were just too many revs, and as each human fell, they grew more and more outnumbered.

A figure stumbled in toward Riony and she drew the short sword from her belt again, shooting back to her feet.

Not a rev this time, but she wanted to skewer the man anyway.

"Zade! Come on. Prove you aren't the worst person

ever and help me get this damned manacle off!"

A trickle of blood ran down his temple, and he looked at Riony, distracted, then looked at the half-cart she was still attached to. He blinked a few times and then waved a hand holding a burning athame at the broken timber.

"Where are the Hjelzahns?" He was already turning away, scanning around the gloomy camp.

Riony yanked on the chain, rattling it loudly. "Forget them and your stupid bounty! Is that really worth more than saving my life?"

Zade turned his eyes back her way. "So you can keep fighting against the people who were trying to help you? Who were trying to help those children? This is the world we're trying to keep them safe from!"

Zade gestured at the clashing humans and undead all around them. "If you can't see that, now, in the midst of all of this ... if you can't admit that we need the dragonlords to keep us safe, and repay them in kind, then you aren't worth anything at all."

"The kids were safe in the undercity! We all ... Zade, ZADE! Come back here!" Riony screamed at him as he sprinted away.

Do I just have the kind of face that begs people to leave me alone to die or something? Riony was starting to take it personally.

A gust of wind blew Riony's hair across her face. The sound of wings made her cringe, and she turned to seek the shadowdragon's form against the darkened sky.

It had remained, lingering above, but it wouldn't come back again, would it? There were at least a few newly dead bodies around, and Riony's mouth twisted at the idea of facing such fresh corpses.

But the shadowdragon's wings didn't stir the air and dust.

The pounding of massive hooves snapped her attention back to the ground. That bovin had her in its sights again, charging directly at her and Dracuni.

Oh sparks, not again.

Riony grabbed the strap of her pack in one hand and wrapped her other around the chain, trying to drag her half-cart out of the path of the rampaging beast.

Riony's surroundings brightened in a flash of warm orange, and she turned her eyes upward. Panic shot like lightning through her clammy hands and she bucked at her chains.

She was in no way fast enough. Not to get clear of the charging bovin rev or to avoid the massive ball of fire lancing down from the sky toward her.

TWENTY-FIVE

*D*ragonriders.

Kess edged herself out from the gap between a tent and a woodpile she'd squeezed herself into when everything got razed. Heat touched her cheeks as the bovin rev went up in flames. It barreled on like a flaming boulder from sheer momentum, before it slumped into a burning heap on the ground, not far from the smashed remains of a cart.

A jet of white liquid flame splashed across the camp, and screams went up as a few humans were caught in amongst the mass of targeted revs.

A snowflame! Kess shimmied farther out, her eyes fixed on the sky.

Two dragonriders were within view, their majestic

steeds hovering on vast, leathery wings. The dragons' vivid scales shimmered in the glow of the fires beneath them.

Two etherflames, one orange and one red. Basic. Solid fire-breathers for dealing with undead, which made them a dragonrider staple, but big and slow, hard to maneuver.

The riders shone as bright as their steeds, their armor forged from the very same scales. Lighter and more flexible, but so much stronger than the simple metal that had been favored for forging armor during the war and was so easy to come by now.

Only the worthy could wear dragon scale armor. Kess watched every movement and action of the two etherflame riders, her gaze ravenous. The tamed steeds could do nothing on their own. The heavy metal spike hammered into their foreheads made sure of that obedience.

Every action, every command, came from the rider. The way they angled their weight, squeezed their grip.

Kess's hands tingled, as she missed that same connection she had with Griskin. The way she would move her body and he would respond, always seeming to know what she wanted, what direction to move and how fast.

She turned briefly toward where he was netted, thankfully safe from flames, for now. She'd get back to him soon.

Griskin wasn't tamed, though. He was as wild as they came, but still Kess had mastered him as her steed. *Only*

more proof that I'm ready to ride a dragon!

Sometimes, Kess wondered whether a dragon had to be tamed in order to ride it. She'd been underestimated her entire life. How those people would be humiliated if she became the first rider to fly an untamed beast!

First, I need a dragon, any dragon, tamed or not, to prove them all wrong. Maybe I'll get lucky and one of the riders will be knocked off.

Kess scanned the night air, trying to catch sight of the elusive snowflame.

A hybrid of a snowshimmer—sleek, solitary, smaller-sized mountain dragons—and the big etherflames from the plains. They'd never interbreed normally in the wild, but the breeders who provided the dragonriders with their steeds had worked out how to get viable offspring with the best features of both parents.

Smaller than etherflames, they were fast and nimble, and their breath weapon was without compare for clearing out revs. The only thing that made them rare was their very short lifespan.

Still, they were the kind of dragon that only the best dragonriders would earn. The kind she would have one day.

There! Kess craned her neck as it sped across the camp again, laying down another stream of white flames.

For a long moment, Kess couldn't tear her gaze away

from the dragons and their masters, her heart pounding in her throat.

The air crackled as the dragons unleashed streams of searing fire that erupted from their gaping maws, engulfing the undead in a cleansing inferno.

The entire camp was going up in flames. The woodpile Kess hid behind, already half-charred, scavenged from burned forests, smoldered and sparked.

But she remained frozen, transfixed by the deep yearning she'd known her whole life, to become what she was destined to be, what every Heithorn should be. Heat licked her arms and face, and she imagined what it would be like to be up above the burning earth, riding among those fearless ranks. How it would feel to command the awesome power of those beasts, tamed and under her complete control.

Someday, she would join those ranks of dragonriders. Nothing would stop that from happening.

Especially not burning to death in this stinking slavers' camp.

Kess dragged her body across the scorched earth, her fingertips blackened by soot. She had half the camp to clear to get back to Griskin. She could get there, but not fast, and the fear that she'd get trampled, set upon by the undead, or hit with a jet of fire left her sheened in a cold sweat.

Intense heat radiated from all around, and the scent of

burnt flesh and decay filled the air. The undead creatures withered and crumbled under the relentless assault, their faltering growls reverberating across the camp.

The dragonriders had turned the tide. Slavers who had fled or hidden were coming back, picking through the fire and smoke to gather anything they could of value that remained.

Mostly, that meant the escaping children scattered all around.

Nobody seemed worried about a small, solitary girl, edging her way along the ground.

Through the haze of smoke, Kess spotted a figure lying motionless ahead on her path. A warning of caution flickered in her mind as she crawled closer. She was right on top of him before she could identify the body as Iarl, the slaver leader.

The sun blesses me. With a wry grin, Kess sat up and reached out to search the man for her vial of silvernix.

She patted his chest, feeling a small bump to one side under his ragged jacket.

As she pulled the fur-lined fabric apart, the man's eyes flickered open, filled with malice and rage.

Kess hissed, scolding herself for not checking he was actually dead first. She'd already made that mistake with Pony.

"Trying to pillage the dead?" The slaver's hand shot

out, grabbing around her reaching wrist before she could withdraw it.

A surge of adrenaline fired through Kess's veins as his clammy fingers squeezed her skin. Depending on how injured the man was, he could still easily overpower her. She opened her clenched fists, holding her palms up in surrender.

"No, sir, I was trying to see if you were still alive, if I could help you."

"Ha!" Iarl barked, then winced. He let go of Kess, both hands clutching at his side. As he squeezed there, blood pressed through the fabric and stained his fingers.

"Where have you got the silvernix? You can use it for your wounds, so you don't end up dead after all."

His eyes went wide. "Yes. The silvernix! Where ..." Fumbling around with shaking fingers, he pulled Kess's coin pouch out from where she'd felt the lump.

Kess slowly brought her hands down and stared at the injured man. The flicker of fire shone off his sweaty forehead and his breaths came fast. As another burst of flame went up nearby, he cringed away from it. Kess held him in a steady glare.

"You're right. I wasn't going to help you. But I've changed my mind. I'm going to give you a swift death, which is more than a slaver of children like you deserves, and then I'm going to take what's mine."

"You, little girl? Ha," he grumbled, lips curled in a painful smile as he tugged the pouch open. Coins spilled out onto his chest as he groped inside. "What are you—"

Kess had a sharp bone dagger lanced into the man's heart as fast as lightning. "And no. Not even silvernix will save you."

He stared at her, mouth open and eyes confused as she leaned her body weight onto the blade, pressing the rest of the way in slowly, holding eye contact the whole time, until the light in his eyes went out.

Kess tsked. "People always underestimate what I'm capable of."

She left the dagger there—she had plenty and could always make more. Plucking the pouch from his still fingers, Kess checked inside. There it was, her bottle of unicorn blood.

She quickly scooped up what she could of the scattered sovs as well.

"Yuck." She grimaced, wiping the man's blood off them on the sleeve of his shirt.

Bringing herself upright again, Kess looked across to her target—Griskin. Without him, it felt like half of her was missing. Not just the ability to move faster, but the way she understood his body language, as though she shared his superior senses. She felt so much less without him.

Kess hiked her legs over the dead body of the slaver leader—just an obstacle now in her path—then crawled forward on her forearms.

Sparks and smoke gusted around as a dragonrider swooped low, scattering embers across the ground. Kess snarled as they singed holes into her leather bracers and gathered under her stomach, burning through her shirt, but she kept moving.

Movement rushed through the haze straight toward her and she froze.

A human rev, skeletal and engulfed in flames, stumbled before her.

The creature's charred bones crackled and glowed, its skeletal frame twisted and contorted in its final moments as it collapsed.

The heat radiating from its burning body seared the air, filling Kess's nostrils with the acrid scent of smoldering bone and seared flesh.

Flames danced hungrily across the creature's remains, devouring it with relentless fervor. The crackling of the inferno drowned out the distant sounds of battle, leaving only the roar of the consuming fire echoing in her ears.

She watched, a mix of fear and fascination gripping her, as the flames lapped at the creature's brittle form.

Her breaths came shallow and rapid, her body trembling

with a mixture of relief and lingering dread as the revenant stilled, the false life the shadowdragon had given the corpse burned away in cleansing fire.

That scourge that the Alderkin cursed the land with— Kess could feel her hatred for the blight spreading being deep in her gut. Her parents had taught her the history of what Elundrae used to be like before the shadowdragon came into being, drawing the undead from the earth.

How the Alderkin had cursed humans with it when it was clear they had lost the war. How dragonfire was the only sure way to cleanse the undead, no matter the collateral.

And how they never allowed Kess to become the dragonrider she'd been born to be, so she could help to save their land, too.

A shadow passed over Kess, and she looked up, hoping for another view of the snowflame darting by.

It wasn't there. Even the etherflames had moved from their hovering position, backing away.

Their job was all but done.

But the shadow over Kess deepened.

She rolled onto her back for a better view, and her jaw trembled and breath stuck.

The shadowdragon was descending ... again.

But why? There were some freshly dead that it could raise, but Kess had never seen nor heard of it touching

ground in the same place twice so soon apart.

It's smoky, swirling wings flapped without sound or substance, and the bright spots of its eyes shone like red stars against its void-black head.

The camp went strangely, eerily silent as it came to rest on the ground. No cries or wails this time, only a mute, clenching despair from everyone who observed. A desperate pang of mourning speared through Kess again, as it did the last time the cursed being touched ground.

And the shadowdragon roared.

The sound shuddered through Kess's chest, rattling her heart within her rib cage.

A deep growl grumbled from behind her. Iarl's white-eyed corpse jolted and convulsed. Kess hissed between her teeth. She really didn't want to have to kill him twice.

Then another more terrifying, crackling sound came from between her and Griskin.

She turned her head slowly, not wanting to see what the sound was coming from, because there was only one thing close enough, and it couldn't be. It couldn't ...

The still smoking human rev that had collapsed before her twitched and juddered.

Kess could only shake her head at it in denial. It had been burned. It was burned and it should never be able to come back again.

All remnants of flesh had been scorched from its bones, leaving only a horrific soot-blackened skeleton. Ashes flaked from it and fell like snow as it clawed itself off the ground.

Now the crying and screaming began again, a cacophony of terror rising all around from the remaining humans. Because all around, the burned revenants had impossibly come back from the dead ... a second time.

Kess wailed through clenched teeth, tearing across the ground away from the new and old revenant bodies she had found herself between. She had to find shelter, somewhere to hide again. But where could that be, with the whole camp aglow with raging dragonfire?

Where could that be, in a world where burnt revenants could rise again?

A deep, dark thought shook Kess to her core. The curse of the shadowdragon was worsening. How? And why? The Alderkin were all gone, their race and their magic destroyed entirely in their war against the dragonlords.

If they were the cause of the shadowdragon, why was it getting worse *now*?

Twenty-Six

The overturned half-cart that Riony had sheltered behind as the world went up in flames now felt like less shelter than a parasol made of cobwebs.

The dead had come back to life. Again.

Riony wished she was closer to the shadowdragon so she could punch the thing in its face. Had anyone even tried that before? Maybe it was the one thing that would end this depths-damned curse for good, but nobody had ever dared.

Riony would dare. She'd love to punch that shadowy serpentine cloud in the face right now.

As much as she hated dragonriders, at least they'd had the revs under control. Riony had time to catch a breath, time to try, and fail, to pick the lock on her manacle with the tip of the short sword she'd pilfered, as the revs burned to ash around her.

And now they were all twitching back into life again.

The shadowdragon took wing, churning like a living tornado of nightmares back into the evening sky.

If only the damn cart had caught on fire too, at least then I might be free of the thing. If a little singed.

Dracuni bleated at her from the open pack near her feet, and Riony eyed the ashy, smoldering revenants that shivered back to life before her. The bovin, for starters, but also a hawk and a human skeleton and Colber—the skinny slaver, not long dead.

Somehow, he disturbed her the most. Still too warm, too squishy, his dead white eyes not far enough removed from a still-alive human.

Riony stood, pushing her bag and Dracuni behind her, between her ankles and the solid wood of the cart. In desperation, she jabbed the sword into the joint where her chain was bolted to the broken timber, trying to cut or lever herself free. With a bright clang, the tip of her sword snapped off.

"Sparks!"

There was no time to find another weapon as the first revenant lunged for her. Her grip tightening on the hilt of

her even shorter short sword, she wished for the reach of her dragonguard longsword as the quick moving skeleton's boney fingers clawed for her face.

Riony cracked an elbow into its bare skull, knocking the lower half of its jaw flying. Ash eddied in the air behind it.

It stumbled back only to be replaced by the hawk, tattered, smoking feathers barely giving it enough lift to fly. It flapped in bursts, withered claws and fractured beak angling for Riony's neck.

Getting the sword between them, she swung like a bat, sending the undead bird soaring across the burning campsite.

And still the attack continued, both Colber and the human skeleton together now, grasping for her in unison.

The bovin had roused itself too. The crumbling, ashy joints seemed to reform like a strange, dry clay as the massive skeleton pulled itself together. Shaking itself off in a wave of smoke, Riony had her first break when it charged off in a different direction.

But the other two revs in human form wouldn't stop.

The ashy skeletal one reminded Riony so much of the one that had taken down the slaver ambush yesterday. Had it been burned and revived too, at some point? How long had this been happening? And how could these reborn revs be killed?

Nothing Riony did seemed to do more than barely keep them and their bloodthirsty jaws off her flesh for more than a moment. And sometimes it didn't, and their claws sliced ribbons across her arms and chest.

She met them with fist and sword, elbow and knee, forehead and feet. The blade of her sword sliced through brittle bones and spongy flesh.

The clash of steel against bone reverberated through the air as Riony unleashed a flurry of strikes, parrying and dodging and trying to push the relentless creatures off her just long enough to breathe. A gust of smoke stung her eyes and she fought blindly, tears streaming.

The revs didn't stop, didn't slow. Her brawling limbs and broken sword weren't enough to put them to rest again, if anything even could.

Across the campsite in the direction of the cages came a shrill scream. A voice Riony knew too well. *Lyrrin.*

Between the snarling, snapping faces of the two revs that had her pinned, Riony looked out, trying to spot her sister.

When the dragonriders had arrived, the slavers had taken the opportunity to gather their scattering slaves, rounding the children up as Riony worked frantically to free herself and get to Lyrrin before them. She'd lost track of her sister then.

She spotted the two delvers first, standing near the

gaping hole in the palisades that the bovin had charged through earlier. A smaller figure ran behind them—Benjin, probably—out through the broken barrier. Yelling and the clash of steel and the bright red of the burn magic in Yoskars staff cut through the din.

And even through the smoke, Riony could see the bloodless pallor of their faces, the whites of their wide eyes.

Aishena turned then, her gaze cutting right through the chaos and meeting Riony's. Despite her arms till swinging and muscles still burning, Riony felt time seemed to stop as they looked each other in the eye.

And then Aishena and Yoskar turned and fled.

Riony wasn't even surprised this time. Everybody of sound mind was running now. Riony would be too if someone had just taken a depths-forsaken second to unchain her.

Some bold slavers kept fighting and rounded up what remaining children they could into the cages. The big red dragon—etherflame, probably, but only dumb Kess cared about that sort of thing—had its claws clamped into the top of the cage and was lifting the children who had been stuffed back inside to safety.

The safety of slavery, at least.

Amidst the chaos, Riony felt the impact of bony fists and claws breaking through her defenses and pummeling her body. She gritted her teeth, fighting through the pain.

She heard a shriek again and Riony's head swiveled, pinpointing the sound.

Lyrrin!

A man with ragged golden curls had one of her sister's arms gripped in his, dragging her toward the second cage. *Zade.*

Lyrrin bucked and squealed in his grip. As Zade grabbed her around the waist to toss her in through the open cage door, Lyrrin's little arm shot out.

Her ungloved claws slashed across Zade's face. His roar of pain rose over the other wails and screams.

Riony's nose scrunched up. *Good girl, Lyrrin. Hurt him good.*

"I'm trying to help you, you little freak!" Still gripping the small child, Zade roared again and swung her small form against the metal bars of the cage. The steel clanged against Lyrrin's skull, and she went limp in his arms.

Riony's burning body went cold all over.

She fought in a frenzy, twice as fast, twice as hard, unaware of any pain or exhaustion or anything other than trying to clear her path to Lyrrin.

Riony's teeth clenched so hard she thought she might break her jaw, and tears ran down her face from eyes abused by smoke and pain.

Stupid. I was so stupid. I should have gone to her first.

She glared at the bag at her feet that held Dracuni. She couldn't do it. She couldn't look after them both. One responsibility was already too much for her to handle and she was getting everything wrong.

Aishena and Yoskar had it right. Just help themselves and stay alive. She couldn't fault them, really, since they'd managed to get themselves and their brother out of there. And what had Riony done?

Riony's parents had died from trying to help too many people. She should have learned their lesson and just focused on herself and her sister. Then she could have moved faster. Then she wouldn't have had to make efforts to hide what was in her pack and get messed around by Kess.

Then she might have had Lyrrin back already, and that dead man walking, Zade, couldn't have *hurt her*.

Riony's muscles strained, her body dripping with sweat. She couldn't keep fighting much longer. Her body was ready to crumple in on itself and give up completely, no matter how much willpower she used to try to keep going. And still the two revs that had her pinned wouldn't stop.

Dracuni mewled up from the ground, seeming to match Riony's rising distress and Riony growled back at the needy thing.

Zade tossed Lyrrin's limp body into the cage with the few other children that had been rounded up again.

The red dragon lifting the first cage of children had them just off the ground now, and panicked slavers were running after it, trying to leap up and grab hold of the outside of the cage, to be lifted away from the revenants too.

As the first etherflame dragon cleared the way, the second orange one moved in, angling around on huge leathery wings to get its claws onto the top of the remaining cage. The one that held Lyrrin.

Riony grunted as she tried to drag the half-cart forward, pushing against the two revs to clear ground at the same time, to get herself across the burning camp to Lyrrin before she was taken away.

But her muscles felt more like sacks of water at this point, wobbly and watery and weak. There was no way she could drag the heavy timber all the way through the campsite battleground in time.

Bright-white light scorched Riony's eyes, and she twisted to the side.

A stream of scorching liquid flame burst around her as the snowflame dragon swooped by.

The two revenants tumbled away, knocked back in the wash of fire.

Riony smashed backward into the half-cart behind her. She crumpled to the ground, dangling from her chained arm. Drawing deep, gasping breaths, her lungs filled with heat as the very dirt in front of her burned.

Hanging from the chain, Riony's face pressed against the timber, close to the ground near her open pack that had toppled onto its side. Dracuni peered out from within. The bright flames glistened in its wide eyes as it whimpered, moved to climb out of the bag closer to Riony, then circled back in again to hide.

The white flames formed a wall around where Riony huddled beside the broken cart. The snowflame's fire licked close to Riony's leg, and she pulled her foot away before it could burn.

Riony thumped her free fist onto the ground beside the bag. Her arm shook as tremors racked her overused muscles. She didn't even know if she had the strength to stand again.

"I should have gone to Lyrrin. I should never have brought you home from that cave." Riony's voice broke, the words too wrong, too painful. But she was so angry and so hurt and so left behind and so not enough to save anyone, even herself, that the words rushed out of her.

Dracuni's eyes widened, and it bleated and backed away from Riony into the pack.

Riony scrunched her face up and sniffed away a sob. Opening her fist, she reached out and cupped Dracuni's cheek in her hand. "I'm sorry. I didn't mean it. This isn't your fault."

Waves of worried emotion pressed into Riony's mind, and Dracuni clawed at the pack, as though trying to dig out through the leather walls to escape out the other side.

Riony pulled the pack closer, curling around it. "Don't worry. The revs won't come for you. If you can wait it out, try to run at the end, when it's all over."

When I'm gone.

Dracuni blinked at her, then looked to where her arm hung above her head, manacle heavy on her skin. The newborn bleated louder and scrambled more desperately. Riony reached for it, and it licked her palm as it dug little claws against the blanket it was tucked beside.

A surge of worry came again.

"Me? You're worried about me?" Riony's voice rose into a squeak.

With a big kick of its back legs, Dracuni unearthed the athame that Riony had left in the bag to show Lyrrin, back before everything fell to the depths.

Dracuni bleated again, circled around on the spot, then stilled again.

Picking up the athame, Riony gave the creature a half smile. She'd forgotten it was in there. Whether Dracuni thought it could help or just wanted it out of the way to be comfortable again in its hiding space, Riony didn't know.

But it was something. An offhand weapon to use with

the broken short sword. That might improve her chances a little. Or maybe she could pick the lock on the manacles with it, since it was slimmer and pointier than the sword had been.

For one moment, Riony wondered whether the blade was an offering from Dracuni, one to take some of its blood. Riony probably looked awful, bleeding from multiple gashes, but it was her insides failing her now. Would it heal her worn muscles? Riony wasn't sure that was something silvernix fixed.

Regardless, she looked into the lilac eyes and soft scales of the little creature and knew she wouldn't do it.

"I won't cut you, okay? I want you to know that. I won't ever cut you to heal myself. I promise." The vow felt easy to make. Whether it was because Riony had little hope of getting out of there with or without unicorn blood to heal her, she wasn't entirely sure.

Holding the athame near her face, she nodded at it, took a deep breath, and prepared to fight again.

"Shame it's out of charge, because this cutting rune would have come in handy right about now." Riony rubbed her thumb over the sigil, tracing it out.

And the athame glowed into life.

Riony startled so hard that she launched onto her feet and almost landed in the surrounding flames.

"What the sparks?" The athame had been out of charge,

she was sure. It had sputtered out in front of her eyes when she first found it.

Alderkin relics didn't just start working again. Once out of charge, they were done. Only Alderkin had the knowledge of how to recharge them, and they were all dead and gone even if they could have been persuaded to share.

But the cutting athame glowed a yellow as bright as the sun.

Riony gulped, held her breath, and ran the tip of the short crystal blade across her chain.

It sliced straight through with a soft sizzling sound. The remaining chain clattered free against the side of the cart.

Riony's body zinged with energy at its newfound freedom, as though shedding the weight of the half-cart gave her a second wind.

She glanced around. The two revs growled, skirting the wall of fire between her and them, waiting for the flames to die down so they could renew their attack.

Riony tightened her grip on the cutting athame. She wondered how well it might slice their heads from their necks and whether that would lay the things to rest.

Across the camp, the orange dragon had secured its grip on Lyrrin's cage and pumped its leather wings. The cage shook as it inched off the ground and the children inside whimpered and screamed. Riony didn't hear Lyrrin's voice.

Bending, Riony righted her backpack, tucking Dracuni carefully in and lashing the opening closed again. "Thank you, little one. I guess it's lucky I saved you, after all."

The straps of the pack had been cut below the buckle, but there were still a few notches in the remaining length. Riony pulled the cut sections out and rebuckled them.

Hoisting the bag onto her back, Riony then grabbed the broken short sword in her other hand. She climbed onto the pile of timber that had been the cart. Tensing her legs, she said a small prayer to the stars and Amma Moon, then launched herself over the white wall of flames.

She struck out at the two waiting revenants, hitting one with the cutting rune and one with the short sword. She didn't slow to see what damage she inflicted, only needing to clear her path.

Her arm muscles had borne the brunt of the fighting and heavy lifting earlier.

Now it was her legs' turn. They still felt fresh enough to run. And she put everything she had into moving faster than she ever had in her life.

She just had to get to the other side of the burning camp filthy with undead before Lyrrin's cage was too high for her to reach and she lost her little sister forever.

TWENY-SEVEN

Riony barreled across the campsite, vaulting over burning bodies and dodging away from skittering revenants. A skeletal horse galloped by, passing in the opposite direction, snorting flames and streaming smoke behind it.

The orange dragon flapped, beating its wings hard with the additional weight of the cage and the children it held. Wind gusted across the camp, blowing in Riony's face, pushing against her like a barrier trying to hold her back.

A dark, shadowy shape leaped onto the dragon's tail, scampering up its back like a bizarre parasite. The dragon screeched and faltered, wings twitching and pulling in as the creature crawled around and up its chest.

Riony squinted at the creature through the heavy smoke, her eyes stinging and raw. A rev. A bear, maybe? Something larger than human, more mobile, more bestial.

It didn't try to hurt the dragon. Instead, it went straight for the rider.

The cry of alarm when the dragonrider noticed the attacker's presence was female. The revenant crawled to the dragonrider's saddle, and metal sung as the woman drew a pair of gleaming swords.

Perched upon the dragon's neck, just above its shoulders and the muscles of its wings, the rider twisted in her seat, flicking a leg upward and swinging herself upside down from one foot to dodge the revenant's claws.

Riony watched in awe as the rider brought herself under and around her dragon's neck and up the other side, climbing its scales like a cliff face, and coming up behind the confused revenant. Her armor glistened in the same sunset tones as her dragon, and her swords clattered against the revenant's back.

Riony knew it wasn't the right time to be forming a new crush, but damn, the rider was impressive.

Without its rider in control, the orange dragon faltered, wings held in place and torso stilling.

Even amongst all the fire and monsters, the dragon had only a dull, glazed look in its sun-bright yellow eyes.

It looked everywhere and nowhere, head bowed, the heavy metal stake punctured into its brain leaving it numb to everything but its rider's commands.

The cage clattered back to the ground as the dragon's wings no longer fought against gravity. The door popped open, and the children inside squealed and pulled it closed again as revs closed in on them. Lyrrin stirred, propping herself up in one corner.

Riony's heart rushed with the warm blood of hope.

As long as the rev kept the dragonrider busy, it was buying Riony time.

Flames exploded to her left, and she dodged right, trying to keep up her pace.

Her path was strewn in bodies and burning embers, and her eyes were drawn to one—small and still moving— crawling with a steely determination in the direction of the netted wolf.

Riony's pounding footsteps slowed.

No. It wasn't worth heading all the way across there to slit the goblin's throat, then stab her in the back for good measure. As much as it sounded like a fun time, she didn't have the moments to spare.

Riony wasn't far from the wolf, though.

Taking a slight veer toward the trapped animal, Riony's lips twitched and curled. She didn't like the feeling that was swelling inside her. It felt too much like pity, and that was something she would never have for Kess. She knew better.

But maybe, maybe it was because she'd regained enough hope to share it around.

Riony had gone out of her way, had sacrificed greatly, to save the little creature in her backpack, even when it had felt like a poor decision. And now freed from her manacle by the athame that still glowed bright in her hand, she felt as though that had been the right decision.

She was so brimming with hope and compassion that it was hard to fight against. Maybe she could go out of her way once more to help another creature.

Stars, I better not regret this.

Riony skidded to her knees in front of the metal netting that pinned the wolf down. He growled low and deep as she raised the glowing crystal blade.

"Do yourself a favor, pup. Ditch the goblin. She's not your friend. She doesn't even know what the word means."

Riony slashed the athame and it sliced neatly through the netting.

"Go on, get yourself out of here."

The wolf twisted, roused into action by the prospect of escape. Riony scrambled straight back up into a sprint as the wolf thrashed itself free, each of them dashing in different directions.

Up ahead, the dragonrider's swords clattered to the ground. The woman's back was pressed against the dragon's neck, her hands gripping the saddle straps beside her head. She curled into a ball as the bear revenant's body smothered her in a whirlwind of claws.

Riony held her breath as she leaped over a spread of embers. If the dragonrider died, what would happen to the dragon? It currently sat like a bird on a perch on top of the cage. Its weight was too much for the shoddy construction and the bars were buckling and groaning, threatening to crush Lyrrin and the others inside.

Then the revenant shot backward, as though blown from a cannon. The rider's legs were both straight out in the air, her arms still grasping the saddle straps at her back. She'd curled in and waited until she had enough leverage on the rev to boot it off her. *Damn, that was bold.*

Riony could begrudgingly see why Kess was so obsessed with dragonriders.

Glancing over her shoulder, Riony saw the tail end of the wolf disappearing behind a cloud of smoke, the silhouette of Kess on its back.

Riony wasn't sure how she felt about that. The wolf deserved better, but it had made its choice.

With the bear rev off her, the dragonrider was already back in her saddle and the orange dragon sprung back to life, wings flapping hard.

The crushed cage groaned and creaked as it lifted from the ground, drawn upward within the dragon's claws.

A couple of adult-sized figures jumped onto it as it rose higher. One clung tight, but the other grasped at a bent bar that sprung free. The man screamed as he tumbled back to the ground. The children inside screeched as the cage swung around, threatening to toss them out of that hole too.

Riony threw the broken short sword to the ground and deactivated the athame, stuffing it down the front of her shirt as her quickest storage option, to free up her hands.

She drew every last bit of energy she had for a final burst of speed. She dashed the last few steps, ran up the burning downed carcass of the bovin rev, still twitching and hot under her boots, using its thick spine as a staircase, and leaped into the air.

She clattered against the side of the cage as it lifted above head height and clung tight.

Her cheek pressed against a bar, and she gasped in relief.

Then a boot smacked into her rib cage.

"Are you *sparking kidding me*," Riony huffed out the words.

The foot shot toward her again, and Riony knocked it aside with one hand, looking up at her attacker.

Zade shuffled away from her, around the corner of the dangling cage. Heading toward where Lyrrin still sat in one corner, looking woozy and teary.

"What are you going to do, Zade? Hide behind a child so I can't break that nose of yours a second time?" Riony kicked her legs out, swinging herself fast around the cage in the way she'd seen the dragonrider maneuver around her steed's neck.

The cage rattled and swung wildly from her weight, and the few children inside screamed. She went around the other side, cutting Zade off before he could reach Lyrrin.

"Why are you still fighting us?" Zade yelled back over the gusting flap of dragon wings. "We need to get out of here! They'll take us to safety."

"You're the one who tried to kick me off! I'm not going anywhere with them and I'm not going anywhere with you!" Riony shouted back.

Zade roared and lashed a fist out. Riony knocked it away from her face with her forearm.

His foot slipped and his swinging arm went wide, pulling his bodyweight sideways. The bent metal bar he held in his other hand creaked and popped. And then it slipped free.

Zade's eyes drew wide, and his mouth gaped in a scream as he fell into the open air. His hands scrabbled forward, trying to grab the cage again, but he fell through the smoke.

He thumped hard on the ground beneath Riony, and the impact cleared the smoke away. He cried out, back arching in pain, but survived. They weren't too far up yet.

Riony turned to yank open the door of the cage when another harsh gurgling scream ripped from Zade below.

The bear revenant was upon him, biting and tearing.

Within seconds, Zade's screams ended, and Riony looked away. She'd wished the young man a special death, but that was a rough way to go.

All she could do now was hope she and Lyrrin didn't go that way too.

The cage swung crookedly again as she wrenched the door open.

"Lyrrin!"

The other children cowered in a corner, clearing the way between her and her sister.

Lyrrin looked up, her blue eyes red-rimmed. Tears stuck her dark hair onto her cheeks and her lips trembled. Both arms shot out for Riony, one hand gloved, one without.

Riony leaned in, scooping her into a hug. The warmth of her sister's small form, clutched close against hers, was a salve to every pain she suffered.

"I'm here. I'm here."

Lyrrin gasped and gulped through sobs. "I tried. I tried

to fight the kid snatchers, and not stop fighting, because I knew that's what you would do."

Riony squeezed her tight. "You did so well. I've got you now. And we're getting out of here."

Lyrrin blinked and looked from the airborne cage at the burning camp below.

Riony followed her gaze. It was hard to judge how high they were now with all the smoke beneath them, but Riony figured they were at least two stories up. The dragon had enough clearance that it began moving away from the campsite.

It would only get higher and faster from there.

Riony separated herself from Lyrrin. Pulling her arms out from her backpack straps, she moved it around onto her front.

"We're going to jump, okay?"

"Jump?"

"It's okay, it's not too high. We'll be scared for a moment, but it's better than a lifetime as a slave."

Lyrrin's little mouth closed tight. She looked into Riony's eyes and nodded.

Riony reached her arms out to Lyrrin again, pulling her in near her chest beside the backpack with Dracuni.

"Any of you lot want to come with us?" Riony asked the other kids.

The few children remaining shook their heads and clung to the corner of the opened cage.

Riony frowned. She didn't like the idea of them being taken away to slavery, but she couldn't force them to do what she was about to do.

Riony heaved up to her feet on shaking legs. She lifted Lyrrin with her, held tight in one arm as she held the cage with the other and stepped to the edge of the open doorway.

Yeah. It's not too high yet. I probably fell farther when I broke my arm.

Riony couldn't see the ground at all through the smoke.

She hadn't been prepared before, to fall a great distance again, not unless it was for something very special, very important. Now she was. This was worth falling for.

She swallowed hard and angled out into the air. Lyrrin squealed and hid her face in her shoulder, her legs wrapping tight around Riony's waist.

Dracuni also loosed a keening sense of fear through Riony's mind. Riony gritted her teeth. She was getting both of them out of this alive.

"Hey, listen to me now. This is important. The most important thing I've ever asked you."

Lyrrin didn't look up but nodded her face against Riony's shoulder.

"Once we hit the ground ... no matter what ... don't worry

about me. Just take the backpack and run, understood? If you only do one thing I've ever asked you to do, do *this*. Okay, little spitfire?"

Lyrrin held still for a moment as the dragon's wingbeats grew faster.

Then she nodded again, and Riony stepped off the edge.

TWENTY-EIGHT

Riony's shirt and cape fluttered like feathers around her as she, Dracuni, and Lyrrin plummeted through the acrid air.

As soon as they were off the edge, Lyrrin was screaming and didn't stop. Riony whipped her head about, trying to get a sense of which way was up, her red hair flicking into her eyes. Her body turned in dizzying circles, tossed about through gusts of smoke and embers.

She brought her knees up, wrapped her arms in, and curled her whole body around the two babies she'd stolen.

She'd taken them on, taken their lives as her responsibility, and she intended for them both to survive.

But as soon as she'd stepped out into the air, she feared

she'd made the dumbest decision of her life, that she'd killed them all. They couldn't have stayed in that cage though, flown back to captivity in a dragonkeep.

That could only end in Dracuni being revealed, taken from her, and forced into a life Riony couldn't even guess at. Who would take ownership of the precious newborn, and what would they do when they discovered its priceless blood?

Lyrrin, with her unique hair, hands, and eyes, wouldn't fare much better.

So Riony had jumped and had to trust in a plan that consisted of only two things: one, hope they weren't really up too high, and two, be the first one to hit the ground.

Stage one already had her shaken. They seemed to be falling forever, with the flame-heated air rushing around them and Lyrrin squealing and Dracuni's **scared, scared, scared** beating her thoughts like a drum.

That probably meant that part two of her plan wasn't going to end well. Definitely not for her. She only hoped she could cushion Lyrrin and Dracuni enough with her body for them to walk away.

And that Lyrrin, for once in her life, would obey her wishes.

Please. Just take Dracuni and run. Maybe Lyrrin would catch up to the delvers, have their protection, make it home, even if she was going home without her.

The crackles of fire and clash of fighting grew suddenly louder and Riony braced for impact. Tears flicked upward out of her eyes into the air. The fiery landscape below expanded, a tapestry of swirling flames and billowing smoke, becoming real and solid and all too close, too fast.

She made contact. Her body smacked against something flexible and leathery, scraping against her back as she kept moving. Hot licks of cinders stung the bare flesh on her arms and flew around her face as she skidded down the soft, burning surface.

They bounced, slid, bounced again, then Riony toppled in a sideways roll off the leather and walloped hard onto the dirt on her back.

All the air woofed out of her chest. Riony closed her eyes and lay still, her flattened lungs squeezed closed like too-tight bellows, refusing to draw breath again.

Come on. Breathe. Breathe! Tears squeezed from the corners of her eyes as she willed her body to keep working.

There was a squeal and sob above her, as Lyrrin wriggled around, and her small hands tugged at the straps of the backpack that Riony wore on her front.

The weight of the bag and Dracuni lifted off Riony. She opened her eyes to see Lyrrin clutching the leather pack in a tight cuddle and wavering.

Working hard, Riony's chest inflated again in the

smallest of breaths. She rasped out her words. "Good work. Go, run! I'm right behind you. Keep going!"

With a nod, Lyrrin took off. Riony wheezed in more air, her compacted lungs struggling to take shape again. She cried out as she pushed herself into a sitting position. Her whole body was going to be one big bruise tomorrow.

She was alive, still alive! But also, *ouch*.

A section of her shirt had caught on fire and she swatted at it, hissing as her fingers sizzled.

Glancing behind her, Riony saw the smoldering wall of one of the slavers' leather tents, tipped to the side and pulled taut. It wobbled, already slackening and slumping after her collision with it, tearing where the flames were taking hold.

Thank all the stars. The odds of landing on that one soft spot in all this chaos must have been a miracle. Riony shook her head at it in awe.

Behind the sinking tent wall, a silhouette moved, obscured by bright arcs of fire and a gust of embers. Riony tensed, expecting it to be a revenant, bracing for it to pounce.

But it turned, moving the other way. It was hard to tell what it was through the haze, large and misshapen, humanoid in some parts, but also not. A shiver ran across Riony's scalp. There was something wolfish about the shape, and its silent, prowling retreat. Kess?

Why would she still be there? She should have turned tail and fled this place the moment she got her wolf back. The silhouetted figure was gone now, vanished into the distance.

Whoever or whatever they were, Riony couldn't know for sure. And she couldn't wait around to find out.

She flopped forward onto her hands and knees, coughing as her winded lungs drew in a big breath of smoke. First, she crawled, then she got her legs under her, moving into a stumbling crouch, then a wobbling jog, until her legs and body worked well enough again to run.

She raced through the burning camp after Lyrrin.

It didn't take long to catch up, since Riony's legs were so much longer than her little sister's.

"Keep going, as fast as you can. I'm with you," Riony whispered. She put a hand on Lyrrin's shoulder, encouraging her on. The open gate of the palisades was just ahead.

There were less sounds now, less screaming. No more sounds of steel clashing against bone. They had been replaced with more disturbing wet chewing noises.

A few revs still prowled through the smoke, but all their prey had fled or already been killed now, and many of the revs seemed to have rambled out into the surrounding wilderness seeking more human life to hunt.

Riony kept her and Lyrrin moving at a fast and quiet pace through the haze, hoping none of the undead would notice that some of their missing prey had fallen from the sky and returned to them.

Nearing the gates there was a glint of metal on the ground ahead.

"Keep going, right out the gate." Riony gave Lyrrin a small push and sidetracked toward the bright strip of steel on the ground.

Lyrrin kept going straight, and Riony flushed with pride. *She's doing so well, and by the stars, she's following my instructions!*

All it took was a long sequence of life-and-death situations. Maybe Riony just needed to replicate these conditions back at home now and then, to keep Lyrrin open to her suggestions.

Home. A destination that was finally feeling possible again. But still so far away. She just had to make it one step at a time.

Riony had hoped that the bright spot in the dirt reflecting the glow of fire was a sword. Honestly, a weapon of any kind would have been a blessing. There were still revs all around, and it was a long, long way home.

When it came within full view, she bit her tongue to avoid letting out a triumphant scream that would alert all the revs to her location. A small happy squeal wheezed out of her anyway as she loped forward, bending to scoop up the abandoned sword as she ran.

Her sword.

The dragon-scale patterned hilt felt so familiar in her grasp, the weight of it as recognizable as family. She had her sword back. She had Lyrrin. And she had Dracuni, still alive, tough little newborn it was. Riony looked up at the stars and all the ancestors they held looking down at her and blew them a kiss.

She swerved back toward the gate, sprinting to catch up to Lyrrin, and they broke out from between the perimeter together.

Riony didn't dare stop running. They left the carnage of the slavers' camp in their wake. She kept her legs pumping and kept gasping out encouragements to Lyrrin every time she slowed or started to lose her grip on the pack.

They ran until they physically couldn't run any farther, and then they stumbled on stiff, wavering legs, blindly through the nighttime forest, through sodden grass onto rocks.

The harsh scent of burning wood and flesh—some of it her own—clung to Riony's clothes and had scorched her nose and throat, but the air now seemed clear.

The night around them was quiet, only a few crickets trilling and the soft gurgle of running water and Riony and Lyrrin's lead-heavy footsteps breaking the silence.

Riony's head spun, dizzy with the hum of exhaustion, but she kept pushing forward.

She hoped no revs had wandered out this far in this direction. She hoped no slavers had come this way either. She couldn't fight either off at this point. She could barely lift a finger.

She also hoped the direction they headed in was the right one to take them home. But even if it wasn't, it was something she could work out after she was no longer busy passing out.

Her body finally gave in, and she folded to the ground, face-first into the dirt.

TWENTY-NINE

A great splash of frigid water across her face roused Riony. She spluttered, and all four limbs flew upward, ready to fight off the next wave of attackers.

"You're alive!" Lyrrin squeaked, stepping out of the way of Riony's flailing fists.

Riony froze, blinked, and took in her surroundings.

Lyrrin stood close, but not too close, to her side, clutching the sodden end of her cloak, wrung between her hands. The pack, still closed, had been left on a flat rock behind her, and behind that, a cliff rose into the night sky, creating a small overhang.

It was dark, only moonlight weakly highlighting the edges of objects nearby. Riony could hear the trickle of water through rocks but couldn't see where it came from through the gloom.

"You *doused* me?" Riony wiped her face with her palms and forearms.

"I thought you were dead! You have blood ..."

"Where?" Riony asked, rubbing at aching and stinging dark smudges on her skin that could all have been bruises, burns, blood, or soot.

"*Everywhere*," Lyrrin whispered, her eyes bright and round.

Riony batted a hand at the air. "I'm fine, just—ouch—have to ... *woof.* Nope. I'm going to stay sitting down."

Riony's body felt like she'd gone ten rounds with relentless undead opponents, then fell onto her back from a great height.

Oh sparks, I totally did though.

She didn't blame Lyrrin for thinking she was dead. She was amazed herself that she was still alive, and there was a weird choking sensation in her throat due to wondering whether Kess had some part of that outcome.

There's no chance. She wouldn't have. Would she? No chance.

Kess had left her to bleed out and die alone in a frozen cave when she had the means to save her. Riony shook her head to herself. No. Hitting that tent wall had been luck, and luck alone.

And if that had been Kess watching from the smoky shadows, she was probably only there to get the front row view of Riony going splat and was sorely disappointed.

But still the lump in Riony's throat remained, images of Kess and Griskin's silhouette swirling in her mind like they did through the ashy clouds.

Riony shivered, the chilled water dripping from her face and onto her chest, soaking her shirt. She wasn't sure if they could dare to get a fire going.

"No sign of revs?" she asked.

Lyrrin fiddled with the wet end of her cloak and looked around with worried eyes. "Nuh-uh. Haven't seen anybody else. It's been really quiet."

Riony nodded. It did feel quiet. She looked over at her backpack, lying still on the rock, and felt no sensations coming from Dracuni. She took a deep breath and swallowed hard.

"Hey, can you bring my backpack over to me? I would get it myself, but ouch."

Lyrrin moved quickly to pick it up, without even an eyeroll or grunt. Riony's lips quirked. She could get used to this, but she knew it wouldn't last.

While Lyrrin brought the backpack, Riony pulled her glow stone from the netted pouch on her belt, activated it, then tucked it down between some rocks so its light didn't spread too far. Just enough soft, cyan luminance for her and Lyrrin to see by.

"I'm sorry I let the kid snatchers take me." Lyrrin meandered back slowly, clutching the bag and looking at the ground.

"It wasn't your fau—*wait*. What do you mean, *let them take you*?"

"'Cause I saw them grabbing Benjin when I was going to go and fight the baby dragon killers."

Riony held the bridge of her nose and sighed.

"And then I followed and saw Zade and some other people grabbing up a heap of kids. And I tried to stop them, 'cause that's what you would have done."

"You think too highly of me, kid."

Lyrrin poked at a loose pebble with her toes. "But you would have! I even punched Zade so hard! Just like you would have! But it didn't stop them. I'm sorry."

Riony coughed out a chuckle, remembering Zade's bleeding nose and blackened eyes he'd blamed on the slavers. "That was you? That was a nice hit."

Lyrrin looked up, beaming. She skittered across the rest of the way and handed Riony her backpack.

"I'm sorry, but that otter of yours isn't in here anymore." Riony shifted around so she could lean against the wall of the cliff.

Lyrrin nodded and a couple of fresh tears dropped. "I

saw him run off. Do you think he'll be okay out there?"

"Oh yeah. That guy? Tough little thing will be running around pilfering food from every pocket he can get." Riony was far more worried about the other creature she'd carried.

Her fingers trembled as she worked on untying the closure to the bag. Her head felt quiet, abandoned, without the added feelings and sensations of the little creature that she was getting used to.

Please be alive, little Dracuni.

There was still no movement from within as Riony reached a hand inside to feel the bundle of velvety scales and floppy wings. She cupped Dracuni's head in her hand and felt a slight wobble as the skin around its large eyes opened.

The newborn let out a weak, dull trill.

"What is that?" Lyrrin asked.

Riony put her second hand into the pack too and scooped Dracuni out onto her lap. "So, what I didn't get to tell you before you ran off to punch delvers and slavers, is that the delvers didn't kill *all* of the baby dragons."

Lyrrin wheezed, inhaling so much, so fast, that Riony was worried she might explode.

"It's a *baby dragon*?" Lyrrin cried.

"Shh! And sort of. Not entirely. I'm not sure."

Lyrrin dropped down next to Riony, cuddling up to her side and cooing at the limp bundle of pale rainbow

scales on her lap.

"Is it okay? What's wrong with it?" Lyrrin asked, reaching out her gloved hand to stroke the baby's cheek. Dracuni opened its mouth again, a silent, wobbly plea.

Hungry. It was so weak now.

Riony frowned, her heart heavy. "It's hungry. But I haven't been able to feed it."

"For this long? Since it was born?" Lyrrin scolded her harshly.

"I tried. I tried everything, but it wouldn't take anything I offered it. And I had so much food before, you should have seen it ..."

"Did you chew on it first?"

"Chew on ... the dragonling?"

"No, the food, silly! It hasn't got teeth yet. You've got to chew up the food for it, like an amma bird."

Riony planted both hands on her face. "Ugh! Of course! But I don't have anything left now, except ..."

Riony checked her belt pouch, and inside were three small bruised and cracked apples. "Stars, I wanted to share these with you. They're kind of wrecked now. I think I landed on them a few times."

Lyrrin gasped. "*Apples*?" She reached for one and plunged her teeth into the browned flesh. "Mmm, it's so good."

She chewed for a moment, then stuck a finger into her

mouth, scooped a lump of mashed pulp out of her cheek, and offered it to Dracuni.

Eyelids drooped, then lifted, then drooped again as the dragonling's snout twitched. With a tiny bleat, it opened its mouth, and Lyrrin stuck her finger straight in. She giggled as the newborn suckled on her, slurping off the chewed-up fruit.

Dracuni's eating!

Riony huffed an uncontrollable laugh of relief. "That's gross."

"You're gross." Lyrrin giggled back.

"I want a turn." Riony bit off a big chunk of apple, grinding it between her teeth. She sobbed happily when Dracuni lifted its head to take the messy fruit off her fingers.

Hungry. More hungry! The thoughts came through loud and clear as the little creature's appetite and strength came back.

"You're going to be okay, little one. We've got you." Riony spoke as she chewed, preparing to feed the newborn again.

She and Lyrrin took turns, laughing and chewing and feeding the baby unidragon, and sometimes taking a bite of apple for themselves as well. The three small apples were gone too fast, and Riony regretted the wealth of food scattered on the ground back at the slavers' camp.

No chance she was going back for it, though.

Dracuni was now sucking on the wet hem of Lyrrin's cloak, eyes drooping into a contented sleep. It felt warm on her lap, and with Lyrrin tucked in beside her too, Riony no longer shivered.

She hadn't meant for her little family to grow, but she was happy that it had.

Lyrrin seemed to have grown so much, too, in the last couple of days.

Riony scratched Dracuni's forehead around the base of its single horn, and whispered to Lyrrin, "So, the really special thing about Dracuni—"

"Aw, that's such a cute name!"

"—is that it—well, she, I think she's a she—she has blood like unicorn's blood."

"What? How can that be?"

"I don't know. I used Grand-Amma's silvernix on Dracuni's egg because it was broken, and then ... then the little critter was just born like this. I found out when she healed me." Riony held up her once-broken arm, stripping off the tattered remains of Lyrrin's bandaging.

Her sister gasped. "You could heal yourself again now! You could be all better! Except..." Lyrrin's excitement faded quickly, and her frown returned, eyes searching in thought.

Riony shrugged. "I sort of promised Dracuni that I wouldn't do that. Which, honestly, I'm kind of regretting right now. Even my bruises have bruises. But I just couldn't, you know? I couldn't hurt her."

Lyrrin nodded vigorously. "That's what I thought, too. Just after I thought you could be healed, I remembered that it was her blood that heals, and you only get blood when you get hurt. I don't want to hurt her either. She's too cute! And only a baby."

"That's why Dracuni has to stay our secret. Bigger secret even than your hair and your fingers, okay? We can't let anybody take Dracuni and hurt her."

Lyrrin lifted her hands in front of her, one glove missing, revealing the sharp blue-tipped claws. Her bottom lip trembled. "I'll try. I promise I'll do my best. But ... Some people saw ..."

Riony put an arm around Lyrrin and squeezed. "It's okay. You did what you had to do to survive. We found your markers; that's how we followed you."

"You did?" Lyrrin perked up.

"Yup. Sometimes taking action is more important than staying secret at the time. We'll work the rest out as we go."

"What was it Pabba used to say? Big dreams, bold deeds?"

A hot sting rushed into Riony's nose and eyes, and she sniffed it away. "Yeah ... something like that."

Lyrrin nodded, folded her arms in, and snuggled closer to Riony. Sighing a soft release, Riony let the tension seep

out of her body as she relaxed back against the stone behind her and even dared close her eyes for a moment.

The slip of feet on pebbly ground clattered through the dark.

Riony shot upright. She slid Dracuni off her lap and back into her bag in one swift motion, then gestured for Lyrrin to stay quiet as she reached for her sword. She stilled and listened.

"Shh!"

"You shh!"

A small whimper.

"Would you all be quiet? Sparks!"

Riony got to her feet with a muffled groan, sword drawn in front of her and Dracuni and Lyrrin behind. She frowned and squinted toward the surrounding darkness.

"Aishena? Was that you?" she called in a loud whisper.

As though materializing from the black background, Aishena stepped out over the rocky ground toward them. "Yes, it's us. You can put your sword away, tamebrain."

Riony lifted her sword point higher. "I don't know if I want to. What if, and hear me out, what if I get to stab you once for each time you abandoned me?"

"Not everything is about you." Aishena held up her hands, the manacle and long chain still dangling from one.

"It felt a lot like it was about me when the abandoning

was happening. Come on. Just one little jab. It will make me feel much better."

"We had to get out of there to save the kids." Yoskar's voice pierced through the darkness.

He stepped forward, trailed by a huddled group of a dozen or so children.

Lyrrin scampered to her feet and squeaked. "Benj! Cammi! Leeu! You all made it!"

She rushed forward into the group of children, hugging and gossiping.

Riony huffed and lowered her sword. "Sorry. Looks like you two did the right thing. I guess I'm kind of used to people *not*."

"Fair. We kind of just wanted to take Benjin, but they all came as a set together." Aishena rolled her eyes at the tight huddle of whispering children.

Riony watched as Lyrrin moved through them, checking the faces. She watched Lyrrin's joy as each teary, sooty, relieved face met hers.

Riony's heart ached for how she had scolded Lyrrin for not staying in their rooms all alone. How the child kept sneaking out to spend time at the orphans' den.

It was never just disobedience. These were her friends.

Yoskar leaned heavily on his staff as he moved in closer and propped himself against the cliff wall with a sigh.

"Benjin said they wouldn't have gotten out of the cage to us if it weren't for Lyrrin. No idea how she managed to cut through those bars though."

"Yeah, I don't know how," Benjin added, his eyes locked with Lyrrin's.

Lyrrin's lips were pressed together, and she hid her one ungloved hand under her cloak as everybody looked to her.

Yeah, no idea, I'm sure. Riony winked at the delver's little brother and gave him a small nod.

She reached into the front of her shirt and pulled out the athame she'd stashed in there. She chucked it over to Aishena. "She had this."

Aishena held the athame up, angling it to get enough light to read the rune. "A cutting athame? That has charge? How do you two own something like this?"

Riony smirked. "We all have our little secrets."

Aishena stilled. "I suppose we do."

Smiling again now, eyes sparkling in the dark, Lyrrin stepped next to Benjin. "Benj kept watch for me, so I could work without the kid snatchers seeing me."

Benjin made a big *aw-shucks* gesture, and his eyes kept turning back to Lyrrin every few seconds.

"That's still ours, by the way." Riony snatched the athame back out of Aishena's fingers, worried about how the delver was practically caressing it. "But I can get those things off you, if you want."

Riony gestured to the manacles still weighing down the delvers' arms. Activating the rune, the area blazed with yellow light.

"Did you see where Zade ended up?" Aishena asked, eying the athame in Riony's hand.

"Yeah. I saw him again, after the shadowdragon touched ground a second time."

Silence fell over all of them as the questions and the horrors of the moment resurfaced.

Riony cleared her throat. "He didn't make it."

Taking care not to slip and amputate Aishena's arm— while also fantasizing about it a little—Riony sliced the manacle lock. The chain clattered onto the ground.

"I never did like him." Aishena rubbed the raw skin where the manacle had been.

"Yeah, I *did* notice the open hostility. Never thought you'd be the one with the well-refined instincts, though."

Aishena shrugged her angular shoulders, flinching slightly as she looked to Yoskar as though for approval, but he offered none.

"Sorry I didn't get your weapons back off his corpse for you. Could have made a nice gift. Maybe make you realize you're sweet on me, after all," Riony said as she turned to work on Yoskar's cuff.

"I've got plenty more athames back at home." Aishena huffed and rubbed her wrist. "It would take far more than that to win my affections."

Yoskar's manacle fell free, then Riony turned the magically sharpened tip of the glowing crystal toward the band of iron that still clasped her arm, despite the chain being removed earlier.

"So, you mean something a bit more like journeying through the perilous aboveground with you, saving you and your brother's life, breaking you free from your chains, not stabbing you after you abandoned me. Something like that?"

"Not even close." Aishena smirked.

"Wow. High standards. That's hot."

"But ..." Aishena's eyes softened, and she tilted her head. "Maybe it's enough for us to put in a good word for you with Brishan. Get you a head start when the next delver trials come up."

Riony's jaw dropped and she nearly slipped and cut her own arm off. The manacle fell away. Swallowing, she slowly and carefully deactivated the cutting rune. "You'd do that for me? Really?"

With the light extinguished again, the area seemed much darker, and Riony could only just make out Aishena's shrug. "I mean, you did okay. And yeah, we do kind of owe you."

"A debt must be repaid," Yoskar agreed solemnly.

"I would kiss you on the mouth right now, but I respect your boundaries."

"Gross!" Lyrrin scoffed.

"You're gross," Riony shot back, grinning toothily.

Aishena made a show of ignoring Riony now and herded the group of children into shelter under the overhanging cliff. She didn't suggest a fire, either, but the sheer number of bodies and the barrier from the breeze seemed to keep everybody warm enough.

"Oh. Also, we found this." Yoskar removed his backpack and rummaged around in it. When he pulled his hand back out, he held up a wriggling sausage of pale caramel fur by the scruff of its neck. "Or rather, it found us. Caught it sniffing for food."

"*Sir Butterfur Spelunkychunks*!" Lyrrin gasped, running in to snatch the cave otter. She cuddled him tight and giggled as he skittered through the opening of her collar and hid in her shirt, chittering angrily.

Benjin added quickly and ardently, "Which we *weren't* going to eat for dinner."

"Well ..." Aishena muttered.

"We weren't!" Benjin snapped back.

Aishena's eyes sparkled. "All these hungry children ..."

"I will stab you in your sleep," Lyrrin hissed.

Riony chuckled and settled her tired body back onto

a rocky seat.

"Some food and some sleep. We've got a long way to go back tomorrow." Yoskar pulled a bundle of flatbread from his pack—the parchment wrapping gnawed through in one corner by the cave otter—and shared the food with everybody.

"Dibs not keeping watch," Riony said, her eyes heavy.

"I will," Aishena replied, still at attention at the front of the group.

Riony nodded and settled in as best she could on the uneven ground, her pack and Lyrrin tucked in beside her.

It would be a long trip to get back to the undercity with all the additional children in tow.

But once they were back, they would be safe again. That's what mattered.

Safe from that dispersed group of slavers, from dragonriders, from seeing Kess ever again, and from the revs, and whatever was going on with the revenants coming back to unlife a second time.

We will be safe again once we get back to the undercity ... won't we?

Riony shivered. The hard lump in her throat had remained, as though she'd breathed in part of the shadowdragon's smoky form, a piece of its curse now embedded in her, turning all her insides into fear.

THIRTY

Griskin's fur reeked with the musky tang of smoke residue. Kess leaned into him, her scraped and burned fingers digging deep into his scruffy coat, holding him tight, as they prowled through the darkness, hunting their prey.

She didn't ever want to be separated from her wolf again. At least, not until she had her own dragon to ride.

Kess had come so close to losing everything. Her wolf, her silvernix, even every belonging she carried on her person and in Griskin's saddlebags. She nearly lost her life in that madness of returned-again revenants.

Most of what she lost she got back. And Kess seethed at the fact she had Pony to thank for that.

It didn't make sense. That Pony would help her, in

any way. When the world was being razed every which way around them, why had the intolerable woman spared a moment to help her?

Technically, Kess supposed Pony hadn't helped *her*. She'd helped Griskin. Which only gave Kess what she needed by association. *Pony always did have a soft spot for dumb animals. Or basically anything in a helpless damsel situation.*

That Pony had only been helping the wolf was a much easier to stomach answer than any other option. Like that Pony had helped her out of some kind of pity. Or literally any other emotion. Yuck.

Regardless, Pony's actions put Kess in an awkward position. Honor demanded a debt repaid. Kess may have been exiled from her dragonlord home, but she still lived by that code.

Luckily, the moment presented itself sooner than expected when that ridiculous woman threw herself from the sky.

Kess considered them to be even now. Which was good, because her ex-slave wasn't off the hook for ruining her chance to get her own dragon. Kess intended to follow through on her threat to destroy everything in that redheaded monster's life in return.

Maybe she would start with the little brat that Pony called a sister. *There's no way they're related. I wonder where along the line she adopted the little runt. And why.* The very concept made Kess's lips twitch.

That was why—the only reason why—Kess had Griskin following their scent. The tightness in her throat and gut drove her on, a horrible, strange feeling, a maddening need for revenge.

It took some time after fleeing the slavers' camp to lose the bear revenant that got on their tail.

Kess's fault, that one. She'd lingered too long to watch and see whether Pony had survived the fall. She needn't have. Either outcome was good. If the falling woman survived, the debt was repaid. If she didn't make it, oh well, how sad.

The undead bear's feral, unyielding chase led Kess and Griskin crashing through the surrounding brushy woods. They skirted the remains of the camp, getting tangled and scratched in the sharp thickets before coming up against the river.

They raced downstream along the pebbled shore, the bear close behind, until they hit a sheer drop that the water tumbled over.

Kess and Griskin leaped from rock to rock, a dance of fleeting fur, in a moment Kess felt must be what flying was like.

The bear rev hadn't the mental capacity or agility to

follow their precarious path. It crashed like a mad berserker into the white waters and was washed over the edge of the high falls.

Free to return to her goal, Kess turned Griskin around. He picked up Pony's scent again back near the camp and they avoided any other run-ins with remaining revenants as they followed that trail.

The moon was high by the time Kess heard the soft giggles from Pony and the little girl. Griskin licked his lips, his skin shivering beneath Kess's fingertips as they neared their prey.

"Shh, boy. Quiet and careful now."

Griskin's paws moved silently over the rocky ground along the path between the river and the mountains. Kess's eyes weren't good enough to see more than some vague movement ahead, under the overhang of a cliff, but Griskin froze, foot lifted, eyes locked.

"That's them?" Kess clenched her teeth. She wasn't sure she could take Pony on one on one, even with Griskin on her side, from what she'd witnessed that evening. The woman was a beast.

"What under the sun are they laughing at?"

Pony had the little girl tucked in close, under an arm, and there was something else there. Something moving on her lap.

The otter was long gone. So what was it?

Directing Griskin to the side, they climbed up through a jumble of boulders opposite where her old slave sheltered.

With a pat to his head, Griskin settled in, silently between the large rocks. The view from there was good, and a soft cyan light glowed around her ex-slave, giving Kess a better look.

The thing on Pony's lap was small, smaller than a cat, and in the cool-blue light, it shimmered with a soft iridescence. Not in the way fur might, but in the way scales did.

Kess's heart set off into a sprint. Could it be?

It was! It was a baby dragon.

The unblessed woman did have a baby dragon all along!

Kess almost threw all of her bone knives then and there, rained them down into the eyes and necks of the woman and girl. Her desire for revenge only grew, but she pushed it aside.

She was going to take that baby dragon, and she was going to take it alive. Whatever cruelty she paid out onto Pony would be an added bonus after Kess had what she wanted.

But for that, she was going to have to wait.

"Come on, go to sleep, you must be exhausted," Kess whispered, as though the wind would carry her words over

and convince Pony to rest.

And once they were asleep, the dragon would be hers.

And maybe she could cut a throat or two at the same time. No, just one. Better to have the giant oaf wake up to find everything she'd tried to protect gone.

The tightness in Kess's stomach grew unbearable. This must have been it, the pull she felt, that gut instinct. It was telling her she was right all along about what Pony had hidden in her bag. That what she always wanted was right within her sights.

Griskin's skin trembled, and he sniffed the air.

Kess cursed, and the two of them ducked lower on their rocky lookout.

It took a few more moments before Kess could hear the footsteps Griskin had already reacted to. And then voices.

Those razing Hjelzahns. Kess looked between the approaching group and Pony, who scrabbled around now herself to face who approached.

Kess bit her lip and grunted. Maybe she should have acted sooner. Even with how soft-pawed Griskin could be, she doubted she could sneak into a camp of that many.

Leaning into Griskin's fur, she rubbed the side of his neck and whispered barely louder than a breath, "Never mind. We know now where what we want is. We'll get it, sooner or later."

A little longer wouldn't matter.

Kess tugged softly on Griskin's fur, and he lifted and turned, slipping them away into the shadowy night. She could bide her time. She was good at that. She'd waited her whole life already to have what she deserved.

Kess would have her own dragon, and she would have her revenge on *Pony* soon enough.

THIRTY-ONE

Riony's muscles hadn't hurt so much since their journey aboveground a couple of weeks ago. She trudged up the final couple of steps to their high-level rooms and sighed happily as their newly repaired front door rolled smoothly into the wall.

She hurt but was grinning like a fool. At least until she looked inside and found Lyrrin and Dracuni gone.

"Lyrrin? Lyrrin?" she called out once into the room, and once out of the room, over the steps and apartments below her that cascaded down from their level on the highest tier of the massive carved stalagmite. The glow stone in the living room, still activated, cast a cyan light over the unoccupied room, through to the small bedroom beside it.

On the messy, scrunched-up blankets, Sir Butterfur Spelunkychunks turned anxious circles, around and around in the middle of the sleeping area, but otherwise Riony was alone.

"Where are they?" Riony asked the cave otter in a worried whisper. Did Lyrrin go to see her friends at the orphans' den? No, she wouldn't have. She knew she wasn't supposed to leave when she was on duty looking after Dracuni, and she took that duty seriously.

She can, and did, spend as much time with her friends as she wanted when it was Riony's turn to look after Dracuni. The two sisters had come to some agreements when they got home, and Lyrrin was enjoying, and rising to, new responsibilities and freedoms.

But even if Lyrrin's judgment had lapsed and she'd left, where was Dracuni? She wouldn't have taken the little unidragon hatchling with her. Even if Dracuni wasn't getting too big to hide in a bag.

Riony grasped her hair and turned a full circle around in the doorway. "Sparks, *where are they?*"

A muffled, stifled giggle replied.

And then the blankets at one of the ends of the sleeping area were tossed into the air, and Lyrrin jumped out, cackling with mirth. "Peekaboo!"

At the other end of the bed, the blankets flicked up as well. Dracuni flung them off her head and bleated a soft, trilling roar. She bucked on her four claws like a baby goat and flapped her weak floppy wings.

Happy!

That was a new sensation Riony was getting used to feeling from Dracuni, after those first couple of days of only fear and pain and hunger. Happy was a nice feeling to share.

Sir Butterfur seemed in on the game too, leaping higher in his looping track and chittering at them both.

"Are you sparking *kidding me*?" Riony exhaled into a shout. "You guys scared the … mushroom farm manure out of me!"

Lyrrin only chuckled more, pulling a blanket back to her face, dropping it up and down in front of her over and over as Dracuni bleated in glee.

"She loves it! It's her favorite game," Lyrrin said.

"It's … a little bit adorable," Riony begrudgingly admitted and pressed the square stone switch to close the door behind her. "Hey. I got you something."

Riony dropped her pack in the corner of the room, rustled around in it, and pulled out a still-steaming bundle. She unrolled the parchment wrapping and held out a fried rope worm on a skewer to her sister.

"We haven't had these in ages!" Lyrrin grabbed the stick, and chomped her teeth on the other end, slurping and licking her lips. "Ow, still hot! But so good."

Riony had one for herself as well. She smiled as she bit the end through the crisp fried skin to the tender, fatty, highly salted meat.

"I figured we deserved a treat," she said around a full mouth. "We have something to celebrate."

Lyrrin stopped chewing. The stick dangled from her hand as she seemed to remember where Riony had been that day. She inhaled sharply. "Did you *get in*?"

Riony grinned smugly. "You're looking at the undercity's newest delver."

Lyrrin squealed and bounced on the spot, setting Dracuni off as well into another round of bleating. The unidragon half galloped, half tripped across the messy blankets to be beside Lyrrin to be part of whatever this new game was.

Riony sat down, leaning against the wall and sighing into a stretch. The trials were hard, but mostly a bunch of climbing and weightlifting and working with ropes, making sure the new recruits had the constitution to deal with the rigors of delving. Which Riony had, in spades. Passed with flying colors and had a good word from the Hjelzahns put in for her on top.

The trials didn't even involve a single riddle or fight to the death with other contestants. Not nearly as exciting as Riony had imagined the trials might be. Although, it wouldn't make much sense to kill off new recruits before they even started. Delving was a risky enough job as it was.

She took another bite and grinned at her sister's excitement. "I'll be starting next week, once I've got some gear fitted for me. Going to get me some of those sweet custom-made delver leathers!"

"We're going to be so rich!" Lyrrin squeaked. "We can have fried rope worm *all the time*."

"We can have all the treats, all the time."

Sir Butterfur stood up on his hind legs at the sound of *treats*.

Riony kicked her boots off, watching as Dracuni circled Lyrrin, little snout chasing the smell of the meat on a stick Lyrrin had forgotten in her excitement. "It will mean more food in general, which will be good, with two growing mouths to feed now, and yup ... there it goes."

Dracuni had Lyrrin's rope worm in her mouth, slurping the entire thing off the metal skewer.

Lyrrin gasped. "No! Bad Dracuni! Stop it." She tugged back, but only came away with a bare stick.

Dracuni's teeth had come in after her first week. Just needly little nubs so far, but enough to demolish a sausagey

worm. The little unidragon was definitely omnivorous. As of that point they hadn't found much that she wouldn't eat, once they worked out how to feed her.

Lyrrin's shoulder's slumped. "Are there any more?"

Riony took another savoring nibble of hers. "You snooze, you lose, kid."

With a pathetic whimper, Lyrrin pouted toward Riony.

"Oh, all right. Only kidding. Here." Riony held out the remains of her fried treat to share with her sister. Sir Butterfur came sniffing around too, skittering between them as Riony handed the food over to Lyrrin.

Riony tossed the wrappers to him. Plenty of salty fat drippings on them to keep him busy.

Riony licked her fingers, then wiped them on her thighs. "More money, more food. But it's also going to mean more responsibilities. I'll be away working a lot, so you're going to be stuck here with Dracuni more often too."

"I don't mind," Lyrrin said, patting the unidragon on the neck as she tried to snap up the food again.

"That means less time with your friends, less time with Benjin."

"Oh." Lyrrin frowned a little, the pout returning.

"I mean, it's not like we can hire a babysitter. It's got to be one of us with Dracuni, all the time."

Lyrrin's expression firmed. "I know. And it's okay.

Dracuni is so special, and she's so cute and lots of fun. I don't mind if I'm alone with her. I want to look after her and keep her safe."

Riony smiled, but her insides turned with a combination of pride and worry at the huge responsibility and sacrifice she'd placed on Lyrrin's tiny shoulders. It was hard enough of a burden for her to carry herself.

Lyrrin brightened. "Plus, it gives me more time here to keep working on my runes. I had an idea just this morning about trying out some different runes on stuff that is already charged, like a glow stone."

Riony worked on stretching out the sore muscles in her arms and sucked air through her teeth. "You be careful messing around with that stuff. I don't want you blowing our house up."

"We're going to need a new place soon anyway!" Lyrrin skipped over to the doorway between living and sleeping areas and pulled the curtain aside.

There were a couple of charcoal smudges on the doorframe there. Height marks from when Riony and Lyrrin first arrived at the undercity and rented these rooms. Then a couple more as they'd gotten bigger over the years. Now there were also a bunch of lower markings too, cut into the stone.

Riony leaned in and looked at the scrapes. "Because you're working on scratching our walls down?"

"Because Dracuni is growing so fast! This is how big she was when we got home"—Lyrrin pointed to the lowest mark—"and this is how big she is now!" Lyrrin pointed to one twice as high up the doorframe.

"Whoa." Riony reached out and ran her fingers over the carved notches. She hadn't realized Lyrrin was keeping track of Dracuni's growth. The care in that made Riony feel warm inside. But she also found her forehead creasing and tension running up her neck.

The unidragon had grown that much already?

She and Lyrrin had managed to keep the creature hidden easily enough so far. Neighbors just assumed Lyrrin had dragged some new cave creature home as a pet, and Dracuni had mostly only ate and slept.

Only in the last few days had Dracuni started getting active, trotting around their rooms, wanting to play, and to play hunt.

And if anything, she was only getting more and more hungry. Riony had scrambled and called in every favor she could when they got back to keep them in food.

To those who had the privilege to care, Riony and the delvers had come home as heroes for having saved at least part of the batch of stolen children, and she'd received some value from that too, a few gifts of thanks here and there.

Now that Riony was going to be a delver, she didn't

have to worry about earning enough to keep them fed, but she did worry about how that much food was going to make Dracuni grow and grow.

Riony's dream of becoming a delver had come true, but she wasn't sure for how long. Could she and Lyrrin keep Dracuni, and the unidragon's precious blood, secret in the undercity for much longer?

It was still easy to remember Dracuni's mother very vividly. Riony had had a rather up close and intimate view of the seasong dragon as the creature had crushed the life out of her. She was sparking *immense*.

Just how big was Dracuni going to get?

TO BE CONTINUED
IN
LEGEND OF THE DRAGON SOUL

GLOSSARY

Including pronunciation guide

CHARACTERS

Riony Eyfarr (Ree-OH-nee AY-far) – Rolanian, Daughter of Eylin and Farrad, born when servants to the Gyrstein Dragonlords, then sold on as a family to the Heithorn Dragonlords, and since living as fugitive slaves. Trained as a midwife and herbalist. Sword enthusiast.

Lyrrin Eyfarr (Li-rin AY-far) – Daughter of "The Guest", an unknown dragonlord woman, and unknown father. Taen and Elgarthan? Has some unusual features. Likes animals and magic.

Kessara Heithorn (Kess-AH-ra High-thorn) – From the once wealthy Heithorn dragonlords with strong dragon riding traditions, estranged. Taen. Rides a wolf

Dracuni (Drak-YOU-nee) – Unique hybrid between unicorn and dragon, created from the use of silvernix on a broken dragon egg, and something more?

Griskin (Griss-kin) – Large gray wolf, male, for some reason abides Kess's company. .

Aishena Hjelzahn (AYSH-en Hyel-zarn) – Delver, Middle sibling of three (remaining), fifth generation heir, grayglim in training. Taen.

Yoskar Hjelzahn (Yoss-kar Hyel-zarn) – Delver, Eldest sibling of three (remaining), fifth generation heir, Alderkin rune expert and academic. Taen.

Benjin Hjelzahn (BEN-jin Hyel-zarn) – Youngest sibling of three (remaining), fifth generation heir. Taen.

Zade Avrin (Zayd Av-RIN) – Worker at the Orphans' Den. Rolanian.

Brishan Ulfaran (Brish-arn OOLF-ah-ran) – Taen ex-grayglim, Master of the delvers.

Kife Heithorn (K-eye-f High-thorn) – Elder brother to Kessara, dragonrider. Taen.

Dragonguards/riders — Those trained to ride dragons, generally for combat purposes. Either born to or hired by Dragonlord families who own the dragons.

Dragonkeeps — Walled in cities protected by dragons. The Dragon King has built and gifted a dragonkeep to each of his first generation heirs.

Dragonlords — Those who have the riches and resources to own their own dragons. Not necessarily royalty.

Delvers — Undercity dwellers who brave the dangers of the Alderkin depths to salvage useful artifacts to be sold in the undercity. A risky but lucrative profession.

Breachers — Undercity dwellers who brave the aboveground world to scavenge resources, highly dangerous but sometimes required.

Silvernix — Unicorn blood. Miraculous healing qualities, a single drop can cure a body from near death. Can only be stored in dragon glass, otherwise loses potency within minutes. Opalescent liquid.

Alderkin (ALL-der-kin) – a secretive and powerful race of elven humanoids. Masters of rune crystal magic. Extinct.

Alderkin War – A twenty year war between the Alderkin and the Dragon King's forces, ending thirty years prior to the events in these books. Prompted by the human's slaughter of unicorns, and the Alderkin's attempts to protect them.

Alderkin Depths – Massive underground cities once inhabited by the Alderkin. There are five known Alderkin Depths across Elundrae.

Alderkin Runes – Magical symbols carved into crystal items, which, when somehow charged, allow for a range of magical functions. The runes must be traced in the right sequence and direction of strokes in order to be activated and deactivated.

Undercity – A human settlement, established in the large upper cavern of the Central Alderkin Depths, as a refuge from the dangers of the aboveground world.

Revenant/Rev/Shadow Revenant – Any undead creature raised by the Shadow Dragon's curse. Generally defeated by fire or dismemberment.

Shadow Dragon – a cursed and mysterious creature of smoke and sadness that brings the undead blight to the land of Elundrae. Wherever the Shadow Dragon touches ground, the dead rise.

Taming – The ceremony in which all dragons are subjected to in order to be domesticated, similar to a lobotomy. Performed not long after birth on captively bred dragons. Utilizes silvernix in the process.

Athame (Ah-Thahm-Ay) – A dagger of varying size, made from crystal, and powered by various Alderking runes for utility or combat.

Dragon Glass – Glass manufactured with the use of dragon's fire to melt the base ingredients.

Unicorns – Ethereal, horned horse-like creatures. Driven to extinction in the race for the riches of their blood.

Elundrae (Ell-Un-Dray) – The continent in which the story takes place. Nearest neighbouring country being Elgartha, across the seas to the East.

Taens – Generally dark-haired and light-to-mid-brown skin-tones, Taens were once a warrior like clan of horse-riders, taking residence through the north-west of Elundrae. When the Dragon King rose to power, Taens became favored and more likely to become dragonlords, and soon became the dominant race across the land.

Rolanians – Once ruling large cities throughout Elundrae, most Rolanian settlements were destroyed as the Shadow Dragon curse spread through the land. As very few Rolanians became dragonlords, they had to buy into protection from those who had dragons, often at the cost of their own freedom. Generally presenting with a warm array of darker skintones, and often curly hair ranging from blonde, through reds and browns.

Elgarthans – A sea-faring race, pale skinned, they will visit and trade with Dragonkeeps for the riches of steel and glass provided through dragon labor, but rarely remain in Elundrae due to the dangers.

Herbs

Corpsefoot – used for contraception, dangerous in high doses.
Shillgrue – to condition leather
Hennen, Tinctoria – for hair dye
Carrowmy – culinary

Genjermint – sleeping tea

Plumeberry – tart, seedy berries, poison detox.

Morass Mercy – powerful sedative, causes headaches and hallucinations during prolonged usage.

DRAGONS
Natural subspecies

Snowshimmer – Mountain dragons. Whites-blues, medium sized, fast build for snatching up rare prey. Big talons, lightning breath attack, rare and solitary. Used in industry for power and interbreeding.

Seasong – Sea dragons. Silvers, greens, blacks, largest size, big lungs creates big surge of air/sound to stun schools of fish, and bigger mouth for feeding. There are tales they once sang, but never have in captivity or once tamed. Mostly used for interbreeding and beasts of burden.

Etherflame – Plains dragons. Golds and reds, large size. Fire breathing for clearing grasslands/cooking herds, and big wings for hovering. Blood itself is flammable, and is aerosolised in breath weapon. Most common dragonrider mount.

Treedart – Forest dragons. Yellows, browns, purples, camouflaged scales. Smallest type, with concentrated fire bolts for individual prey. Considered pretty basic by breeders and dragonlords, mostly used for interbreeding. Main/only dragon still in the wild because of size.

Dragons

Interbred selective breeding species

FlameSongs – Etherflame/Seasong cross. Largest size, high-capacity fire-breathers, used mostly for industrial uses, not used as mounts because their unstable nature means they can spontaneously explode.

Shimmerdart – Snowshimmer/Treedart cross. Small size, with small ball lightning darts, dangerous for single targets but not great against mass undead, bred for speed as scouts/communications/assassinations.

Snowflame – Snowshimmer/Etherflame cross. Medium-large size, white "liquid" fire, fast, considered a great dragonrider mount, but short lifespan as breath weapon deteriorates their health fast.

Etherdart – Etherflame/Treedart cross. Medium size, tough but slow, big fireballs. A basic combat dragon.

Seashimmer – Seasong/Snowshimmer cross. Large size, cold, icy breath used in ice making and food storage industry.

Treedart/seasong – don't interbreed successfully.

Animals

Bovin – A large (twice human height) buffalo or yak style creature, docile, used to be in large herds that supported wild dragons. Moved into farming for captive dragons.

Dreer – Deer with Armadillo like scales, that grow as large as giraffes. Also popular prey for wild dragon populations in the past.

Cave Otters – A large sized otter with specially adapted claws that allow them to climb sheer walls easily, pale colors to match limestone surroundings.

Owlettes – Cave dwelling owls that feed on small rodents and insects within the caves, the size of a small hand.

Glowflies – firefly-like bugs, finger sized, live in large swarms and light up when disturbed.

Rope Worms – Just a worm, but much larger.

Olm – Just like real olm, but larger than human size and carnivorous.

Cave Spiders – Head-sized spiders, nonvenomous.

ALDERKIN RUNES

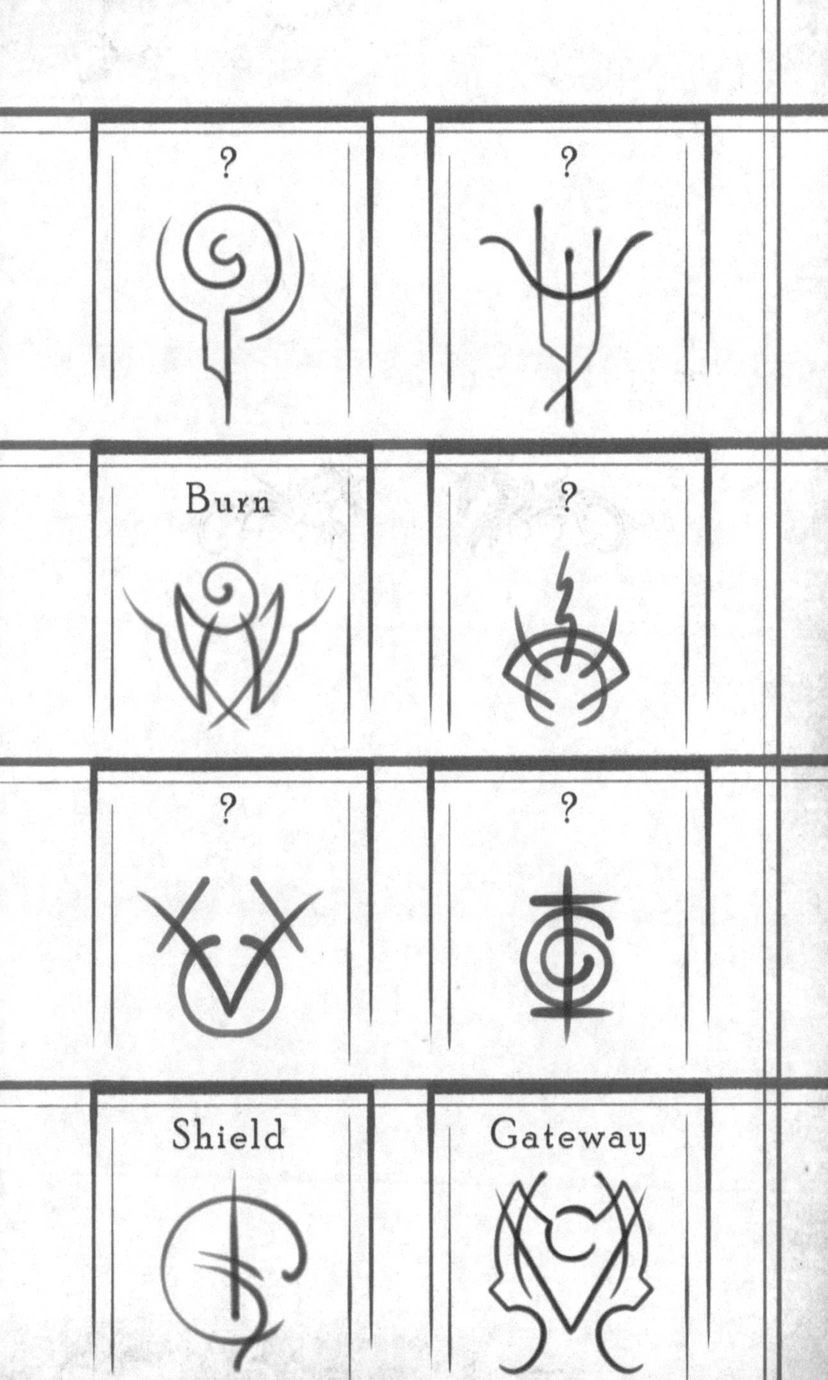

?
?
Burn
?
?
?
Shield
Gateway

Tree Dart
Sea Song
Snow Shimmer
Ether Flame

About the Author

PROFESSIONAL DAYDREAMER, SELINA A. FENECH writes "adorably dark" Epic and Urban Fantasy for teens and adults. Filled with sweet and quirky characters, laugh out loud moments, and perilous adventures, her magical worlds are perfect for readers who love daring twists and happily ever afters.

A cancer survivor determined to live life to the fullest, she is an escape room enthusiast, avid gardener, foodie and self-proclaimed geek, residing in Australia.

In addition to literature, Selina applies her unique take on the dichotomy of light and dark as a professional fantasy artist working under the name Selina Fenech and has published many illustrated books, oracle decks, and colouring books.

Find Out more About Selina

OFFICIAL WEBSITE: www.selinafenech.com

Memory's Wake Trilogy

A modern girl lost in and hunted in a fairy tale world.
An illustrated young adult portal fantasy with
Arthurian and Victorian themes.

Empath Chronicles

Teenagers with superpowers fueled by emotions ... what
could go wrong? A young adult superhero romance.

More Books by Selina A Fenech

Beshadowed

You have been lied to. Werewolves, vampires, ghosts ... they aren't what you think. What is really lurking in the dark? A spooky urban fantasy.

Heartsblood

Her blood is irresistible, but is it worth the cost? A vampire romance for adults.

www.ingramcontent.com/pod-product-compliance
Lightning Source LLC
Chambersburg PA
CBHW010546170726
48285CB00011B/2782